LIONHEART

LIONHEART

Robert Taylor

Book Guild Publishing
Sussex, England

First published in Great Britain in 2014 by
The Book Guild Ltd
The Werks
45 Church Road
Hove, BN3 2BE

Typesetting in Sabon by
Norman Tilley Graphics Ltd, Northampton

Printed and bound in Great Britain by
CPI Group (UK) Ltd, Croydon, CR0 4YY

A catalogue record for this book is available from
The British Library

ISBN 978 1 909984 63 9

To my wife, Jane, and my family for their unstinting support.

And to Vanessa Feltz and Lyn Bowles of BBC Radio 2 for their early morning inspirational words.

1

Sir James Walters marched, almost at the double, into the broadcasting studio of BBC Radio 5 live. Although now in his sixties, he still held the gait of a soldier: close-cropped silver hair sat atop a tanned and chiselled face; the body still erect with shoulders back and chest jutting forward like the bow of an old battleship. He took in the scene; a round oak-effect table stood in the centre with various cables running to and fro and three microphones positioned equidistant around the circumference, one with a computer screen and keyboard. Three chairs with blue fabric coverings were stationed in front of the microphones, which each had a pair of headphones lying nearby.

A woman in her mid-thirties held a hand outstretched to greet the tall man as he entered. She was a striking looking woman with green flashing eyes and shoulder-length brown hair framing a high-jawed face that betrayed a pound or two of excess weight, but nothing a few good sessions in the gym couldn't sort out, Sir James thought.

'Sir James Walters, I presume?' she asked.

'Yes, ma'am,' the man answered, taking the proffered hand. Um, he thought, a strong handshake and an eye contact of steel that he admired – no doubt a powerful inquisitor.

'My name is Mary Lawrence. Thank you very much for coming; it's much appreciated. I present the phone-in programme that starts at nine o'clock. Are you familiar with its format or would you like me to go through a few things?'

'Yes, ma'am. I am indeed familiar. Even though I generally listen to Radio 4, I listened to all of last week's shows on the iPlayer over the weekend.'

'Ah. Good!'

A compliment would not go amiss now, he thought. 'Indeed, I was impressed, ma'am. You are a strong advocate.' He smiled, showing his stunning white teeth which, set into his tanned features, and with his silver hair and sharp charcoal suit, clearly cut in Savile Row, split by a strong blue silk tie and matching kerchief in his breast pocket, indicated he was clearly of some substance. 'I must say, with your looks and style, I cannot believe I haven't seen you on television?'

She felt a satisfactory warmth around her neck and loosened her grip on the warm hand. Many men, and even some women, had flirted with her. Most she had found false and without depth, but here was a man as old as her own father who was charming and sophisticated. But she would not be distracted, not be swayed, from grilling him if it became necessary to get to the crux. Utter charm had never won over Mary Lawrence in the past and it was not about to now.

A feminine cough allowed her to re-gather her composure as the second combatant entered the studio. 'Ah! Colin. So nice to see you again,' she greeted the newcomer. Turning to Sir James she declared, 'This is Colin Hunter. Colin, Sir James Walters.'

The two men shook hands. 'Nice to see you again, sir,' Hunter greeted the older man.

'And you, um, *Mr* Hunter?' enquired Sir James. 'Or are you still serving?'

'Plain mister will serve absolutely fine, sir,' Hunter returned. 'How is Lady Isobel?'

'Ah! It appears you two already know one another?' Mary interjected.

'Indeed we do,' admitted the younger man. 'General Walters, as was, was my commanding officer in the Balkans in the nineties. The best in the business.'

2

'I see,' said the phone-in host.

'And, if I may be so bold as to say, Major Colin Hunter was one of the more proficient officers on my staff. Do you remember that hideous man, the so-called colonel? Lukic was his name, I think.'

'Ah! Yes. I believe I do. The beast of Southern Bosnia?' remembered Mary.

'The very same,' Sir James agreed. 'Major Hunter went in on his own and took him out. An action that earned him a very well deserved George Cross.'

Mary looked uneasily through the glass at her production team for reassurance. Her notes told her none of this. It was too late now, for in a few minutes they would be on air. 'This seems to be a mutual admiration society rather than one which is about to debate the pros and cons of British involvement in Afghanistan!' Mary was looking for the confirmation she needed that it would be a worthy debate.

'Don't worry,' assured the retired general. 'We are clearly on opposite sides of this battlefield.'

They took their positions and waited for cues as the Breakfast Show began to wrap. The phone-in jingle started and, at the same time, as she had opened every show for the past three years, Mary Lawrence made her welcoming announcements. 'My thanks to Richard and Shannon for the Breakfast Show. Now it's our turn. I am Mary Lawrence and welcome to this morning's phone-in. Today is Monday the thirtieth of June 2008 and at nine thirty, after the news headlines and sport, we will be taking calls on last night's historic Spanish victory in the Euros in Vienna. First, though, we start with events in Afghanistan. On Saturday, three more of our soldiers died in an ambush in Helmand province. After the news I will be joined by the spokesman for *Bring Them Home* and a supporter of government policy in Afghanistan. That's all after the news with Caroline Holmes.' Mary flicked off her microphone and waited for the news to finish before the end of the sports headlines would cue her in again.

'Thank you, George,' she said at the end of the sports bulletin. 'Right, then. On Saturday afternoon in Helmand province a routine patrol turned into a bloodbath as three British soldiers and five Afghani troops were ambushed and killed by Taliban militia. Once again it has opened the debate about Britain's involvement in this seemingly unwinnable war. Colin Hunter, himself a former major in the army who has seen action in the former Yugoslavia, is here to represent *Bring Them Home*, the organisation vehemently opposed to our involvement in the war. And, to counter this, we have retired general Sir James Walters, who has seen distinguished action in the Falklands, the first Gulf War and the Balkans: conflicts, it is said, that had the backing of the ordinary man in the street. Sir James knows the grief that the families are going through, for his son, Colonel Nathan Walters, was killed in action in 2005 and never saw his own unborn son.'

Even though Sir James knew the introduction was going to mention his son, he still felt the pain of his lost child. He clasped his hands together on the table with his microphone cradled between them like a lost soul looking for comfort, closed his eyes and offered up a silent prayer for Nathan.

Mary started with Colin Hunter. 'Colin, an ex-soldier your-self, you are a man who is used to following orders. Why should now be any different?'

'No. That's not what we stand for. *Bring Them Home* firmly believes we are now involved in a conflict we cannot win. In fact, if we were there for another hundred years we would not win. In the Balkans it was justified as it was on our own doorstep in Europe and we knew who the enemy was. Here, our poor lads are on a hiding to nothing; one minute we're facing uniformed militia, and you know who's on who's side, and the next a civilian with a backpack saunters up to you to ask a question and – Boom! – you're a goner. Bring them home.'

'That seems fair and logical, Sir James?'

'Mary. May I correct one thing?' asked Sir James.

'Yes. Yes. Of course.'

'I was not a supporter of our government sending our troops into Afghanistan. But, now we are there, I believe we should finish the job. We now have a democratically elected government, increased women's rights, education for all, a burgeoning economy, among other things, and I feel we cannot desert them now. If we left now, the sluice gates would be reopened and the Taliban and Al Qaeda would flood back in. At present, they are dispersed around the world with no real base to launch attacks against our cities and towns.'

Colin took up the baton again. 'Um. Yes. That's right. We don't disagree with that view, except we believe Afghanistan is becoming a lawless society and by withdrawing we would only make it more lawless. But, bring our boys and girls home and defend our realm from within.'

'Sir James,' Mary intervened. 'Should we care what happens to the people of Afghanistan? If we brought all of our troops home, and from Iraq as well, surely we'd be better equipped to protect our own people with the manpower that would become available?'

'I see the argument, but I don't agree,' allowed Sir James. 'I maintain that if we pull out we shall leave a vacuum that will suck in all the enemies of the West, who, in turn, will rain their terror down on our towns and cities. Also, what would you do with the members of the democratically elected government and their associates?'

Hunter countered, 'We have trained their security forces for long enough now, and I am sure they are fully capable of filling the hole left by our men and women.'

'A fair point, Sir James?' the presenter enquired.

'Umm! I don't believe so. But if I can just finish my point?'

'Of course,' she agreed. 'Please continue.'

'Thank you. In addition to the politicians and bureaucrats of the present government, there are also the girls who are now getting an education, the women who may educate them, the women who run their own businesses or have risen to positions of responsibility in commercial organisations. What happens to them?'

'What do you think would happen to them, Colin Hunter?'

'I am sure there would be some disruption. Maybe it would return to the old ways but I am afraid to say this is not our concern.'

Up to this juncture, the debate had been held with civil recognition of the other's views, but Sir James was beginning to fret and started to tap his right index finger on the table. His former subordinate was just beginning to get under his skin. For Christ's sake, he thought, a soldier's position was to obey orders, and Hunter should understand this more than most. Even in retirement. Questioning the army's position could undermine the morale of those in the field. He continued to tap his finger as if to emphasise his point.

'Some disruption?' he sneered. Raising his voice slightly, he continued, 'I'll tell you exactly what will happen. There will be executions, public and private, of all forms, imprisonment without trial, amputations, floggings and other brutal punishments. That is what will happen if we bring our brave troops home. And that, in my opinion, is unacceptable!'

The lovey-dovey start was waning. Good, Mary thought. Bring it on!

'Sir James infers...' began Hunter, his eyes widening in disbelief that his former commander was showing signs of letting his normal implacable mask slip. He believed it was the burden of Nathan's death rather than anything he had said himself. Hunter conceded, in his own mind at least, that it must be difficult to put on a show in such trying circumstances

Mary held up her right hand. 'I think it's about time we went to the phones. First up, we have Albert from Dorset. Good morning, Albert.'

'Aah! Umm! Good morning, Mary.' Albert spoke in the slightly clipped tones of a more formal education. 'Please forgive me. I am slightly nervous. I am now eighty-seven years old and was a young officer at the Normandy landings in 1944. I have to tell you, I am with the general on this one.'

Feeling calmer at the thought of others continuing the debate, Sir James let out a long breath to help regain composure. 'Thank you, Albert,' he said.

'Can you imagine,' continued Albert, 'if we had had these open discussions during the war what the effect would have been on the morale of our boys back then? Discussions did take place in private, but I am sure it would have been treasonable to have held these discussions on the wireless.'

'Times have changed,' observed Mary.

'But not always for the better. The reason they have changed,' continued the old soldier, nerves seeming to have vanished, 'is that people like me and those that served with me or under me did not question what we had to do. Mr Hunter – I shan't oblige him with his rank – is a disgrace and people like him should not be given airtime until after the conflict is over.'

Hunter rolled his eyes at the jibe. He had heard it before and, no doubt, would hear it again. 'Okay, Albert. I hear what you say, but I am not in the army anymore and plain Mr Hunter or Colin will be fine,' he countered calmly. 'All of us around this table and beyond owe you and your comrades a great deal of debt. And it's because of what you did that we can have these open discussions. No one is disputing that.'

'Exactly,' interrupted the caller, now raising his voice to emphasise his disdain for the *Bring Them Home* campaign. 'And you should not be encouraging these brave lads to question their duty, which is exactly what you are doing.'

'If I could just finish? There is no way I would encourage soldiers of any era to question their duty. No way! But that doesn't mean we can't have the discussion about the ethical or moral side to this war. If you like, we are conscientious objectors who, if I am not mistaken, were around in your day.'

'They were not, sir, given a platform like this.' There was now a real anger in Albert's tone.

Sir James sat back in his chair and admired the coolness with which his opponent was dealing with the caller. Indeed, he thought, Colin Hunter was demonstrating the very qualities that had made him stand out above his contemporaries when under fire in the Balkans.

'I am still of the opinion that you are wrong, and as a former soldier you also have a duty to your old mates.' The voice had now quietened slightly but was quicker.

'My point exactly,' beamed a victorious Hunter. 'My duty is to the soldiers out there in theatre, the soldiers out there who have not yet died or been mutilated in some horrendous suicide attack. Bring 'em home.'

'Just hold the line, Albert,' Mary requested of the caller. 'We have Rameez from Burnley on the phone. Good morning, Rameez.'

'Mornin', Mary,' replied the broad Lancashire accent.

'Rameez, you are an Afghan national and don't agree with Sir James and Albert?'

'No. I don't.'

There was silence as Rameez searched for the words.

'Go on,' Mary encouraged.

'Well… Well. They should come home. And, I don't agree that these people are brave. They are occupiers of a foreign land and they should expect hatred from the people they are trying to rule over. And, what sort of country sends women to war?'

'That's another discussion for another time,' Mary put in. 'Sir James, would you –'

'No, it's not,' Rameez exploded with a ferocity that had the three around the table exchanging glances. 'That's all part of it. Bush and Blair want the liberal ways of the West imposed upon

8

my people. My people are a proud people where everyone, including and most importantly of all, women, know their place.'

Mary moved uncomfortably in her seat. 'Our so-called liberal ways... I'm sure the term liberal has not been used of President Bush too many times. Anyway, as I was saying, our so-called liberal ways allow women like me to do jobs like this. Do you object to me working?'

'Actually, yes, I do object. You should be at home.'

Sir James held up his hand and Mary nodded to him to comment. 'Hold on, Rameez. James Walters here. If I may be so bold? You don't sound much like an Afghan national. Your accent suggests a man brought up in Lancashire.'

'I can't help it that my father was so short-sighted as to settle in this God-forsaken land with its promiscuous ways.'

'If you were in your homeland at this moment and the Taliban were still in control you would not be able to ring a phone-in like this and express views opposite to the regime. Is that correct?'

'You and your like are trying to force my people into a way of life we do not care for.'

'Can I come in?' asked Albert.

'Go ahead, Albert,' said Mary, now feeling she needed to be alert for fear of what this hothead from Burnley was going to come up with next. She could feel a fire inside. How dare this idiot put the entire female gender down like this? She wanted to declare Hunter the winner and let the bloody people get what they deserved. On the other hand, though, Sir James was right: if women were to prosper, the troops had to stay.

'I can't believe what I am hearing,' Albert started. 'The man has just given us all the reasons we need to stay and –'

'Shut up you blithering old fool,' blazed Rameez.

'That's enough Rameez,' refereed Mary. 'If you are going to make it personal I will have to end the call.'

'Okay,' the seemingly reluctant caller agreed after a short pause and some deep breaths.

'Thank you. Please finish, Albert?'

'Um! Yes. Sorry! Where was I? Ah yes. The General is right. All the peoples of Afghanistan should be equal and given the same chances that we expect for ourselves. And if that fellow thinks it is such a wonderful place he should take the next plane. Then he can decide which is the better society.'

'Trust me. I will go back and celebrate with my people when the imperialist powers of the US and UK have been expelled and the crops grow well on the blood of your so-called heroes.'

'We will stay until we have the job done and my son's death will not be in vain,' Sir James added.

'Just listen to the hoity-toity general,' sneered Rameez. 'I wouldn't mind betting that you're from a long line of imperialist conquerors.'

'If you mean am I from an army background, yes I am. My father was a soldier and my grandfather before him. And I am proud of my son's service.'

'I'm sure you are,' Rameez went on with a sarcastic tone. 'I wonder how many countrymen of mine he murdered before he got his just deserts? And, if I had my way, I would urge my countrymen to rise up and kill your whole fuckin' family.'

The last few words were not broadcast. They were replaced by a couple of trailers for programmes scheduled for later in the week.

A stunned silence befell the three participants. Never in her years of broadcasting had such a threat been issued on Mary Lawrence's watch. 'Wow!' was all she could manage.

Neither Hunter nor Sir James responded.

'I'm so sorry, Sir James,' said Mary, the apology cutting through the tension.

'You okay, James?' asked Hunter, seeing that the tanned features had turned a ghostly white.

'Umm... Yes. Yes I am. Thank you.' Sir James let out a breath before continuing. 'A young man of conviction, I would suggest,' he added with a wan smile.

'Indeed – we have other callers lined up, but I would totally understand if you didn't wish to continue,' said Mary.

Sir James emptied his glass of water and, wiping his mouth, said, 'I am happy to continue. Do we finish with young Rameez first?'

'We can't take that chance. We'll move on to someone else.'

'I wouldn't mind being able to have a conversation with the young man away from the mike and try to understand his perspective,' said Sir James. 'Anyway, I have faced real live bullets and shells before and not given up. I am not about to start now.'

'Colin?' enquired Mary.

'Yeah. Yes. I will as well. And, I'm with you, James. I'd like to understand the young man's angst as well.'

The producer came through the studio intercom. 'Mary. We'll take some early news headlines and sport. Rameez has gone. We'll try to get him back. Sir James, would you have a quick word with Albert and let him know you're all right?'

Sir James agreed and assured Albert he was in fine fettle and thanked him for his concern.

The producer could not get hold of Rameez. Sir James and Colin Hunter were not sure how hard he tried.

After the news and sport, the debate continued for another fifteen minutes or so without any controversy or threat. The two old soldier friends then left together after a series of hand-shakes, cheek kissings and goodbyes. Outside on the pavement, Hunter pulled a slip of paper out of his pocket.

'That isn't what I think it is, is it?' asked a surprised Sir James.

Hunter nodded.

'How did you get it?'

'Slipped one of the young lads a twenty while you were charming the delectable Ms Lawrence and he wrote the number down for me. Are you game for a little chat?'

'Maybe. I'm not sure.' The older man scratched his head

before sighing and continuing. 'Colin, while we were in there I did a bit of thinking. I know we disagree about the war, but I know we are agreed that our young boys and girls are putting life and limb on the line. I'm thinking of making a point to go and visit all the bereaved families from now on. Will you join me in a united front?'

'I'll give it some thought but I think not. I think that if my organisation were to see me doing that, they'd think I'm offering support to the war. But, we must speak again for we have much common ground.'

'I understand. Give my love to Emily.'

'Of course. And likewise give my best to Isobel.'

Eight days later, Rameez ul Shafiq was reported missing. He left his parents' home to meet a friend in Burnley town centre. He never arrived. It was a newsworthy disappearance following his now well-publicised spat with Sir James. The newspapers and other forums were full of tireless speculation about the missing man. There was talk that he had gone to join a terrorist cell in the UK or even in Afghanistan for training and would be back to wreak his revenge on the streets of Britain. Others said he had been kidnapped and murdered by a home-grown neo-Nazi group. Rumoured sightings led to nothing. It was as if he had simply disappeared into the atmosphere. Police investigations drew a blank except for one thing: Rameez ul Shafiq was not an Afghan national as he had claimed in his short broadcasting career, but a third generation British Pakistani. Until that day in June 2008 he had seemed as English as English could be. He supported Burnley Football Club and even England at cricket. He enjoyed a pint with his mates, white and Asian. His ethos was moderate in the extreme. No one will ever know what tipped the scales that morning. He left two grieving parents and two distraught younger sisters.

2

Three years later, in July 2011, a black Volkswagen Transporter looked out of place outside the glass-fronted headquarters of the London *Echo and Post*. Sean Bryant noticed it when he had taken a cigarette break earlier in the afternoon. The trees with fluttering leaves planted in gaps in the pavement, and surrounded by cast-iron protective grates, were not out of place; the smokers in the office doorways under grey-blue clouds of tobacco smoke were not out of place; the aroma of coffee wafting on the summer breeze from Starbucks across the street was not out of place; the hubbub of London hanging in the warm air was not out of place; but the black VW was.

The van had arrived in the early afternoon and was parked on the red line running along the edge of the road. The line depicted Transport for London's Red Zone, an area of the capital designated as no parking and no waiting except under permit. The van displayed no such permit. Police cars drifted by seeming not to notice the black hulk obstructing the busy traffic and traffic wardens had wandered past not even bothering to stop and write a ticket. Bryant sniffed his roll-up. No, it was definitely his favourite Drum shag. He was not hallucinating after all, but what was making this gleaming black incongruity invisible to others, especially officers of the authorities?

Bryant drew hungrily on his cigarette as if it had been denied him for half a lifetime, not just a couple of hours, and wondered what the van's purpose was. The driver's side window was down and he could hear that two men, both dressed in black polo shirts with company insignia on the breast, were listening to tennis commentary from Wimbledon. He couldn't make out who was playing, for all he could hear were the thuds of racket on ball and the shrieks of the female players – as they summoned every ounce of energy into the orgasmic climax of a shot – interspersed with cheers and applause from the crowd.

He reflected he'd never been to the Wimbledon fortnight but now he would go. Someone in the sports department would blag a couple of tickets for him and he would take Amelia, a decent club player herself, as part of their wedding anniversary celebrations. Eight years, he thought. Where had all that time gone? Then he smiled as he remembered an old boy from the village had said: 'You think it goes quick now, boy. You wait 'til you get to my age!' A wiser phrase there couldn't be. A bucket list. That was what he needed. In the few days off, he and Amelia would write that list.

A man from the business section of the paper joined Bryant as he was nearly at the end of his roll-up. Ian was a great fat lump about five feet six tall, and probably the same around his wobbly bulging waistline. Sweat had already appeared on his receding forehead just from the exertion of getting to the smoking area. Bryant exchanged meaningless pleasantries with the business journo as the fat man wheezed his way through a filter-tipped full-strength Marlboro.

They talked about the weather; apparently a very hot few days was forecast. They talked about the black van; Ian reckoned it had been there for about an hour and a half, or at least four Marlboros which, give or take a minute or two, was one every twenty minutes. What on earth was the van doing? The fat man came up with a plausible explanation.

'I know,' he said. 'The Olympics are in about a year's time, I think. I reckon it's part of an ongoing security exercise by the organisers.'

Probably, thought Bryant, and returned to his desk to put the finishing touches to his feature. One final read-through and it was done. He clicked the submit button to file his copy at the editing desk, closed his laptop and headed for the exit. A couple of goodbyes as he made his way, a collision avoided with a woman on the stairs reading copy and slurping coffee, and he was back on the pavement at 7.10 p.m. At last, a few days off!

After checking the time on his mobile phone – he was part of the increasing trend of not wearing a watch – the only decision left was a beer at a riverside hostelry and then the train, or the train and then a beer in the Fox and Hounds' garden in the village. No contest. It would be getting dark as he arrived home. The charms of the riparian hostelry calling him through the sound of the city would win out on this occasion.

He plucked the pre-rolled cigarette from behind his ear and flicked the cheap lighter into flame. He sucked on the lit tobacco, drawing it deep into his lungs before exhaling the exhaust. His fat friend had probably done seven or eight Marlboros in the time he had been back at his desk. The sanitised world of the commercial indoors was now a blight to a smoker's working day. Since smoking had been banned in the workplace, fag breaks had probably added half an hour to the working day. He chuckled at the thought of his fat friend; he probably didn't even have time to go home!

The van was still there. This time, though, there was a man leaning against its side, just in front of an open door which revealed a luxurious interior with tanned leather seats in a conference layout, four or five, he couldn't see them all. The man wore a similar black polo shirt to the others he had seen, but wore a charcoal suit jacket and trousers like a fashion throwback to the eighties. He wore dark glasses and had an earpiece curled around his left ear. He appeared to be speaking into his jacket lapel.

A feeling of unease came over Bryant. The hairs stood up on the back of his neck and a lump formed in the pit of his stomach. He looked down the street toward the river. Out of the corner of his eye he noticed a front passenger getting out of the vehicle. His heart pounded against his ribs. He turned and headed back toward the security of the office lobby just as a fresh-faced cub reporter was disappearing in through the sliding doors.

'Will! Hold the doors, mate.'

The youngster looked round before stepping back into the line of the doors to prevent them from closing. Another man appeared from his left and came between him and Bryant. Will recognised him as one of the paper's senior feature writers. He had hardly talked to his esteemed colleague since he had joined the paper and yet, here he was addressing him as 'mate'. Bryant seemed perturbed by something and as the other man approached, raised his left hand to thank the young man although his assistance was not now necessary. Will went inside and the doors slid closed.

Bryant had breathed a sigh of relief as the young man he could remember only as Will had stepped back into the line of the doors. Then a man came into vision from his right and blocked the route to safety. He had raised his left hand to indicate that Will should hold the doors. To his dismay Will gave a polite nod and stepped away allowing the doors to slide closed. God's sake, Bryant thought. The idiot didn't get the message!

Bryant spotted the CCTV camera above the doors and guessing it had an unobstructed view of the cigarette in his right hand, dropped it onto the floor. He hoped that someone, when reviewing the footage, would spot the gesture and realise it was at a moment of distress.

The man produced a warrant card from his inside jacket pocket and flourished it in Bryant's line of view. The jacket was open just enough to show off a holstered pistol. That had been deliberate and the flap of the coat was not dropped until the man was sure of its effect.

The effect was instant. Jesus Christ! Bryant thought. Fuck me, this is serious! His mouth had now gone dry and he feared for his life. For Christ's sake, stay calm and you'll be all right.

'Mr Bryant? Mr Sean Bryant?' the man enquired politely.

'Yes, I am.' It was as much as he could answer.

'It wasn't a question, Mr Bryant. We know who you are.'

'Oh!' Jesus! It was as if his mouth was full of flour.

'My name is Captain Ben Morgan of the Civil Protection Group.'

'Oh!' Bryant gasped again.

'You are to accompany us to our headquarters for questioning.' Morgan indicated the open van door with his free hand and said matter-of-factly, 'Shall we?'

The pair climbed into the back of the van, Bryant taking one of the comfortable leather-clad seats to which Morgan gestured. Another man got in behind and slid the door shut. Four downlighters in the ceiling came on as the door closed. Bryant heard the front passenger door slam shut and the van glided away into the evening traffic.

'Looks like you could use some water,' said the captor.

Bryant nodded. 'Please.'

The other man grabbed a bottle of water from a small refrigerator and a glass from a cupboard above. Bryant glanced around at the well-appointed interior and was impressed with the quality of the finishes: deep pile carpet, the leather seats and real wood cabinetry. He felt reasonably secure; he didn't believe they would spill his blood in such plush surroundings.

'Thank you,' he managed to say as the libation was placed in front of him. He poured some of the water into the glass and took a relieving gulp.

'As I said, my name is Captain Ben Morgan.' Tipping his left hand toward his colleague, Morgan continued, 'And this is

Neil Ramsey. I expect you're wondering who we are and what we want with you.'

Bryant began to feel a sense of relaxation. Morgan appeared affable, cool and collected, so Bryant replied with more confidence: 'You could say that. Yes.'

'Have you heard of the Civil Protection Group before?'

'No. I can't say I have. What do you want with me and where are we going?'

'Mr Bryant, I will set the agenda.' There wasn't exactly menace in Morgan's tone, but an assertiveness borne out of what Bryant assumed was army officer training. 'We'll let you know who we are and then we'll have time for some questions. The Civil Protection Group, or CPG, is one of the leading security companies in the world. Long before I joined the company we started installing domestic security alarms back in the seventies. The history is contained in this DVD.'

Ramsey placed the DVD on the table and slid it across to Bryant. He picked up the case. The front consisted of an outline map of the world with various regional offices pin-pointed. Various icons of the security world were scattered around the perimeter, such as alarm boxes, fencing, safes and weapons. Peering out from the middle of the cover was a very attractive young woman with wisps of blonde hair strategically shaped under an army-style combat helmet. She wore full combat body armour and brandished what Bryant took to be an automatic assault weapon. The uniform was entirely black and each part bore the same insignia as the two men's polo shirts, now clearly in view. The woman's blackened face indicated a veiled threat. The eyes, though, were something altogether different. They were the colour of a bright summer's sky and, in this context, shone out like deadly lasers seeking a target. Nobody, thought Bryant, could sport such deadly-looking eyes. He was convinced the picture had been doctored for effect. It worked!

'From these humble beginnings the company has gone from

strength to strength. You can see it all in there. We now cover all aspects of security including personal protection and corporate security, hence our interest in you. One of our clients feels threatened by you and wants us to find out why you attacked them in this feature you just submitted for tomorrow's *Echo and Post*.' Morgan held up a wad of six or seven A4 pages.

'God!' uttered Bryant. 'Where'd you get that from?'

'Not difficult. We simply hacked your computer,' Morgan smiled. 'I believe it's a technique that some of your colleagues use. I'm quite sure you wouldn't stoop so low.'

The last few words were true. Bryant hated the mess in which his profession had become embroiled. In his mind, phone and computer hacking were not the tools of a true investigative journalist, any more than burglary or torture was, and should not be tolerated in any quarter. Burglary was against the law, torture was against the law, and hacking was against the law. If you get caught doing any of them don't claim you were just doing your job and tar all good honest journalists with the same brush. Punishment should go right to the top as well. Any direct link found to the owner of a news organisation should mean that the officer should face a court martial as well as the trench-fighter.

Morgan continued, 'Anyway, we sat in here and watched every keystroke you made. And, when you filed your copy we got ourselves ready for you. You could never have escaped. Oh, and if you're wondering, it didn't arrive at the editing desk. It came here via your main server.'

'So much for our state of the art firewall protection or whatever it's called,' joked Bryant.

'Ah, yes,' said Morgan. 'It is state of the art. And very, very good. I must admit to a slight conflict of interest here. We provided it to your organisation. Bit naughty, I know, but our client believes this is a matter of national security.'

Bryant smiled.

'Sit back. Enjoy the corporate blurb on the DVD and we will resume in forty minutes or so.'

'Forty minutes? How long's the journey then?'

'Two and a half, three hours, depending on traffic.

After another ten minutes or so the van came to a stop. After a few seconds it rolled forward slowly. Bryant sensed it had moved inside. His heart began to race. National security? He reflected on Morgan's statement. This is it. His palms were sweating and his throat felt as if it was constricting.

Morgan sensed the apprehension in Bryant and moved to reassure him. A narrow smile played on his lips as he thought about playing with his victim as a cat would toy with a mouse, but then sighed, 'Don't be alarmed. We're not about to cut your throat or anything hideous like that. We've only stopped for some planned maintenance.'

Peculiar, thought Bryant, an organisation like this, that had planned his abduction in such fine detail, and here it was stopping for maintenance.

He returned to the DVD which featured the laser-eyed woman selling the company's wares, from the simple intruder alarm for semi-detached homes in suburbia to personal protection for celebrities and high-powered business executives, and to security for global sporting events and government and military installations. She took the viewer through the history of the organisation from the sale of their first burglar alarm in a small town in Hertfordshire to the security provided to dignitaries at the soccer World Cup in South Africa in 2010.

While watching the film, Bryant was aware of activity around the van, activity he couldn't identify. There was a whirring sound like a giant hairdryer. There was a crinkling sort of a sound like someone scrunching up aluminium baking foil. There was the distinct sound of a drilling-type machine and numerous sounds of scraping on concrete, which could have been step ladders being dragged around. In short, he had no idea what was going on.

After a while, he wasn't sure how long, but before the end of the video, the sound and feel of the engine being gunned took his attention. The van reversed and turned to the left before moving forward and stopping, perhaps at a junction, before pulling away once more. He was then aware of the sound of traffic again. A few turns left and right and they seemed to be on their way.

The film ran its course.

'Now, Mr Bryant, we don't want any alarms raised with the lovely Amelia…'

Bryant snapped. 'It's not the lovely Amelia to you. To you, my friend, she is, and will remain Mrs Bryant. Understand?'

Morgan was taken aback, and quickly withdrew the familiarity. 'I am sorry, sir. I was just trying to…'

'Well, don't.' The very mention of his wife's name had conjured a vision of their bucolic bliss in the Suffolk village of Oakshott, the family dream home near the picturesque Norman church; Amelia sitting on the swing chair sipping a chilled Pinot Grigio; the two children, Poppy, aged seven, and Daisy, just turned six, playing in the back garden – even his beloved white Labrador, Elsa, laid out in the sun keeping the expenditure of energy to a minimum. Bryant's eyes pricked at the vivid image. He shook himself free of the reverie.

'We don't mean to keep you for long and don't want your family to become worried and do something silly like alert the police. I believe we have covered our tracks extremely well, but we don't want them sniffing around anyway. Will you be kind enough to send a message to your wife and let her know you've been detained on business and will be taking a flight somewhere tonight. Let's say for four nights. You'll return Sunday. We already know you can go at short or no notice if a story demands it. Okay?'

Brilliant, thought Bryant. Absolutely brilliant. He couldn't believe his luck. He reached in his pocket and pulled out his mobile phone. Glancing down at the screen, he saw he had two messages, both from Geoff Woodcock. 'Two messages from my editor,' Bryant announced.

'Read them. No. Don't read them. He may request read notices. No. Leave it for now. I'll give it some thought.'

'As you wish. Now, what do you want me to write?'

'Anything you like. We'll look at it before you send it anyway.'

Bryant thought about sneaking a look at Woodcock's messages, but shied away not knowing what sort of surveillance equipment his captors had on board. He didn't need to read the messages to know that Woodcock would be marching up and down in the corridors between the desks in the newsroom shouting, 'Where's Bryant? That's the last time he writes for us. He's finished.' Every senior member of the staff had been threatened with the sack at some stage, usually a couple of times a week. To his knowledge, Woodcock had never actually fired anybody. Once the paper was out on the streets the editor changed from a snarling Rottweiler to a cuddly poodle. He smiled at the contrasting images and started to text his message to Amelia.

Bryant tapped out the message and handed the mobile to Morgan.

Morgan read the text. 'Sounds plausible,' he said and pressed the send button. Morgan took his own phone from his pocket and after a short delay gave Ramsey an instruction. 'Send for Walker to come forward, please.'

A few minutes later, the van rolled to a halt and the side door slid open four or five inches. Morgan handed the mobile phones to a gloved hand; a motorcyclist, Bryant pondered.

'Can't be too careful,' he said to Bryant. 'Don't want the boys in blue knocking on the door the minute we get there.'

Bryant had tried to get a peek through the opening to see if he recognised any landmarks. Not a thing. It was just an anonymous street on the outskirts of London. The shadow of the van was on the driver's side but that didn't really tell him anything apart from the van was facing north. It could have been facing north in Wimbledon or Romford or Brentford.

At nearly 10.00 p.m., the van came to a stop. After a muffled exchange of words from outside, it moved forward a few metres. It stopped and moved forward again, this time for twenty or thirty seconds. The door was opened by an armed man with the same familiar uniform as his captors.

'After you,' said Morgan to Bryant, indicating the open door with his left hand.

Even though it was now 10.00 p.m., the sky was not yet fully dark, but all he could make out were shadows. A building, fencing, car park. Lights were on in the building and he was faced with a revolving door that might be found at a hotel or office lobby. Above the door there was a black granite stone with gold-block writing announcing Plantagenet House.

Bryant took a few steps toward the door before holding back to wait for Morgan. He turned to see Morgan was only a couple of paces behind. Bryant's eyes widened at the shock of what he saw. Words caught in his throat, but eventually came, loud and clear. 'Jesus Christ. No!'

3

Amelia Bryant took her place in the queue at the Oakshott village post office, two from the front. She had received her husband's text message on Wednesday at 8.03 p.m. Poppy and Daisy were both in bed, the washing up was done and at the time, she was sitting in the conservatory reading the evening newspaper. Sean was expected home around 9.30 p.m. She wasn't expecting anyone to call so was sitting in her evening comfies: a pink T-shirt and light grey pyjama bottoms. Her right leg was tucked under her. Life was good. Their eighth wedding anniversary was now less than a week away and when Sean arrived home that evening he wouldn't be going back to work until the Monday after the anniversary.

Then the text had arrived. The double ping of the alert had drawn her from her reverie. She placed her glass of red wine on the window sill, pushed the paper to one side and went off in search of her iPhone. Unlike many of her friends, she hadn't made it an extension of her arm and was always putting it down in the most obscure places. She paused in the doorway between the conservatory and the lounge, cocked an ear and waited for the second alert. Ah! There it is, she thought, raising her right index finger in the air as if she had solved some great conundrum. It was on the hearth next to the coal scuttle. God knows how it got there? *One message: Sean*, the screen announced. She pressed the read button.

Sorry hun. Gotta go to Libya. Col G wants to talk to the

world through the EP. C U Sun. Got passport b4 u ask. Love XX.

'Fuck you, Sean Bryant,' she whispered. The words had been heard only by Elsa who raised her head from the floor with a quizzical look on her face, as if she were asking, 'Wanna talk about it?'

Amelia just smiled at the apparent concern and when no further words were uttered in Elsa's direction, she rested her big head on the floor and yawned at the apparent fuss. How many times did Amelia have to put up with this treatment? Other wives at the tennis club spoke about the control they had over their men. How? She couldn't imagine anyone controlling Sean.

Amelia immediately regretted cursing her husband and reddened slightly at the selfish thoughts about having to cancel the anniversary dinner on Saturday as it dawned on her that the message contained two code words they had worked out. The third code word in the message was passport.

Amelia went upstairs to the main bedroom and opened the bottom drawer of Sean's bedside table. There lay his passport. He was in trouble. Next to the passport was a small notebook, about A6 in size. She worked her way through the pages until she came to the end of the notes. The first nine pages had notes that had been crossed through, the meanings now redundant. She remembered how she had laughed at the thought of having these codes between them after he told her the story of how he helped put three armed robbers behind bars in the West Midlands three or four years before they met. She wasn't laughing now, but summoning all of her self-control to remain calm.

She ran her finger down the columns of recently concocted codes looking for the true meaning. The secret meanings were updated to reflect long-running news stories. 'Libya' meant Sean had been abducted and 'Col G' meant he wasn't sure why. If G had been Gaddafi written in full that would indicate it was the armed robbers who had him. Amelia mused for a moment about who else it could be. Sure, some of his forthright writing had upset politicians, sports personalities and other celebrities, but without doubt all would move on within a short time and forget about it. In short, she could not think of anyone. Sean had always told her that all publicity was good. Remember, he had said, today's newspaper is tomorrow's fish and chip paper. A smile played on her lips; she had no idea that newspaper was once the wrapping for takeaway fish dishes. How unhygienic! Yuck!

The leader of that small band of thugs had threatened to kill all those who had given evidence against him resulting in a fourteen-year sentence. Randolph Soames had now been out of prison since April, having served eleven years. It was judged that he was no longer a threat to society. Bryant did not agree and had many sleepless nights after he learned of the release. He could still remember the wild rant and the deathly glare from the dock as the three men were led away.

Soames had received the longest term of the three. Fourteen years seemed fair. Stephen Patrick had been given a nine-year term and released from his incarceration in 2005 and as far as Bryant knew, had been as upstanding a citizen as one could be after his earlier career choice. He managed to get menial employment which he would keep for a time before the employer was tipped the wink about his previous. Bryant was convinced that the then-still-imprisoned ringleader had been behind these tip-offs in a bid to keep Patrick onside.

The third member of the gang was a young black kid called Dwight Carter. Carter had been the getaway driver, doing the job even before he had passed his driving test. When the sentences were passed down, Carter was two weeks short of his twentieth birthday. He was given five years. The sentence had shocked Bryant and the policeman who led the enquiry.

Shortly after Bryant had graduated as a journalist from

Portsmouth University he had taken a position as a trainee reporter with a provincial newspaper close to his home town of Ledbury in Herefordshire. He had met the copper while playing football for a Sunday league side and they had become good friends. Although only five years Bryant's senior, the policeman already held the rank of detective inspector and, in Bryant's opinion, was destined for the very top.

One night, Bryant had been due to meet the policeman in a Ledbury town centre pub, but a message was given to him from behind the bar that his friend had been delayed at work and would not be making it that night. There was only one other person in the pub. A bright-eyed black kid was playing darts on his own.

'Fancy a game?' Bryant asked.

The kid, who was actually only two years younger than himself, viewed him with suspicion. 'Why?' he eventually asked, the Birmingham accent easily detected, even in the one word.

'My mate's stood me up and I've got a whole pint to finish before I go.'

'And you don't mind playing with a no-hope black kid?'

'No. Why should I?'

They played darts, they drank some beer and a friendship grew. Dwight Carter had maintained he was a student: a student, however, who was not sure what he was studying. One night it would be brickwork and building, the next something to do with cars. Eventually, one night, the truth came out. They had met for a drink in the pub and were sitting at the bar, each with a pint of lager. Bryant rolled a cigarette, lit it and noticed out of the corner of his eye his new friend was captivated by a news story on the small portable television perched behind the bar.

'What's up?' Bryant asked.

Carter raised his right hand to quieten him.

Bryant turned to the TV, but the volume was low. 'Nick,' he

summoned the barman. 'Turn the volume up, mate.'

There had been an armed robbery at a village post office, the latest in a series of similar raids on small convenience stores, garages, pubs and the like going back over three years. The difference this time was that there had actually been a shot fired – and there had been a group of young children in buying sweets on their way home from school. The shot had narrowly missed a small girl. Police were seeking two black men and a white man in connection with the robbery.

'She pissed herself. It was horrible,' said Carter, taking a slug from his beer.

'What?' asked an astonished Bryant.

Nothing more needed to be said. Tears were rolling down Carter's face. Bryant was sure nobody else had heard.

'Come on, mate, let's go get some air.' Bryant helped the youngster to his feet.

'Is he all right?' asked the barman.

Bryant nodded. 'Just feels a bit peculiar. Needs some air.'

By this time, Bryant had his own flat in Ledbury so the pair headed there. They sat on the worn armchairs Bryant had acquired from an uncle. 'You make it sound like you were there?'

Carter leaned forward, elbows on his knees and chin resting in his hands. He sighed: 'I was. Um, I've been at 'em all for the last three years.'

Carter went on to explain how he was normally the driver, but had persuaded Soames he wanted more of the action. Soames agreed as the job was a small rural post office and Patrick drove the car. The shop was empty until the school kids had come in. At the sight of the stocking-faced thugs they began to scream. Soames fired a shot to quieten them. One of the little girls began crying and shaking, the colour drained from her face and a pool formed at her feet. As Carter looked on, an image of his young niece danced across his thoughts. From that moment he wanted out; it was time to change!

Bryant and Carter agreed they would set up a meeting with the copper where a deal would be done to protect Carter if he gave evidence against his accomplices. The policeman took the deal to his seniors who ratified it, but the judge had not read the script and sent Carter away for five years.

After the court case, all Bryant wanted to do was go to his friend and say sorry. But he never saw Carter again and Carter never saw his twentieth birthday. Bryant was sitting alone in his flat when the news came through that Carter had been murdered in prison. Not a single person was ever convicted of the killing, but Soames openly bragged that he was behind the death. The crook made it clear that he was not a man to be messed with and let it be known from inside his cell that the journalist and copper were also on the list. Soames and Carter were sent to different prisons, but Soames's brother, Charlton, and Carter were in the same one. The rumours would not go away. The message was clear and loud: no one messed with Randolph Soames.

Amelia handed her letter to the postmaster and asked for recorded delivery to the now Detective Chief Inspector Duncan Cobbold of the London Metropolitan Police. It was Friday, so she didn't expect to hear anything until the following week. She had made many attempts during the previous twenty-four hours to contact Cobbold on the mobile number she had for her husband's friend, but to no avail. Plan B was the antiquated postal system, but it would have to do.

From the post office she crossed over the road and walked along to the primary school. It was brightening after a dull misty start. Des Leadbetter, the jolly publican of the Fox and Hounds, was sweeping down the forecourt of the pub.

'Morning, Des,' Amelia greeted from the other side of the road.

'Mornin', Amelia. 'Ope yer keepin' well.'

'Fine, thanks,' she lied and waved. 'Have a good day.'

He leaned on his broom and reciprocated the wave before turning back to his work.

Amelia continued, passing the little duck pond before turning into the school gate. Gillian Francis, the head teacher, looked up from her desk and came to welcome her. Not really protocol, but the two women exchanged cheek kisses.

'Amelia, how are you. Nothing we've done, I hope.'

'No, good heavens, no.'

Gillian had been good friends with Amelia and Sean for more than three years. Her divorce from Craig had been acrimonious. Most of the village had taken pity on her and seen Craig as a lazy good-for-nothing who gambled and drank away her salary. The pair had been declared bankrupt and Gillian had moved into the old schoolhouse which, luckily for her, had been vacated by the retired caretaker. The move had, in effect, made her neighbours with Amelia and Sean, even though they were on different roads and were parted by about 250 metres of field. Gillian had remained loyal to the village that had given her a supporting shoulder, despite county encouraging her to take a larger school with less successful OFSTED inspections. Her school had been marked good with many aspects outstanding. And that was the mark she had given to the village with which she had now fallen in love.

The friendship had preceded Poppy starting school. Amelia and Sean had been prepared to find another school for the sake of the friendship, but Gillian would have none of it and they set out a way forward that either party could walk away from without risking the bond built up over the years.

'What is it, then?' asked Gillian.

'Oh God, where to start! Gill, can I speak in confidence? I mean strict confidence.'

'Of course,' said Gillian, getting up from her chair and closing the door. 'Go on.'

'Sean's disappeared.' She let the words hang in the air for a few moments.

'When? How? I mean. I only saw him Wednesday morning when I was out jogging.'

'Remember we told you about the coded messages.'

'Yeah. I do.'

Amelia pulled out her mobile phone and flicked through the messages and passed the gadget to her friend. 'This came through Wednesday night.'

Gillian read it. It meant nothing. Shaking her head she asked: 'What does it mean?'

'He's been abducted. But he doesn't know why or by whom.'

'And you think it's Soames?' Gill knew the history of murder and threats.

'Can't be anyone else.'

'He's a journalist. It could be.'

'Anyway, Gill. What I really want – and I know you wouldn't allow it anyway – is that you won't let anyone else take the girls in the evening, no matter how well you know them or trust them. If I'm not here, I won't be far.'

'Consider it done.'

'Thanks.'

Amelia turned off The Street into Church Lane, still carrying the weight of worry. A blue Mercedes saloon was coming up the road and slowing for the junction. She made eye contact with the driver and shuddered. A black man smiled back. She quickened her step and broke into a trot as she approached home. She didn't pay any attention to the farmer in the field taking crop samples, checking readiness for harvest.

Curtly Richardson sat on a sun-lounger on the foredeck of Deck 5 on the Seabourn Cruise ship *Legend*. He had boarded at the southern Italian port town of Sorrento as a special guest of its captain, an old friend, William Bathgate. A waiter had just delivered a generous port and a cup of Americano coffee. That sat on the squat table to his side. He was stretched out on the lounger, necktie of his black tuxedo suit undone. Formal dress, he reflected. That was the last time he would fall for that one. Apart from him there had been only one other man in the restaurant dressed the same. And that was the captain, a so-called friend! Others were dressed formally simply by draping a complimentary jacket over the chair. Nearly 500 euros!

Then, there had been the infernal Esther Lowbender. Esther had been a guest at the captain's table for dinner and Richardson had had the misfortune of sitting next to the plump Floridian.

'Curtly!' she had exclaimed at Richardson's introduction. 'That's a funny name.' And after no one joined in with her hysterical cackle, and to reinforce the point, 'My word. So it is. A funny name!'

'You can call me Curt,' he said sharply.

She had been polite enough, but had dominated Richardson's evening like a young puppy brought a rawhide treat. Even the red wine had failed to shut her out. He exchanged the briefest of conversations on his beloved cricket with an Englishman across the table then heard her say, 'My husband says cricket is the stupidest game in the world. You play for days on end and no one wins.' The cackling laugh was this time accompanied by pig-sounding snorts. Richardson peered back at the Englishman, seeking a safe harbour in a known port. The other man turned away to strike up a conversation with a total stranger. Richardson got the message and glugged a three-quarter glass of red.

'My husband says too much red wine gives you gout!'

I bet your bloody husband is sitting at home in the sublime silence of an early Miami evening drinking gallons of the stuff, and at the start of each glass raising a toast to absent friends.

'What do you do for work, Curt?' Esther asked when Richardson was nearing the end of his dessert and was dreaming of a getaway.

'I'm a civil servant,' he replied. Indeed, he was a public servant in the employ of Her Britannic Majesty. A pen-pusher behind a desk he certainly was not. In truth, he was one of only half a dozen crack pairs brought together to protect British interests at home and abroad. They had one commander, an ex-policeman named Duncan Cobbold, who held the title of Detective Chief Inspector. Apart from Cobbold, they were responsible only to one other, and that was the Home Secretary. Each pair was made up of a policeman, in this case Richardson, and a Special Forces operative, as was his partner, Michael Jones. The pair had just been on baby-sitting duty at a summit in Rome that was discussing the Middle East. An ex-British Prime Minister had been attending with Richardson, and Jones added to his retinue as extra eyes and ears. The summit passed without incident. The former PM left for a break in Tuscany, Jones had headed back to England and Richardson, after phoning his old friend, the sea captain, had boarded a train for Naples and then a local rattler to Sorrento.

'My husband says public servants are a waste of money and that is why the world is in such a financial mess.'

Richardson balled his fists under the table. He was well trained in all methods of keeping cool in stressful scenarios. This woman, however, was testing his resolve far more than any terrorist had ever done. This was his private time.

'Does he, indeed?' Richardson snapped. 'And, pray tell, what does he do?'

'Oh. He's an investment banker. And very important too.'

'Sometimes,' Richardson started thoughtfully, 'it might be worth the important investment banker looking in the mirror and debating the truth of the causes of financial ruin. I'm sure if he is as intelligent as you make him out to be he will find the true reasons.'

'Oh! He often discusses it with all sorts of people including poor folk. He always wins the argument as he is very strong. We all know that poor folk cause financial angst for the rest of us. That's what my husband says, anyway.'

'A bully more like,' Richardson whispered to the captain,

before turning back to Mrs Lowbender. 'I would like to meet your husband, madam. I believe educated debate can play a part.'

'He wouldn't discuss it with you. He thinks black folk are less intelligent and doesn't like them too much.' Mrs Lowbender didn't realise she was being offensive and hadn't even noticed that the rest of the table had stopped talking and were concentrating on the exchange between the gentle Englishman and the inbred bigot from Florida. Oblivious, she continued, 'I, on the other hand, think there is a place for men like you.' She affectionately stroked the man's massive bicep.

He didn't reply, but turned to Bathgate and asked, 'Apart from my suite, where can I go for a bit of lonely and tranquil peace?'

So here he was on the outside foredeck just below the bridge and under the stars. The sun had slid into the oily sea beside Vesuvius two hours earlier to be replaced in the heavens by an almost full moon. He had been staring at the silver avenue running from the horizon when the waiter appeared with his order.

Richardson had fallen in love with Sorrento. Or had he fallen in love with Augusta, the beautiful dancer he had met only two nights ago? After travelling to the end of the suburban line on a rattling train with nothing more than a shoulder-bag, he had strolled to the hotel along the Corsa Italia, through the Piazza Tasso, named after the famous Sorrentine poet, and on into the lanes of the old town. He passed a church in which a wedding was taking place, where the accents were clearly of a Welsh origin rather than Italian, and onto the Hotel Tramontano perched on cliff tops with a panoramic view of the Bay of Naples. On the edge of the old town he had seen a theatre with posters advertising a performance about Sorrento life. After freshening up in his suite, which had a sea view from the balcony, he made his way back to the theatre and bought a ticket.

34

That evening he had set out early to grab a bite before the show. He found his seat after a glass of wine in the terraced bar. The auditorium was by no means full. The seating, spacious and comfortable, was in three banks with two aisles. He found himself sitting in an aisle seat closest to the right-hand walkway. The show got underway with rousing renditions of many Italian classics. He even recognised some of them as they were knitted into the tale of daily life in Sorrento. The fishermen set sail into the Bay of Naples to cast their nets, before returning to sell their catch in the old market place. The story, all in Italian, was not difficult to follow, and the final scene was a Sorrentine fiesta. The dancers spilled over from the stage and into the aisles. Now he knew why the audience had been seated along the aisles rather than in the centre. His toes were tapping, roughly in time with the beat. An attractive woman dancer took position next to him. He didn't want to make eye contact, for fear of being dragged to his feet and proving what a useless dancer he was, but the girl's eyes were full of a fiery vibrancy that had him captivated and then captured. He didn't want to dance, but before he could fend her off he was on his feet and whirling around. Although a fit man, Richardson had the dancing ability of a man with two right legs made of iron. However, the girl took control, her firm hold steering him in the right direction like an equestrian would guide a horse. Lights whirled about. Her fiery dark eyes reflected the light in flashes of sparkling reds and yellows. The brilliant smile, which could have lightened the room alone, had him mesmerised. The music stopped. Richardson and the girl faced one another, applauding. He affected a bow of sorts. Her, a low curtsy.

'Grazi, señor,' she said.

'No,' he replied. 'It is I who should thank you!'

He regained his seat and continued applauding until his hands were sore. The audience was then invited to join the cast on the terrace for some complimentary champagne. Richardson took his glass and made his way to the railing at the back. Stars twinkled in the sky. Lights flickered in and around the bay. The great hulk of Vesuvius slept. He was in a dreamy stupor, but he was aware of a woman by his side. The fragrance gave away her presence first. He turned to see that same captivating smile.

'I never tire of this view, Englishman.'

'I understand why,' he confirmed. Indeed, it was breathtaking.

She sipped her wine. 'Are you on vacation, señor?'

'Sort of. I've just finished a job in Rome and came down here for a couple of days. The day after tomorrow I will meet up with a cruise ship and disappear.'

The smile changed to a scowl. 'That is a shame. Sorrento, it is so beautiful.'

'Yes. I agree,' he said, sipping his wine.

'What are you going to do? What do you mean to see?' she enquired, moving closer.

It was a heady cocktail: hairspray and perfume mixed with her own sweet scent.

'I don't really know,' he said gazing in the direction of the dormant volcano. 'I wouldn't mind going up there.'

'Me as well,' she replied. 'I go with you. Tomorrow?'

And so they went to the top of the mountain and looked back at Sorrento. They went to Pompeii and looked back at Vesuvius from the ruins of the Roman forum. It was a hot and dusty day and a shower was as welcome as a rainstorm in a drought. He returned to the theatre and watched the spectacle all over again. He had the same seat and danced with the same girl. After champagne on the terrace they ate at Augusta's favourite rooftop restaurant. The following day, they wandered through the old town and Richardson got kitted out for the cruise – case, tux, shoes, shirts, even deck shoes.

The goodbye had to come as sure as the sun rose in the mornings. As inevitable as parting was, the hurt was so painful. Richardson knew he had found the woman with which to share his life. They had been together for a paltry two days, but he knew. It was like blundering into a huge rock on a country lane; you couldn't move it and you couldn't go round it. He had never before felt like this, yet they weren't even lovers. He knew there was room on the ship, for Jonah had turned down an invite to cruise, quoting his young age as a barrier. She declined the offer, pragmatically, putting contract before love. Not instead of love, she had assured him, for her heart would dance for him every night.

They watched the tender bouncing its way across the bay from the ship. They held one another. He promised her he would return later in the summer. She promised him she was already counting the days. The parting kiss was not even a kiss of lovers. The tender chopped its way back to the ship. He could still return with it. The distance was still swimmable and he could throw himself in the sea and make his way back to her arms. He stared at her picture on the screen of his mobile. No one noticed the teardrop from an eye of granite fall to the picture.

All it was now was a sweet memory.

'Ah! There you are.' It was the loud and slightly tipsy Mrs Lowbender. 'The waiter said you were out here. I've bin lookin' for ya.'

'Oh,' was all the acknowledgment he could muster.

'My word,' Mrs Lowbender exclaimed, pointing at the bow of the ship with her wine glass, the contents of which were sloshing from side to side. 'The pointy bit.'

'That's the bow,' he corrected with heavy disdain.

'Will you do me the honour, Curtly?' she slurred.

'Honour?' he queried. Like throw you overboard, he thought. After all, it would make the rest of the cruise more pleasant.

'Let me climb up like the woman in *Titanic*?'

Innocent enough, he thought, but he was keen not to indicate there was any chance of it going any further. 'If you must.'

'I must,' she insisted then took a none-too-straight line to the pointy bit and climbed up on the railing. 'Hold me, Curt. Hold me real tight, now.'

Seeing how precarious her actions were, he held his arms around her podgy middle. She extended her arms out like a floundering bird trying to take off. Then she started to sing. Apart from it being out of tune, lacking melody, and being the wrong song altogether, it was perfect.

'Everything I do, I do it for you,' she blurted. He didn't have the heart to tell her it was the wrong theme.

His mobile phone rang in his trouser pocket and he was suddenly forced to juggle his grip on the cut-price Kate Winslet with fumbling for the phone. He glanced at the screen – it was Duncan – then pressed the answer button. 'Duncan, how are you?'

He lowered Mrs Lowbender to the deck, loosening his grip as he did so. An unexpected wave sent her sprawling to the floor like a freshly landed fish with legs. As much as she tried to coerce her legs to stability there was no reaction.

'Fine, thank you,' replied the technical chief of the UK Home Security Team. The only person Duncan Cobbold answered to was the Home Secretary. He could never be brought before parliament to answer for his actions for one simple reason: officially, the Home Security Team did not exist. All of its operatives were paid by their former employers. In the case of Curtly Richardson, Hampshire Police. Michael Jones, the SAS.

'Good. I hope this is a social call? But I suspect not.'

'Very perceptive. You should go far!'

'Ha bloody ha!' Richardson watched his companion regain her unsteady feet.

Cobbold went on to explain that Sean Bryant had been

38

abducted. By whom they weren't sure. Randolph Soames was the only one in the frame at present, but most were agreed that the means by which the kidnapping was carried out was well above the Soames' station. Soames, however, was also on the missing list, as was the other surviving gang member, Stephen Patrick. Cobbold had reviewed the CCTV tapes from the *Echo and Post* and was convinced it was not Soames and Patrick. But they needed to be found and eliminated from enquiries.

Cobbold went on to brief Richardson about what he expected him and Jones to do. A Sea King was already on its way from Brindisi, and should be over the *Legend* in less than forty minutes.

'I'd better pack my bags?'

'Don't worry about that. Just get changed out of that penguin suit.'

'What? How do you...?'

'It's above you. Pretty amazing, isn't it, this satellite technology. Give me a wave.'

Richardson involuntarily looked into the heavens.

'Nice smile! Who's your friend, by the way?'

Richardson turned to Mrs Lowbender, who was now managing to stand unaided. 'Esther. Give my friend, Duncan, a wave.'

Mrs Lowbender wore a puzzled look. Richardson pointed skywards. She looked skywards. He waved to the empty darkness. And, after a further moment of confusion, so did Mrs Lowbender. Her legs immediately gave way as another wave moved her centre of gravity and she hit the deck like a blancmange falling off a table.

Richardson, hearing Cobbold chuckling down the line, ended the call and bent to help his unwanted admirer. 'Have you got any of that stuff left?' she slurred again. 'It must be good.'

Richardson bade farewell to his sea captain friend, giving him assurances that there was nothing in his luggage that would embarrass the upright sailor. He changed into black jeans and black polo shirt and made his way up the central spiral staircase and aft of Deck 8. Bathgate had slowed the ship to a couple of knots and before long, the whirring, chopping sound of the aircraft's blades could be heard. The yellow monster hovered above the stern deck. Richardson climbed into the harness dangling on the rope and to the astonishment of the passengers who had gathered at the commotion, was whisked away.

Mrs Lowbender ordered some more wine.

Richardson touched down at RAF Wattisham in the early hours after a two and a half hour flight from Brindisi. Michael Jones was there to meet him.

'Hey, Jonah. I can't say it's nice to see you. But here I am anyway.'

The smiles exchanged were warm. Jones tossed Richardson the car keys. Richardson gunned the engine and they headed to the sleepy Suffolk village of Oakshott, no more than five miles away. After a short stop at a rented house, Jones acquainted Richardson with the area – roads in, roads out, woods, streams, that sort of thing. Richardson dropped Jones off and after allowing him a few minutes to gain position posing as a farmer testing a cereal crop, drove off.

He went past the church on the left, followed by a small farm, open fields on the right. The Bryant home, an attractive two-storey detached house with garage, was next on the left. Richardson continued along Church Road toward the village. A woman was walking towards him on the opposite side of the road. Well, I never, he thought; is that who I think it is? Richardson bent to get a better look at Amelia Bryant as he drove past. Eye contact was made. All that was reflected back was cold fear. He looked in his driver's side mirror and watched the woman break into a jog.

4

'I think I spooked her,' Richardson said into his phone. He was sitting in his blue Mercedes in the Fox and Hounds car park.

'How so?' Cobbold asked.

'I don't know really. Um, we just made eye contact. There was a primeval fear in her eyes. They instantly lost their sparkle and she was on her way.'

'Um, I'm gonna have to get you in there. I guess she thinks you're Randolph Soames stalking her.'

'Just 'cause I'm black. Jumping to conclusions a bit, isn't it?'

'Just look around. How many blacks do you see? A bit thin on the ground, I would say! Yes?'

'Okay,' Richardson agreed. 'Who are the kidnappers? And where are the deadly duo? And another thing. Why are you so sure that Soames is not behind this? He's the only one with motive.'

'True. Remember, though, Bryant is a journalist. They tend to be pretty effective at dividing opinion and making enemies.'

'Tomorrow's fish and chip paper, though!'

'Huh! I'll bring the disks with me and I'm sure you will come to the same conclusion. It isn't Soames.'

'Where is he then?'

'That's another matter,' sighed Cobbold. 'And for sure, he needs to be caught. Anyway. I'll text you when you can call on Mrs Bryant.'

Amelia had fumbled with the key at the door before the lock

clicked and she let herself in. The door locked, bolted and chained behind her, she slumped on the doormat, her back against the door, sobbing. She tried to pull herself together, but all the will in the world couldn't bring her out through the fence of fear that had engulfed her in the last few minutes. Was that Randolph Soames she had just seen? She rubbed her eyes and wiped her nose with her palm. God, she was scared.

The shrill of the phone ringing in the study made her heart skip a beat before racing ahead ferociously. The study phone was too exposed to the outside. She climbed the stairs and took the one in the bedroom.

'Hello,' she rasped.

'Hello, Amelia,' the caller announced with a calm assuredness. 'It's Duncan Cobbold. How are you?'

'Oh my God, Duncan.' She collapsed on the bed with relief and started to chunter, trying her best to sound in control. 'I've just posted you a letter. How did you know so quick? He's here. He's after me.'

'No, Amelia, he's not.' Cobbold tried to reassure, but his words felt hollow.

'How do you know?' she shrieked. 'I've seen him with my own eyes. Only five minutes ago. He's here, I tell you.'

'No, Amelia. Listen.' He tried to be more assertive. He needed to quell her hysteria and soothe her angst. 'I have men on the ground keeping a watch over you. They were going to keep up the vigil until I could make it up there. You're not in any danger. The man you saw is one of my best. His name is Curtly Richardson and he and his partner, Michael Jones, will be popping by very shortly.'

'I'm so sorry, Duncan. You must think me such a fool. That bloody man.'

Cobbold surmised the last comment was aimed at Amelia's husband. But it might have been Richardson or Soames. Who cared?

'Just to let you know, I won't be around to receive your

note. Woodcock from the *Echo and Post* alerted me. Richardson will fill you in with the rest when he gets there. I'll see you in the next few days.'

Amelia took a handkerchief from the top drawer of her bedside table and dabbed her eyes and cheeks. She went through to the en suite and splashed her face with cold water and dabbed again, this time with a towel. Holding the hankie scrunched up in her palm, she returned downstairs. At the bottom tread the doorbell rang. A glimpse in the mirror and a final wipe of her unmade face and she opened the door.

'Good morning, ma'am,' said the tall black man with the shaven head. This time the face appeared gentle and open, the smile wide and dazzling. How could she have mistaken this affable fellow in front of her for a wicked, scheming murderer?

'My name is Curtly Richardson, and this is Michael Jones.' He gestured to the other tall man standing slightly to his right and behind. 'We work for Duncan Cobbold. And, Mrs Bryant, I'm sorry I spooked you earlier.'

'That's fine,' she smiled, a sense of security returning. 'Please come in.'

The two men entered, Jones running his eye over the front door to ensure it was secure. He noted it to be unusually thick, with four sturdy hinges, a star-key operated bolt top and bottom and a generous five-lever lock. Good, he thought, seeing Cobbold's advice at work.

'Please excuse the kitchen,' Amelia apologised. 'Let's sit in the conservatory. Tea, coffee, anyone?'

Both men accepted.

'Do you have any news?' Amelia asked from the kitchen.

'Nothing substantial,' said Richardson. 'We're not really abreast of the investigation. Cobbold will be here in the next day or so, so I'm sure he'll fill you in. At this time we are only here to look after your security.'

A tip-tapping on the tiled floor was followed by Amelia

bringing through a tray of coffee, cups and biscuits. A very attentive Elsa, the golden Labrador, was in close attendance.

'Hope you don't mind dogs, guys,' Amelia said in a manner that hinted a negative reply was tough.

Coffee served, biscuits dished, and Elsa dutifully sitting in front of Jones who took the first biscuits, Amelia sat down on the wicker sofa.

'I know that Sean and Duncan have been very close over the years,' Amelia stated. 'But did any of you guys know my husband?'

Jones made his excuses and left, using the security of the property as a reason.

Richardson placed his mug on a coaster on the low window board. 'I've met or rather seen him on a number of occasions, but only when I've been involved with Cobbold. I've never actually spoken to him for a long time. So, I s'pose, I don't really know him. I have read some of his articles, though.'

'What do you know about the gang who have Sean?'

Richardson caught movement from the corner of his eye and turned his gaze in the direction of Jones, who was now in the garden testing the strength of fence posts. Richardson reckoned the property was reasonably secure, but knew that Jones would find something to fault. Watching Jones for those few seconds had given him time to consider his answer. He did not want to frighten Amelia any more than she already was. Her face was still betraying the fear of an hour ago.

'Well,' Richardson began, sitting back and interlocking his fingers, as if in deep thought. 'Firstly, Cobbold doesn't believe it's Soames and Patrick who have Sean. He says Sean's abduction was extremely professional and involved too many men. He's seen the CCTV footage from outside the newspaper's offices and he's bringing us a copy to look at.

'Anyway,' he continued. 'To be honest, from what I know, Stephen Patrick is a reasonable bloke. Just got caught up with the wrong people. Thought it was cool to be black, even though he's white. Could say he got caught up with the wrong sort of blacks.'

'Sean wouldn't necessarily agree with you. He always maintains that the lad who died in prison was a good bloke and if things had worked out better and, to be fair, as planned, he would have got on with his life and made something of it. Apparently, he was very bright.'

Richardson smiled and shook his head. 'I've heard that as well. Cobbold reckons he's probably the most intelligent person he's ever met.'

'And brave,' added Amelia.

'None braver,' agreed the policeman. 'Died a martyr, I would say.'

'Are you mocking me, Mr Richardson?'

'Good Lord! No. No, not at all. But whatever people think of Dwight Carter eleven years after his death is irrelevant. Our friend Dwight could have helped more if he had plucked up the courage to do something about it earlier. Who knows? We might not be sitting here now if he had.'

'Are you not sympathetic with him, then?'

Richardson pondered his answer as Jones reappeared with a set of steps and a coil of barbed wire. 'Never really thought about it, if I'm honest. I tend to look to the future rather than dwell on the past.'

'What's he doing?' asked Amelia, cupping her mug in both hands and staring in Jones's direction as if transfixed by the devil on horseback himself trotting up the lawn.

'Just making the back garden more secure.'

'Why?'

'The regular police have lost contact with Soames and Patrick.'

Amelia didn't answer, but the concerned look in her eyes made Richardson elaborate.

'It's quite ironic, actually. We were following their every move for a while. Cobbold thought them a threat a while back. We knew exactly where they were and what they were planning from monitoring their mobile phones. We hacked their texts and voicemails, listened to their conversations, and knew where they were from their phone signals. Then, when the phone hacking became big news a week or so ago, it stopped. Even the dumbest of thugs can change their tactics.

'There is absolutely no question about it, Soames wants Cobbold and Sean dead.'

Amelia gasped. Even though she and Sean had discussed it, it had never seemed real. It was now. 'He won't want to kill me? Will he?' she asked weakly.

Richardson averted his gaze. 'That might be the case, but Soames believes Cobbold was only doing his job. And, in a perverse sort of a way, he sees Sean as an interferer, and has threatened you all.'

Amelia placed her mug on the coffee table and slumped back in the chair and blew out her cheeks. Her heart had missed a beat. She thought the teary floodgates should have reopened, but the utter shock had blocked the ducts and the tears never came. It felt as if her heart had bounced up into her throat and was choking off her breath.

Richardson knew he couldn't have told her of the deaths that Soames had planned for her and the children. Sean himself would be last, though, with a bullet to the head. The last images he would see on this earth were the bloodied, tortured and mutilated corpses of his dearest Amelia, Poppy, and Daisy. The only advantage the police had over Soames and Patrick was that the latter didn't know where Bryant and his family lived, nor did they know who Bryant was married to, even if he was married, or if there were any children.

Amelia composed herself. 'Why don't you just arrest them?'

'A fair question. The trouble is, Cobbold has had to call in favours to get the phones monitored. The authorities wouldn't sanction the tapping. Therefore, because the bugging is, in essence, illegal, they cannot be simply arrested. The Home

Security Team has a nearly bottomless pit when it comes to budget, and with the Home Secretary's approval, here we are. Soames and Patrick will not get through.'

Richardson went on to explain how every way into Oakshott was under guard. All roads had hidden cameras linked to a central computer with state of the art number plate and facial recognition software. Every car number registered in Oakshott was already stored on the computer, as was the name of every person on the electoral roll. Any suspicious vehicle or person would be identified before they had even passed the camera. If there was still any doubt, an unmarked car would be sent to investigate. Only as a last resort would vehicles or people be intercepted and questioned.

In addition, there was a visible police presence made up from a combination of local and special units sent by New Scotland Yard. In effect, Oakshott was surrounded by an impenetrable blue fence.

Jones entered the conservatory. 'That should do it. If they get through, one of them will get a nasty shock when they grab hold of the top of the fence.'

Amelia winced.

John Connelly was now back in a prison cell, this time it was for stealing a car. It was alleged he had breached his parole conditions, so had been remanded prior to going to trial. It wasn't easy to get by after coming out of prison and even sitting in his cell, there was a sense of security; three meals a day, a warm room with a roof over, and clean bedding – certainly more acceptable than a shop doorway on a bitterly cold February night.

Randolph Soames had told him to get rid of the car after his job was complete, but who would find out? The number plates had been changed. The copper had agreed with the Irish rascal that it was not against the law for an Irishman to be driving a BMW on a 2009 plate. But where he did have a problem was that the index number was registered to a pink Vauxhall 200 miles away. Connelly had rolled his eyes toward the sky and proffered his wrists for the handcuffs. He hadn't been out for six weeks.

He had been offered £1,500 cash from Soames for carrying out the easiest job he had ever done in his life. This bloke, a reporter called Sean Bryant, had wronged Soames in the past and he now wanted to know everything about him. The only clue was that Bryant worked for the London *Echo and Post* as an investigative journalist. Not the smartest bunch in the world, Connelly had thought when he found a photograph of this so-called top journo on the paper's website. Armed with this image he set off in pursuit of his prey. It took about a week all told.

On the first day, he had been standing across the road from the *Echo* office and seen who he thought was Bryant coming out for a cigarette. To confirm his target, he had wandered across and asked him for a light. Later that evening, he watched him board a train for Norwich. It was only stopping in three places: Colchester, Ipswich and its destination. Connelly purchased a return ticket to Norwich and got on the train a coach behind Bryant. Fifty minutes later the train arrived at Colchester. Connelly had never even heard of Colchester, yet it seemed as if half the passengers alighted in the Essex town. He had no idea whether Bryant had got off or not for the crowd had been too overwhelming.

Next stop, Ipswich. It seemed the same number of passengers got off. There was Bryant. As the train rolled out of the station, Connelly caught a glimpse of his prey climbing the stairs to cross the track.

The following day, Connelly returned to Ipswich to wait for Bryant to return. Sure enough, same train, same time. This time Connelly saw Bryant hop in a taxi that headed off in the Sainsbury's and Hadleigh direction. On the third day, Connelly stole a car from a village to the north of the town. Not a difficult job, but made easier by a careless woman leaving the keys in it outside a shop. She had even been generous enough to leave the engine running. In a field entrance, Connelly swapped the number plates for the ones Soames had given him.

For the next few evenings, Connelly parked up just along from the railway station and waited. Even though it was now April, dusk made the light murky and it was not easy to spot the target. Then, in the middle of the following week, there he was. Connelly followed the taxi to a beautiful cottage-type house in the village of Oakshott. Got him! Connelly exulted and rapped the steering wheel, whooping in delight.

The following day he returned and took pictures of the house. What a lovely family, Connelly thought, as he watched a woman, two little girls and an intelligent-looking dog on a lead. The girls were carrying bags, which he guessed contained school books and perhaps even lunch. A pang of guilt knotted his heart. He could drive away now and never see Soames again. Trouble was, he had been given only £500 and desperately needed the other £1,000.

Soames was more than pleased with the result and even threw in another £250. Connelly would rather not have known what Soames's intentions were. Almost every night, he had gone to bed with images of the poor innocents, including the dog, trussed and hanging by their feet from butcher's hooks, mutilated beyond recognition above a lake of blood.

He could tell the police; no, he was a small-time crook who didn't want to be embroiled in murder. He could tell the family; no, he just might turn up at the same time as Soames. In the end, he did nothing; he just waited for the television news to tell him that the brutal deed had been carried out.

Soames and Stephen Patrick had now dotted the Is and crossed the Ts and were planning to leave for Suffolk in the next few days.

5

Sean Bryant sat at a picnic table in the shade of an ancient oak as grand as any of the kings of trees. He was puffing on a rolled cigarette. There were three stubbed-out ends already in the ashtray. He was confused. He had now been in captivity for four nights. He should have been going home today, at least that's what he'd told Amelia in the text. He suspected he wouldn't be going anywhere very soon. If it wasn't for his worried family he probably wouldn't care, for the accommodation and surroundings were most agreeable, relaxing even.

The other confusion nagging away inside was his abduction. No mention had been given to it on the television news. Had Amelia understood the hidden message correctly? It was true, she had been appalled by the tale of Randolph Soames and his bullying crime spree in the late nineties. She had been appalled at the death of Dwight Carter and the way Soames had claimed the credit, even though Sean had suspected it to be coincidental and nothing more than bluster on behalf of Soames. But, when they reviewed the secret coding, Amelia was sometimes not as switched on as Bryant had thought she could be.

Still, there was nothing he could do about it from where he was. Amelia needed to do all the running. If he wasn't going to make it home tonight, which seemed more likely as every hour passed, perhaps the concern would grow then. Perhaps, he thought, Amelia had already made contact with Duncan

50

Cobbold, who now walked along curious and secretive avenues and maybe was keeping the whole thing quiet. There was no doubt the *Echo* would refrain from printing anything about his disappearance. Perhaps... Stop it, he chastised himself. Stop beating yourself up. The trouble was, analysis always led to anxiety, and anxiety always led to mind images of Amelia and the girls playing and prancing with Elsa on a sunlit lawn, images that then skipped across his vision.

Then reality dawned. He had no idea of his whereabouts in the country. He didn't even know if he was guest or prisoner. True, if the former, then guesthood had been forced upon him. He occupied a suite, really a large room, on the first floor of Plantagenet House overlooking the entrance gates and a barrier beyond. The complex consisted of two buildings: the guest block, where he was now in residence, and the prison block. The latter was roughly the same size as the first, but if rumours were to be believed, there was no doubting the status of its residents.

There was access to all modern needs except communication with the outside world. There was a television but no computer; there was a radio but no telephones; there were newspapers but no letters. There was a bar with complimentary beverages including beers, wines and spirits. There were other communal areas including television lounges and a library. It was clear that whoever was behind this establishment was not short of a bob or two.

The two buildings were surrounded by trees, an inner ring of conifers and an outer ring of British natives such as ash, lime, beech and birch. Inside the natural barricade was a man-made one in the form of a 10-feet-tall fence with a green liner to it. Bryant suspected that if someone were looking from beyond the trees, the complex could not be viewed. Between the two buildings there was a chain-link fence about 8-feet tall topped with barbed wire. No. A second glance proved it to be razor wire.

Bryant rolled another cigarette and leaned back to take the first drag. He closed his eyes and let the sun shower his face with warmth. There they were again. It was as if the memories of home were imaged on to the back of his eyelids, forever rolling like an unforgettable film. The pictures were not unpleasant, indeed, they were more than welcome, but they did prick his tear ducts. The moisture scrambled the brightness and a darkening mood descended in its place.

'A penny for them?' The voice was female.

'Oh! Um! Sorry. Miles away,' he replied. At least the intrusion had rid him of the swings between a dreamy ecstasy and the enveloping blackness of despair.

'May I join you?' she asked, smiling at the newcomer.

'Yes. Yes, of course. Be my guest. It will be nice to chat to someone.'

The woman's eyes caught the sunlight. They were a piercing blue. Not the same laser-like penetration, but without doubt this was the woman on the corporate DVD of the Civil Protection Group. There was no makeup in the vision now sitting in front of him, but the beauty was still striking. The woman, probably in her late thirties, displayed the effects of years of heavy exercise: narrow waist, flat stomach and femininely bulging biceps. Clearly not a bingo player!

'My name is Sue-Beth Walters, Mr Bryant.' She held out her hand.

He took it. The handshake was firm and not really ladylike. 'Oh!' he managed, pinned by the eyes. 'I'm Sean Brya... Ah, but, you know that anyway.'

Sue-Beth picked up his pouch of tobacco, pulled out a rolling paper and adeptly made herself a cigarette. Bryant flicked the cheap lighter into life and she drew hungrily on the nicotine-drenched smoke. 'Thank you.'

'You're the girl in the video? Yes?'

'I am. I suppose it was made a year or so ago. I guess the CPG will be looking for a new face for their promo videos now.'

'Oh! How come?'

He realised she was dressed similarly to him: white baggy T-shirt, loose-fitting blue jeans and black plimsolls. No insignia on her chest. The few guards, or hosts as they preferred to be called, were dressed entirely in black: polo shirts, cargo trousers and boots. They all bore a CPG insignia upon their chests. There were no such markings for those residing against their free choice at Plantagenet House.

'Simple; because I furnished you with some delicate information about the membership of one of our clients I was unceremoniously booted out of the organisation, and I'm now held as a guest, pending our inductions.' She took another drag on the burning tobacco. 'Or, put it another way, our trials.'

Bryant was even more confused. He lit another roll-up and mumbled, 'I've never met you before.' He would never have forgotten those eyes. He protested, 'This is meant to be my last day. I am supposed to be going home today.'

'There is no such thing as a last day in this place.' She waited for a reaction to the statement, but Bryant's face was blank with disbelief. 'Well. That's not strictly true,' she continued. 'Some, not all, are transferred to the prison block across the way.' She nodded with her head in the direction of the other building.

Bryant didn't need to follow the indication. He had studied the more austere-looking of the two buildings. 'To my original point,' he said, recovering his composure, 'I have never met you. And, who is the client?'

'Second bit first. I thought you would have worked that one out for yourself.' She watched the penny drop, and a slow nod betrayed the realisation. 'The first bit is true. Our only connection is that we live in the same village.'

'We do?' he asked with surprise.

'We do,' she confirmed. 'I live with my in-laws on the way to Ampsley. Do you know Crouch Hall Farm?'

'Ah, yeah. I know. Of course. Walters! Wasn't he a high-up

bloke in the army? A general or something?'

'Army family, through and through. Sir James is a retired general and a nicer man you couldn't hope to meet. He and Lady Isobel have put up with me ever since my husband was killed.'

'I'm sorry,' Bryant said with meaning. He imagined Amelia dead and thought he wouldn't cope.

'He was Colonel Nathan Walters and was the highest ranking officer to be killed in Afghanistan. I was pregnant with Toby at the time. After my maternity leave I went back to the army myself. I was a major. I found it difficult to carry out my duties and was given a compassionate discharge. After a period of inactivity, James knew of someone high up in the Civil Protection Group and with my army leadership background, I was an ideal candidate and was taken on immediately. I've now been with the group for nearly three years.'

'So, what do you know about the Knights Tempest, then?' Bryant asked, knowing that could be the only possible connection they had in common. He had just finished writing the article about them and six of its members.

'Nothing. Apart from the fact that they're one of CPG's clients. They, that's the Knights, suspect I've passed you confidential information about them as a client. At the moment they are very concerned that the identities of all of its members remain a secret, especially the six you were writing about. I have been removed from my duties simply because I live in the same village as you.'

'I'll tell them you had nothing to do with it.'

She smiled. 'Thank you. They won't believe you. You had to get the information from somewhere.'

'I got it from a place in Dorset called Beardstock Manor.'

A glint of recognition flashed across Sue-Beth's face. 'Beardstock Manor?'

'Yeah. Exactly. Why?'

'I was on security duty there. There were no journalists on

the guest list. They were banned. Not that they knew it. But we had to throw out any who tried to get in. Tell me about it. I was in the grounds.'

Bryant sat with his elbows on the table and his chin cupped in his hands and started to recount his version of the evening. He had been invited by an old soldier who campaigned vociferously that British troops should be withdrawn from Afghanistan and concentrated on the defence of the kingdom from within the realm. Walls built thousands of miles away were easy to get round. Using the same amount of bricks at your own boundary meant the wall would be much higher and thicker and, therefore, impenetrable. The name of the retired soldier was Colin Hunter.

'Colin Hunter?' Sue-Beth was shocked. 'He was the contact James put me in touch with for the job here. He was a loathsome sort. His public persona is full of charming bullshit. He seems to have the public on his side with his campaigning to bring the troops home from Afghanistan.'

'Loathsome?'

'Yes. It was when he was interviewing me for the job here. For some reason the "interview" was held in a hotel room. And I agreed to it, but it made me alert. After chatting for a while, he started walking round me, and on the second or third pass he made his move. In a flash his hand was inside my blouse and bra and he had my breast cupped in his hand.'

'You still took the job?'

'As I said, I was alert. He hadn't even caressed the nipple but was thrown over my shoulder and on his back with my knee in his chest. No real damage apart from a ripped blouse where his hand was pulled out and a sting from the twang of the bra. I took his wallet, removed fifty quid, stood and tossed it back on his chest, to pay for the torn clothing.'

'Ouch?' winced Bryant.

'He said I was good and how soon could I start?'

'Anyway,' Bryant continued, 'Back to Beardstock Manor.

Hunter chaired the gathering, which for want of a better description was a sort of political conference. As bizarre, though, as any you could see. And far more worrying.'

Sue-Beth helped herself to a second cigarette. 'I had never, ever smoked until two days ago, but there's a lot of time to kill in here.'

'You roll a mean fag.'

'An old boyfriend smoked 'em and I used to enjoy rolling them,' she smiled, holding her hand out for the lighter.

Bryant told Sue-Beth how Hunter had started the meeting with a welcoming talk and urged the time was right to declare themselves a proper political party that would attract support from the downtrodden middle class. The Knights Tempest would hand back power to the people. There were three types of people in the country: the haves, the have-nots and the have-not-bothereds. Anyone who fell into the last category had no place in society and must be ostracised. Good, honest people were fed up with government interfering and telling them what to do all the time. They wanted to take charge of their own destiny. The continued left-leaning administrations of Thatcher, Major, Blair and Brown had robbed the intelligentsia of their place in society. People who did not pull their weight needed to be punished for it rather than rewarded as the previous administrations had done.

Dinner was then served, followed by port, brandy and cigars. Yes, cigars. Hunter urged as many people who wished to smoke to do so. The Knights Tempest would not be nannied by the state, and it was for the people to decide if they wanted to smoke, not the busybodies of Whitehall; people could make up their own minds about staying in a room where others smoked, not a pathetic bleating doctor on television. The wine of dinner was clearly beginning to have an effect. Inhibitions were flying out the window and for the first time in the evening, there was hearty applause.

The first speaker after dinner was the Duke of Woodbridge.

Cheeks pinkened by wine and port, he strode purposefully to the lectern. He spoke, in general terms, about the fledgling party's stratagem to take the party through to govern within ten years. You only had to go to every public bar in the country, every football ground, every workplace canteen, and you heard it. People were fed up with their hard-earned money allowing the benefit blaggers a life without responsibility, while those who worked and earned were often worse off. It would stop and the scroungers would be put in their place: at the bottom, where they belonged.

Woodbridge said the tables were turning across Europe as well. He welcomed like-minded emissaries from Scandinavia, the Balkans, Iberia, France, Germany and Russia. They all stood and accepted enthusiastic applause from the majority in the sumptuous old ballroom.

There followed short speeches outlining the key points for the economy, health, housing, immigration, welfare, education and, most important of all, crime.

The finale was as chilling as it was theatrical. The head of this national socialist crusade appeared from the wings. A figure dressed in chainmail, with full helmet, a surcoat sporting the bright red cross of St George and a broadsword at his waist, mounted the dais. Applause grew with every step. It grew wild with excitement and the whistling was ear-splitting. The man, assuming it was one, held his gauntleted hands high, pleading for quiet.

A synthesised voice then spoke, still not betraying the figure's gender. It announced that the world was facing its biggest threat in decades, if not centuries, maybe even going back to the time when Richard, Coeur de Lion, the Lionheart, had led the armies of Europe against the evil Saladin and his Saracen hordes. Now like-minded Muslims and Christians were to forget their ancient rivalry and stand together against the new pox that was spreading across the European continent – the pox that was now recognised as the left-wing laziness canker: a lowlife group who lived an undeserved life of luxury on the back of hard work by others.

This evil disease was highly infectious and if it wasn't stopped it would mean communism let back in through the back door. The Lionheart acknowledged that every single person in the room had achieved high net worth by working hard at education and career alike. The fruits of their endeavours were now being ripped from the boughs and handed, yes handed, to those who had never worked hard in their worthless lives. They had never gone the extra yard yet bemoaned their lot; they had messed around in class, laughing at the swats, yet ended up on educational waste heaps; they had shunned the extra few hours at work in favour of a few pints at the pub, yet were embittered at others' promotions; they sneered at the Easterners coming in and cleaning cars for a fiver, yet claimed their jobs had been stolen while sitting on their benefit-fattened arses.

This virus was extremely dangerous. The vaccine had been developed at Beardstock Manor and would now be dispatched to every corner of Europe.

Holding up a freshly filled flute of champagne, the Lionheart proposed a toast to the Knights Tempest and the Final storm-surge that would cleanse Europe of all its ills. A scraping of chairs and the knights toasted themselves and then their Lionheart. The Lionheart left to whence he had come.

Bryant, head buzzing, ears ringing, and eyes disbelieving, excused himself and made for the gents. As he crossed the lobby, there was a stir of patriotic music, beginning with 'Rule Britannia'. Music muffled as if wrapped in cotton wool, he was joined by a man with a permanent grin, possibly intoxicated. Bryant very soon realised the grin was not as a result of alcohol, but of the event.

'The Lionheart. Very good. Yah?' The stranger spoke in a guttural accent, maybe Scandinavian. 'He is so right. Every one of them is right. It was an honour to be here. I will take away many things from this. I will be the first to make my mark as the right fights back.'

'I'm pleased to hear it,' Bryant allowed, doing up his zip.

The Scandinavian was not far behind him, standing at his shoulder as he bent to wash his hands, no attempt being made to utilise the spare basin. As Bryant waved his hands under the dryer, the opening door allowed the music to crash in like a wave smashing the coast. The Scandinavian introduced himself.

Bryant didn't hear due to the cacophony and the thickly accented voice. 'Sorry? I didn't get that.'

'You call me Andy. Yah?'

'Sean,' responded Bryant, reluctantly accepting the proffered unwashed hand.

'I realise they are not the most pleasant of people,' said Sue-Beth as Sean completed the tale. 'I never realised that they were that bad, though.'

'And they intend to field candidates at the next election. If you want my opinion, they are not just bad, they are dangerous.'

'We must stop them.'

'We?' he mocked.

'When we get out of here we need to start to undermine them.'

Bryant leaned forward, elbows on the table and fingers interlocked, forming a triangle. 'We can't do anything on our own.'

'Yes, we can. You're a journalist, are you not? You can write damning condemnations of them and turn opinion against them. You have already connected six very high public figures with them. Seven, if you count Hunter. Come on. What do you say?'

Bryant noticed an electric charge pulsing through her eyes again. The thought of a fight was building in her like a soldier eager for battle. 'We're not going anywhere,' he said. 'As I was telling you, it dawned on me there was a direct link between the Knights Tempest and the Civil Protection Group.'

'I know that,' she said. 'They're one of our cli... *their* clients. That's all.'

'It's more than that,' he said, sweeping his arm in the general direction of the reception. 'The name of this building.'

She knew the name but her eyes followed his gesture anyway. 'Plantagenet House?' she said, puzzlement manifesting itself on her face. 'What of it?'

'How's your history?' he asked.

'Um! Not brilliant. Why?'

'Richard the Lionheart was the second Plantagenet king of England in the late twelfth century. Not a coincidence, I would suggest. I bet you'll find common links between the two. And I wouldn't mind betting that the CPG is bankrolling the Knights. That's different to the original Knights, for they were an extremely wealthy lot from the Middle Ages who helped to finance crusades and such to the Holy Land. I know the call went up for Christians and Muslims to be united, but I don't believe that. This lot are as xenophobic as their twelfth-century counterparts. When you get a mo, read up on some of the carnage left in the Crusaders' wake!'

'Might be coincidence. Obviously, Plantagenet is a strong name as CPG is a strong company and brand. You won't find the identity of any of the main stakeholders a matter of public record. Because of the nature of the work they do, especially for the government, it cannot be risked that anyone could get at them.'

'Convenient,' Bryant agreed.

'Don't worry. At some time in the not-too-distant future we are to be summoned before the great general.'

'That bloke Sharp?'

'The very same.'

'I've heard it said he can be a tyrant.'

'Perhaps,' she said, a glint forming in those mind-catching eyes. 'But he has three weaknesses. The first is that he is an avid fan of his fictional namesake, Richard Sharpe of the Napoleonic Wars. Second is red wine, and lots of it. And third is me!'

'You?' Bryant was startled.

'Yeah. He has an unhealthy and unwanted fondness for me. In short, he wants to shag my arse off.'

That evening, Bryant went to the library before retiring. He was looking for one subject only: the personal leather-bound copies of the Sharpe stories by Bernard Cornwell. He took half a dozen from the shelf. Sure, he knew the television series, but had never read a single one of the books. On the way out of the library, his eyes were drawn to a display of pamphlets and small booklets. One stack was entitled *The Knights Tempest: A Path to Government.* Interesting, he thought, before adding one to his pile of reading.

Sue-Beth had gone on to tell Bryant about the commandant that they had nicknamed Sharp, the one without the 'e'. He had been a career soldier and reached the same rank as his fictional hero. When he was offered the managing executive role at the CPG's research and development headquarters he had insisted on running it along military lines. No one objected as it was manned by about 99% ex-army. He insisted on the rank of general, raising him above the rank achieved by his fictional namesake.

It's likely that the Sharpe of the books would not have approved too much of the 'kommandant' as he was born into a long line of army officers in Leicestershire, inevitably ending up at Sandhurst. Sharpe, on the other hand, had risen through the ranks from a lowly private – once set against a punishment triangle by the likes of Robert Sharp as a result of strategic bravery and, of course, the vacancies caused by a brutal war, to the rank of colonel at Waterloo.

Bravery was not one of Robert Sharp's more valued attributes. Indeed, there was a misted shroud surrounding his honourable discharge from service. Whispers would not go away concerning one deed of bravery. He had led a patrol of five men on a routine patrol in a dusty town in the Iraqi interior when they were ambushed. They sought shelter behind a stone wall. As the insurgents crept toward them like locusts over a savannah, Sharp decided they would go down fighting. He ordered his men to rise up from their barricade and blast the ragheads with metal. They all rose, including Sharp, and went over the top. Sharp soon ducked back down below the parapet. His men were all gunned down. They didn't stand a chance. The whir of helicopter gunships belatedly coming to their rescue drove the tribesmen away.

Back at the field hospital, one of the fallen was still breathing. His breath was shallow, but he was still alive. Sharp was informed of this but refused the invitation to go and see the man, pointing out that he had been wounded himself and needed immediate treatment.

At the military enquiry, it was claimed by a medic that the wounded soldier, who had since died, confided that Sharp had risen with his men but, for some inexplicable reason, had shot himself in the leg. The board of enquiry decided the wounded soldier's evidence could not be admitted as he was probably suffering from delirium. Other testimony suggested the bullet found in Sharp's leg was consistent with his own ammunition, and none of the deceased had similar wounds. The board decided this could not be proven beyond reasonable doubt as it was known some weapons and ammunition had fallen into enemy hands.

Sharp was awarded the Military Cross for his bravery and honourably invalided out of the army. A cover-up to protect an honourable army family? The rumours never went away.

Bryant would bone up on the adventures of Richard Sharpe, but not before he had read the Knights' manifesto.

6

'What do you mean, you've fuckin' well lost 'em?'

Duncan Cobbold had arrived in Oakshott one week after Sean Bryant disappeared and he was not best pleased. The only perceived threat had come from Randolph Soames and Stephen Patrick and even Mercia Police had lost them. It hadn't been difficult to piece together. Since the fortuitous arrest of John Connelly, the threat was very real. Connelly had become indignant toward Soames who had still not delivered the final payment so, in exchange for a police caution, he decided to confess all. He told of the train journeys, the stolen car and the Bryant family home. That was enough to convince Cobbold that Soames meant to cause damage to Bryant. Then Connelly had added, 'Not only Mr Bryant, sir. He intends to kill the whole family, starting with the dog and the wee'uns. He'll do that in front of the poor mum and dad. The bastard! Then he'll rape Mrs Bryant before torturing Mr Bryant until he dies a very unpleasant and painful death.'

Cobbold had seen enough grisly sights in his time, but this, if successful, would be the grisliest of them all. He couldn't bear to think about it. He had immediately tracked Soames and Patrick, by hacking into their phones and computers. First, they had cottoned on that mobile phones were not a safe form of communication since the bloody hullaballoo over the press phone-hacking scandal. It was all very well penalising the press for their indiscretions, but the downside was that organisations like the Home Security Team would lose a dependable weapon in the short term. It was now in the short term and Soames and Patrick had suddenly ceased all communication with one another by phone and computer. Now, to add insult to injury, the dunderheads had managed to shake off the plods of the Mercia force.

Cobbold ended the call and returned his phone to his trouser pocket. 'It's fuckin' incompetent, that's what it is,' he said to no one in particular. He paced up and down in the Bryant living room while Amelia, Jones and Richardson looked on. Repeatedly, he slammed the balled-up fist of his right hand into the palm of the left. His face was red with fury and beads of sweat were forming on his forehead.

Richardson spoke first. 'Um, look, Duncan. There's no need to worry. The whole village is protected better than Buckingham Palace. No one, and I mean no one, can get in here without us knowing of it.'

'I know that. But I'm fuckin' pissed off. It'd be so much easier if we knew where they were.'

'We don't. Let's not fret about it. And if I may be so bold to suggest –'

'What?' snapped Cobbold, fury still coursing through his veins, although now at a slightly slower rate.

'I'm sure Amelia would appreciate it if you could tone your language down.'

'What? Oh. Yes, of course.' Cobbold scratched the back of his head irritably before turning to Amelia. 'I'm sorry.'

'No probs,' she said. 'Tea for anyone?'

All accepted the offer. Jonah, who was becoming bored with inaction, got up and offered to make the beverage.

Cobbold took the vacated armchair and appraised Richardson and Amelia of the progress of the enquiry so far. Jonah popped in and out while tea-making and Richardson filled in any gaps.

CCTV footage had told them very little about the vehicle used in the abduction as its index number was not yet allocated. There were at least six people involved in executing the deed and they all wore identical uniforms with company branded clothing. One thing for certain was that this was not the work of Soames; this was a professional organisation and 'professional' was a word as far detached from Soames as the moon is from the earth. When the zoom device was used on the screen, the images of the logos blurred and could not be deciphered. The vehicle left the congestion zone, heading in the Essex direction. But, the strangest of things, Bryant's mobile phone was traced to an empty office's post box in Chiswick. Needless to say, the CCTV there was not working.

'And, that, my friends, is where the physical trail runs cold,' concluded Cobbold. 'The vehicle has not been seen since last Wednesday evening.'

'Motorway cameras?' enquired Richardson.

'Not all checked yet. But so far nothing.'

'What was he working on?' asked Jonah as he set the tea tray down on the coffee table. 'Hope you don't mind, Amelia. I found some chockie biscuits in the cupboard and it would be a shame to see them go off.'

'Good question for a squaddie,' Richardson chided.

'A special squaddie,' Jonah shot back.

'Have any of you heard of the Knights Tempest?'

'Weren't they in one of the Indiana Jones films?' Jonah joked.

'I thought you had used the intelligence cell for the day,' retorted a smiling Richardson.

'I'll take that as a no, then,' Cobbold interjected, putting an end to the joviality by the tone of his voice. 'In modern terms, according to Woodcock, the Knights Tempest is an underground political party of the national socialist type.'

'Nazis?' exclaimed Richardson.

'If you like,' said Cobbold. 'Once again, according to Woodcock, they are part of a Europe-wide movement that believes now is the right time to start flexing its muscle. Woodcock believes these are the people behind the kidnapping.'

'What's Sean got to do with it?' asked a disbelieving Amelia. One week ago, she was happy being the dutiful wife: kids to and from school, trips to the gym, coffee with friends, even the occasional game of tennis. Now this. She and the girls were now better protected than the Queen. An hour or so before there was only the one threat. Now there were two.

'As Sean was leaving the office last Wednesday he popped in to say goodbye to Woodcock and assured him he had filed copy.' Cobbold leaned forward and helped himself to a couple of chocolate biscuits. 'That copy never arrived. Fortunately, he left his laptop at work. Our people are working on it now. The Knights Tempest has a few influential and celebrity members and Sean was looking at six of them. Seven, if you count Colin Hunter.'

'Who's he?' enquired Richardson.

'One of the bravest soldiers in recent times,' Jones interrupted. 'Can't remember exactly what he did, but it was in the Balkans and he won the Military Cross or something.'

'George Cross, actually. And he's now a leading voice of *Bring Them Home*,' added Cobbold, 'an organisation that wants to end our involvement in Afghanistan.'

'Ah! That's it. Took that Paki kid out a couple of years back,' said Richardson.

'Nothing proved,' snapped Cobbold.

'No smoke without fire. Sounds like a right racist bastard.'

'Enough,' Cobbold insisted. 'Anyway, the other six are Alan Monro, a pop singer from the sixties who had quite a few hits; Jonathan Smithson, extremely right-leaning Tory MP; Barrington Swift, media mogul, as you well know; the Duke of Woodbridge, royal loose cannon; Isabella de Montmartre, formerly Willow the porn actress-stroke-celebrity; and, finally, and most shocking of all, Shona Forbes.'

'The Labour MP?' Amelia put in. 'Scottish, I think. Married to that union bloke. Not exactly a couple we would have to dinner.'

'Former MP. Stood down at the last election.'

'I remember her,' Jones mentioned. 'She did that TV programme with Willow about the porn industry. If I remember correctly, she wanted all pornography banned, but after a week with Willow changed her tune. I think I read she had an affair with her.'

'Didn't make *The Times*,' sniffed Richardson. 'Now divorced from Mick Forbes. Your union bloke, Amelia.'

'How did they all get involved with a Nazi-style party, then?' she asked. 'Nothing in common?'

'Money,' Cobbold stated.

'What?'

'Money. That's what they've all got in common. And lots of it. Apart from that, we're still to find out. Hopefully, the laptop will provide us with some clues. Any questions?'

'Probably loads, but can't think of any right now.'

'Okay. Look. I'm going back to London. The Home Secretary is now taking an interest.'

Richardson followed Cobbold out to his car. 'Keep in touch if you hear anything of Soames.'

'Don't worry. Will do. Just be vigilant. Make sure Amelia and the kids always have you or Jonah with them. I'll be back at the weekend.'

'If he gets through, he'll be in for a hell of a shock.'

'I know,' said Cobbold, squeezing Richardson's elbow. 'She's in good hands. The best.'

The following few days were quiet. Richardson and Jones traversed the countryside around the village. Elsa had never been so well walked – Richardson in the morning, Jones in the afternoon. They knew every path and field, stream and pond, copse and spinney. Jones was on the school run in the morning,

Richardson in the afternoon. A bucolic peace descended on the Suffolk village.

Sunday morning was greeted by a warm sun. By the time the Bryant household had risen it was already high in the sky and a fine day promised. Amelia had felt restricted by the closeness of her protectors. Apart from trips to school for the girls and brief exchanges with other mums at the school gate, and a longer discussion with Gill Francis relating to the children's welfare, contact with other humans was restricted to Richardson and Jones. She conceded that she was probably better protected than the royal family, but did they ever feel the urge to break out and seek the company of others? Or just feel the wind in their hair in a field or on an open moor? They must have done, she thought.

Conversation was easy with Richardson, but Jones? Well, she achieved more reaction from Elsa, and even swore she could hold a more meaningful conversation with the Labrador. Richardson excused Jonah as being in awe of women, particularly pretty ones. Not really sure about the fairer sex.

Amelia found Richardson on the decking reading the *Sunday Times*.

'What are we going to do today?' she asked like a bored young child.

'Same as yesterday,' came the reply.

'Can't we just... well, go for a walk?' she pleaded.

'It's easier to protect you here,' Richardson countered without lifting his eyes from the cricket reports. 'And besides, we can be sure only that Soames hasn't come in by road. He has been missing for a while, so no chances; he could be making his way across country.'

'I thought he was a city boy with no idea of the country?'

'He is. And, while I doubt his ability of finding his way out of a field, we can't be too careful.'

Amelia sighed. 'Can't we just walk out at lunchtime and call at the pub for a bite to eat?'

'No. Jonah'll cook. You've seen; he's a good cook.'

'Please! For the children. They're so fed up.'

'I'll think about it.'

The party set off at just after midday for the stroll to the Fox and Hounds. If travelled directly, the route was no further than a quarter of a mile. This way, up and down dale, it stretched closer to three miles. Jones checked the security of the home and they were off.

Clouds travelled the blueness of the summer sky. Hedgerows rang to the song of birds and a green woodpecker bobbed its way above as if providing air cover for the convoy. They went past the church going down to the little bridge that crossed a still stream and up the other side. About a mile or so further on, the party of Amelia, Poppy, Daisy, Richardson and Jones turned off the road and headed out across the fields. A paddock with three horses in it to the left gave way to a field of green wheat turning gold. Richardson and Jones were very familiar with the topography for they had reconnoitred every square inch and could almost find their way around blindfold.

As they entered a field of barley that, to Richardson's eye, appeared ready for harvest, a couple was walking arm in arm toward them with a black Labrador cross ranging ahead.

'Good morning, Curt,' the man said and nodding to Jones, 'Mr Jones.'

'How are you, Derek?' Richardson answered.

'Not bad. Thank you. You?'

'Very good, indeed.'

'Any sign of these villains you're looking for?'

'Not yet. We're keeping our eyes peeled. As I say, anything suspicious, let me know.'

'I will that. I will that.'

Amelia shot an enquiring glance at Richardson.

'It's our job. We just about know everyone in the village now. As soon as a stranger starts poking around, we'll be on the case. Having said that, though, we're not exactly looking for a particular grain of barley in a barley field.' He looked at the crop as if to emphasise the enormity of such a task, feeling inwardly pleased with the analogy. 'We are looking for a lump of granite protruding from a field of freshly fallen snow.'

'You what?' said a disbelieving Jones, shaking his head as if his partner had lost his mind in going poetic.

'In other words, Mr Soames should stick out like a sore thumb, being the only black man in a village full of white.'

Jones just glared.

'Well, apart from me,' Richardson smiled.

Cobbold was heading back to Oakshott, feeling very content indeed. An amazing stroke of fortune had come his way the previous afternoon. The search up until that point had been concentrating on the black van. But it was as if it had simply evaporated, and the trail with it.

'Get yourself across to Romford Police Station,' the caller had said. 'There's a young woman PC with an interesting tale to tell.'

Police Constable Hayley Brunnings had dismissed the claims of the old man as the rantings of a homeless drunk attention-seeker. Everyone at the homeless shelter in Romford knew that Hayley was a cop, but they also knew she had a heart of gold. After or before work she would volunteer at the centre and would listen for hours to tales of ill fortune and what-ifs. Some of the home's inhabitants would eventually deal with whatever ill had put them there in the first place, but most would be condemned to a life in and out of the centre.

Boxer was one who had fallen into the latter group. A heavy drinker since the age of ten when he had nicked shots of whisky from behind the bar at his father's pub, he was now nearing fifty, but could easily pass for someone twenty years his senior. Hayley recalled the exultation when he told her he had a job on a local building site. Having kicked the booze, he was a shining example of what a loving arm could do. She had given him the same time as anyone else and she believed she had made the difference. Why were the older helpers so much more cynical? Two Fridays in a row he had refused the invitation of his workmates for an after-work beer. Only one, they had promised. On the third Friday he gave in and at 3.00 p.m. he was having his only one. By 5.00 p.m., he had had four more and uncountable scotches and was all over the place. At 2.00 a.m., Hayley had cried herself to sleep, not being able to dismiss the image of Boxer slumped in a doorway in his own vomit.

Now back in the home he had come up with one of his more fanciful stories: a black van had turned white and changed its number plate.

'Well,' she remembered saying, 'It must have been a different van.'

Then she had been at the station and heard colleagues talking about a black van that had disappeared, despite all the modern surveillance. It was a genuine mystery. For the first time, she had gone to the shelter in uniform, but Boxer wasn't there. She and a colleague drove around for the best part of two hours before spotting him trudging along the road. The patrol car pulled up alongside, but Boxer made off. Hayley jumped out of the passenger side.

'Boxer!' she shouted.

Boxer turned. 'Oh, Miss 'Ayley. It's you,' he said with a toothless smile.

'Boxer. You remember you told me that story about the black van that turned white?'

'Yeah,' came the guarded reply.

'Where was it?'

'Not far. Just round de corner.'

Hayley caught a whiff of booze but chose to ignore it. 'Can you show us?'

'You didn't wanna know the other night. What's in it for me, like?'

'I can't give you anything. But there's been an abduction and we think that van has got something to do with it.'

'I don't want yer money. All I wants is you try with me agin. You got me sorted good before.'

'Okay. Deal. Jump in.'

The small industrial unit was in a terraced row of six and appeared to be empty. The owner was found and let them in. The place was spotless. No visible signs of activity. There was, however, an underlying odour like burned or melted plastic. Within an hour Cobbold had joined them. It wasn't much to go on, but it was all they had. Bryant's phone had clearly been placed in West London to throw them off the track.

'It might have worked,' he found himself thinking out loud. 'But, for a smelly tramp.'

Hayley bristled and admonished her superior for such discriminatory language and to her surprise, he apologised and commended her on her work.

As he pulled off the A12 he reddened at the memory of the chastisement from a PC. But it had been deserved. A young officer untainted by time dealing with lowlifes. Even Cobbold remembered ideals and thinking there was good in each human that walked the planet. He smiled as he remembered Dwight Carter.

Memories flooded back, memories of that court so many years ago. Five years. Five bloody years for helping to catch a small-time but extremely violent thug such as Soames. Carter had been rewarded with five years inside. Cobbold had promised he would put in a word and thought Carter would probably get only a suspended sentence. When the judge delivered the sentence Cobbold could not bring himself to make eye contact with Carter. Instead, he fled the court and headed straight to the nearest boozer.

Later that night he ended up at a strip club, reputed to have been owned by an ex-copper. For that reason, the police were more than welcome. The host was always discreet. It was a two-way street, though; a blind eye was turned to some of the more sordid and lewd goings-on that took place upstairs.

Cobbold took a stool next to the bar, ordered a scotch on the rocks and opened a tab. Whisky followed whisky. He didn't converse with anyone. A couple of strippers tried but it was soon obvious that there were no further earnings from that particular punter, so he was left alone. The whiskies continued and the images moved despite holding his head still.

He paid little attention to the entertainment, but when he glanced in that direction he saw there were three women on the stage doing an identical act with a chair. He closed his eyes and shook his head. Two of the strippers disappeared but slowly came back into vision. He tipped another whisky down his throat and stared up at the criss-crossing of the suspended ceiling grid, trying his best to stop it moving. He brought his head down and nearly fell from the stool. He mustered all his concentration and looked around for a toilet. On spying the sign, or rather signs, he got up from his stool and landed flat on his face.

He awoke in a sun-bright room, mouth as dry as a desert and head banging like a pneumatic hammer. He tried to move his head but the pain was so excruciating it was best left on the pillow. Then the stomach started to rumble. He lay back and let the rising inside subside. God, he felt ill.

A woman's voice cut through the misery like an angel calling him from another world. 'You all right, duck?'

Cobbold opened his eyes, but it was no use; he couldn't focus. Through his feathery mouth, he asked, 'Where am I?'

'Don't worry, Duncan. You're in good hands.'

'Water, please?' The words caught in the slurried mix that was his mouth.

'Ah, ha! You're back with us then.' A man's voice cut into the room.

The woman helped Cobbold to a position where he was propped on an elbow. He took some water. It mixed with the contents of his stomach and immediately headed back from whence it had come. The woman expertly moved a bucket into the path of the liquid projectile. Cobbold could feel sweat forming on his torso, laid back and allowed himself to be taken up by a fretful sleep.

Two hours later he came to again. This time he felt fresher, even though he was in a clammy condition. The head pain had softened, albeit still on a scale of six. Better than ten earlier. Recollection was difficult. He remembered dancing lights and loud music. That was it, though, and the music still shook his eardrums.

His nurse told him how he ended up in the bed. After he collapsed, they searched his pockets and found his warrant card. The boss, ex-old bill himself, had insisted he was looked after. His clothes were freshly laundered and on the chair in the corner. The shower and toilet were through the door, but he could stay as long as he wished. The boss had even had the decency to telephone the station and let them know where he was.

Christ! The ridicule.

He eventually made it home and straight to bed. The following morning he was woken by the phone. 'Cobbold,' he answered.

'Oh! You are there? Christ I've been trying all morning.'

Cobbold caught a glimpse of the clock. Bloody hell, eleven o'clock! 'Yes, sir. I'm here.' He wanted to add 'I can explain'.

As if reading his mind, the voice said: 'Look. We know where you've been. Ol' Jack filled us in. You weren't the first and you most certainly won't be the last.'

'Sir.'

'It grieves me to tell you this, but Carter was killed in prison last night. He wanted you to have his possessions. Can you get down there as soon as possible.'

'What happened?'

'Details are sketchy. They will fill you in when you get there.

I can tell you that Soames already knows and is claiming responsibility.'

Cobbold pulled up at the Fox and Hounds and slipped down the side to the garden at the rear. There was Jonah sitting with Amelia and another woman near the sandpit, with the dog curled up under the table. He could see the two girls on the swings toward the back. No drinks on the table yet. Richardson would be in the bar sorting out an order. A pint of orange juice and lemonade would hit the spot. There hadn't been a drop of alcohol past his lips since the night of the court case that had seen a man sentenced for no good reason.

7

Richardson appeared with a tray of drinks and served them up. Two cokes for the girls, orange and lemonade for the guv'nor, a white wine each for the ladies, a larger coke for Jonah, and for himself, keen to be treated like a local, a pint of Adnam's Ghostship. He smacked his lips as he took a slurp. 'Aaah! That's good! Duncan, allow me to introduce Ms Gillian Francis, headmistress at the –'

'Excuse me.' Gillian was indignant. 'Headmistress, indeed!'

'I thought you were,' pleaded Richardson, trying to sense where the offence may have been caused.

'It's the term "headmistress". It makes me sound like a dried-up old spinnie who has dedicated her life to a cause greater than herself. It's now head teacher, so as not to differentiate between the sexes; the cause is not greater than me; my chill time is as important to me as kiddie contact time and, finally, I'm not dried up yet; I just feel like it sometimes.'

Richardson apologised for causing any offence and promised to report for detention. 'Do you still have a cane?' he enquired, suggestively.

'Oh, God, please,' an offended Jones put in, having witnessed the smooth tongue of his colleague on far too many occasions in the past.

'Enough of this frivolity,' said Cobbold. 'Can I talk openly about our enquiry, Amelia? Or do you wish me to remain confidential?' The last comment was linked to a sideways glance at Gillian that only Amelia noticed.

'No. No. You can talk openly. Gillian might be my children's teacher, but she is also a good friend and confidante. Whatever you told me in confidence I would probably share with her anyway.

'Anyway, as we were saying before you arrived, Gillian received a visit from two policemen on Friday.'

'Is that right?' Cobbold asked. 'What did they want to know?'

'They wanted to know the connection between the Walters family and the Bryants.'

'What did you tell them?'

'I said there was no connection apart from the Walters' grandson and the Bryant girls coming to my school.'

'Is that true?'

'Yes.' Both women answered simultaneously.

'Good. Let me know if you see them again. And, trust me, they weren't policemen. Who are the Walters then?'

'He's the retired army general whose son was killed in Afghanistan. Do you remember?'

'Yes, I do. You don't need to say any more. I didn't know they lived in Oakshott.'

Gillian took up the story. 'Yes. I think they moved in about six years ago. Maybe seven. General Walters and his wife bought the place after he retired. He carried on living in London, quite active in the Conservative Party, while she was up here on a regular basis with a swanky architect to supervise the refurbishment. They have never said how much it cost but rumours say one and a half million.'

'Christ! We're in the wrong business, Curt,' Cobbold joked. 'It's Jonah who'll make it wealthy.'

'I think it helps to have a wealthy background,' Gillian continued. 'Lady Isobel has really taken to the village since the house was finished. A few noses were put out of joint in the village construction fraternity because all the tradesmen were brought in from London. Even the local architects had a bit of green-eye as they thought they were as equally competent as a gay from the West End! Afterwards, though, she was brilliant, a real charm offensive, and she's now really popular.'

'And him?'

'Nate, their son, died without actually seeing the house and that really hurt Sir James. I think he had this image of living in one end of the house with Isobel while Nate, Sue-Beth and Toby lived in the other end. Actually, I don't think. I know.'

'Sue-Beth?'

Gillian giggled. 'Yeah. Major Susan Elizabeth Walters. A child of the seventies apparently and the youngest of four. Family loved *The Waltons* on TV and her name was shortened to Sue-Beth and stuck ever since. A tough-nut, though. Went through the mill a bit when Nate died but since then has pulled herself together. Do you remember when those two diplomats were rescued in Sierra Leone or some place? She led the rescue.'

'How come you don't know them, Amelia?' Cobbold had had his interest piqued and leaned forward, elbows on the table.

'Never really mixed in the same circles. I'm not in the WI and she's not in the tennis club; I'm not on the parish council and she's not in the PTA; so on and so forth.'

'Umm, good. Anyway,' the senior policeman continued. 'We have had an extreme slice of good luck in our enquiry.' He went on to tell them about Boxer and how they were now looking for a white van with new plates. 'Plates, incidentally,' he continued, 'that have not yet been registered to a vehicle and therefore wouldn't necessarily trigger a number plate recognition computer programme unless the van committed an offence. It couldn't be registered as stolen. Quite ingenious!'

'How do you know the index number is correct?' Richard-son wondered. 'Boxer is a drunk!'

'Old-fashioned police work. Well, nearly old-fashioned, anyway. After painstaking study of hours of recording, we have now spotted a white van with those plates at a number of sites. What's more, the driver and the front-seat passenger are the same as those in the black van.'

'Quick-drying paint or a different van?' asked Jones.

'Neither. Well, we think neither. A paint job can't be done so quick and the small industrial unit, more the way of a lock-up, wasn't big enough for two vans inside. The great minds of the Met, and I make 'em right, reckon it was filmed with that plastic they use in signwriting and was just melted off with hairdryers or something.'

A waitress approached the table. 'Are you ready to order?'

'Ah. Haven't really thought,' said Amelia. 'But I think it's simple. I believe it's five roast beefs.'

The rest of the table nodded or grunted their agreement.

'Girls,' Amelia shouted at Poppy and Daisy and they came running over. 'Roast beef or chicken?'

'Chicken,' chose Poppy.

'None. I want chicken nuggets, chips and beans,' Daisy demanded. 'And chocolate ice cream for afters.'

'They only do roasts on Sunday, darling.'

'No we can do –' the waitress started, only to be halted by a stony stare from Amelia. But, it was too late and the cat, or rather the chicken nuggets, were out of the bag.

Daisy jumped up and down and banged her hand on the table accompanying it with 'Good, that's sorted then,' and returned to the swings.

A red-faced waitress made her retreat accompanied by a stifled guffaw from Richardson. Any sustainability in the laugh withered on the vine as another of Amelia's Neolithic stares made contact with Richardson's eyes.

Sensing a slight unease around the table, Gillian took up the questioning as if a recalcitrant schoolboy were answering her enquiries.

'Where's the van now?'

'We don't know,' conceded Cobbold. 'We have it tracked

coming up the A12 in this direction, but only as far as Chelmsford. We're checking cameras to all points at the moment. There's no guarantee that it hasn't turned tail and headed back to London.'

'No idea yet who they are? Soames?' asked Richardson.

'Not a chance. Far too professional. That prick couldn't organise a bunk-up in a broth… Sorry, ladies, in a brewery, if the fanny was free!'

Mixed and messed up metaphors, but it brought a giggle.

'Where is the bastard?' Richardson wondered. 'It seems we need to take him out first then go get Sean. The last thing we want is Soames being up our arses as we're trying to get to Sean. That would stretch our resources trying to defend one front and attack on another.'

'I agree,' said Jones.

'The soldier speaks and has an opinion!' Cobbold mocked. 'I thought you were just meant to follow orders?'

'Working with cops for too long,' Jones retorted. 'Nosey bastards!'

Broad agreement was reached that the Soames and Patrick threat was nullified first. No one knew where they were, however, so it was easier said than done. They could turn up that afternoon or the next day or even next year. All they could do was sit tight and wait for something to happen, and there were worse places to sit it out than the Suffolk countryside in summer. Food was enjoyed before retiring to the Bryant residence.

As the sound of chatter died and a summer quiet descended, Richardson swore he could hear the faint but unmistakable sound of leather thwacking on willow. Of course, there was a village cricket ground in the meadow opposite the pub. Of course, it was Sunday and village people would be gathering up and down the country for this uniquely English pastime.

'Can you do without me for a couple of hours, guys?' he asked.

There were no dissenting voices from those awake and he

didn't give a damn about those sleeping off their Sunday lunch. So off he went, past the school and into the cricket meadow. There was a sightscreen in place slightly to the left as he entered. To his right and on the cover point boundary was the red-brick pavilion. There was an unoccupied bench at third man and that's where he sat and watched the home side plunge from a less than promising 46 for 4 to 88 all-out. Apart from a woman selling raffle tickets, he was not disturbed all afternoon.

The effect of the warm afternoon and the laborious display of the Oakshott batsmen made his eyes heavy. Very soon he was slouched in the bench in a cotton-wool land. Bliss. Absolute bliss.

He came to with a start and with it came inspiration; somehow they had to entice Soames to Oakshott. So far there had been no media coverage of the Bryant abduction. Now was the time. It needed to be wall to wall. A well-organised gang operating in London had blatantly lifted an award-winning journalist off a city street and simply vanished with him. Police were mystified as to the reasons and were seeking the help of the public. Witnesses were urged to contact the police, and so on and so forth. Normal bullshit! Generally, though, the police were scaling back their search and Bryant's family were being comforted by friends.

'The theory is that Soames and Patrick will make their move sooner rather than later,' Richardson told the others, 'and then come after the vulnerable Mrs Bryant and daughters while they are at their lowest ebb. They'll get a shock when the comforting friends are two crack members of an armed special ops group.'

'They surely wouldn't be so dumb? Surely?' said a sceptical Cobbold in a less than enthusiastic manner.

'Got a better idea?' snapped Richardson.

'Why don't they just wait until Sean's returned to his family?'

'Come on, boss. You know the animal. He is a bear of extremely little brain and all he wants to do is hurt Bryant and that he can do by getting to Amelia and the kids. Anyways, if he has to wait too long he'll have forgotten what he was meant to be doing in the first place. I swear it will be hook, line and sinker by the end of the week.'

The plan was worked on, a few alterations made and they were ready for execution. Cobbold would see the Home Secretary in the morning and headed back to London, though not before he'd taken a call to say the white van in question had now been on the Orwell Bridge to the east of Ipswich. That left too many options to concentrate a search. It could have headed into the heart of East Anglia or, more scarily, headed to Felixstowe – and the Continent and the world?

Richardson took two phone calls in fairly quick succession. The first was from the raffle master at the cricket club; he had won a bottle of Chablis.

He was staring at a picture on his phone and was totally unaware of Amelia coming out onto the decking to join him. 'Who's she?'

'A beautiful girl I met in Italy. Her name is Augusta.' He let go a deep breath he hadn't even realised he'd held. 'I think I love her. I only knew her for a couple of days, though.' He paused for some seconds. 'Is there such a thing as love at first sight, Amelia?'

'Only for very special people,' she replied in a low tone. 'If it is love and it is returned, you'll be like Sean and I.'

He looked up and saw her eyes glitter. She looked away. 'I didn't realise Sean was like that,' he laughed.

'But you don't know Sean… Do you?'

'No. No, I don't. I just assumed he was a big –'

The mobile rang in his hand. 'A local number,' he observed and answered. 'Richardson.'

'Curt?'

'Yes.'

'It's Des here at the Fox. We've just had two blokes asking around about Sean Bryant and his family. One was white and one was ah, well, um, black, um, like you.'

Richardson smiled. The good folk of the village tried to go out of their way not to offend. 'Where are they now?'

'One of the blokes told 'em to sling their hook and that Mrs Francis was probably the best person to ask and then pointed out her house.'

'I'm on it.' Richardson bolted in through the conservatory doors, shouting, 'Jonah! Come on! Rustle up a couple of plods to stand closer guard on the house until we're back. Bring yer toolbox.'

Standby security organised, the two men were on their way, jogging along Church Road and turning into The Street. Richardson indicated the ditch that ran alongside the road to the right. Jonah sensed a nod and in a single unflustered move-ment they leapt the water onto the footpath the other side like a couple of vaulting ballet dancers. They didn't break stride as they made their way along the grass-covered path to the back of the school house. They hurdled the 4-foot fence at the rear and crouched down behind a shrub in the middle of the lawn. There was no moon, but the English summer afforded enough natural light in July for Richardson to curse.

The un-blinded kitchen window was in clear view. It was apparent that there was plenty of light within to obscure any vision of the outside, for no one inside as much as flinched at the sense of movement in the garden.

Three figures sat around the circular kitchen table. As seen from the garden, Gillian was at three o'clock. And, sure enough, a black man sat at eightish with his back to the window and a white man at noon. Richardson stood. If there was any chance of being spotted it was now.

'What're you doing?' Jones let out in a terse whisper. 'You

only need a car headlight to catch you and you'll give us away. Get down.'

'Nothing to worry about. That's not our friend Mr Soames. Look at them.'

'And?'

'They're a couple of pups. Those two're far too young. Soames and Patrick are older than me. You go and knock on the front door and when she gets up to answer, I'll nip in the back if it's open.'

Richardson took position, but never heard the knock. As Gillian rose to get the door he tried the back door handle. It opened. Careless, he thought, and made a mental note to talk to Gillian about private security. He slipped quietly into the small utility area and through an arch into the kitchen. The two men didn't notice, attention drawn by the front door. Jones arrived in the room first and nodded to Richardson.

The two young men turned in the direction of the nod. 'Jesus!' they uttered in unison.

'You boys need to take more care; you could get yourself shot,' the tall black stranger growled, gun in hand.

'Sorry,' the white kid stammered. 'We were just going.'

'Hold your horses,' Richardson ordered, holstering his weapon.

Jones lent menacingly against the doorframe and Richardson joined the two lads at the table. 'Now then,' he started. 'Who are you?'

'Are you the law?' asked the white lad.

'They're simple rules. I ask the questions, you answer. But, I'll allow you this one. No, we're not the law. We're much higher than that. My name is Curtly Richardson and this is Michael Jones and we work for the government. Now, who are you?'

The same lad did the talking. 'My name is Will Charles. I'm a journalist with the *Echo and Post*, and this is John Churchill; he's a photographer.'

'What brings you to Oakshott?'

'Well, um, nobody actually knows we're here. Look, Mr Richardson, I am really only a trainee reporter and I thought if I could get some sort of scoop about Sean's disappearance I'd get a good pat on the back. John is just with me to take pictures.'

'What do you know about it? Hold on.' A moment of realisation came into Richardson's mind. 'Are you the young man who witnessed the abduction?'

Charles's face brightened at being recognised by someone who was clearly very important. 'Yes. I am, indeed.'

'Look guys' – a more conciliatory tone in Richardson's voice now – 'your description as a couple is very similar to two blokes who have threatened Sean and his family. So, I think it best if you just withdraw from the area before some trigger-happy rookie gets tetchy and takes you out. Give me a card and I'll make sure you get your scoop when we have Sean back in the bosom of his family. In the meantime, we're now look-ing for press coverage, so I suggest you go back and talk to your editor. Woodcock's his name, is it not?'

Charles nodded. Churchill was still frozen in his chair.

'Make sure you get as much coverage in the paper for the next few days. Get Woodcock to speak to my boss, Duncan Cobbold is his name. Woodcock knows him and will confirm our change of heart on press coverage.'

'Okay. Here's my card.' Charles produced a small leather business card wallet from his jeans pocket and handed one to the agent. 'Oh, and there's another thing...'

'Oh?'

Charles reached into a back pocket and pulled out some folded sheets of A4. Richardson unfolded it and scanned it. Six pages, stapled in the top corner. 'Is this what I think it is?'

'Sean's last report, yes,' beamed Charles.

'How'd you get this?'

'Easy. I hacked his laptop and checked a couple of things.'

'Hacked?' Richardson interrupted. The police hadn't managed to furnish him with a copy of the report yet.

'Yeah, easy as you like. First thing we're taught at Uni!' Charles smiled before continuing. 'First, in his sent items there was an email with it attached and sent to File and Woodcock. It never arrived at either destination. Secondly, there it was in his documents, as bold as brass, but no one else had thought to look. Everyone assumed it had just gone missing. You can keep that; I have other copies.'

When Charles had managed to coax Churchill from his chair, the two newspapermen left. Jones followed soon after.

'I know they were harmless,' said Gillian. 'But they scared me. Will you stay for a while?' The question was aimed at Richardson.

He consented and Jones returned to guard duty. Richardson, first of all, lectured the schoolteacher about personal security. She took a bottle of white wine from the fridge and ushered him through to the sitting room. There was a DVD case sitting on the coffee table. Gillian mentioned that she had been about ten or fifteen minutes into the film when the knock on the door had come, and she invited Richardson to stay and watch. Richardson wasn't a great one for films but accepted the invitation. They shared the wine.

After a glass each, the chemistry changed and Gillian snuggled up in his strong arms, admiring the rich contrast between the pinkish white of her arm and the rich ebony of his. She hadn't been held by a man, at least not like this, since her divorce. It felt good.

It was late. The security, the warmth and the wine led to a relaxing feeling coming over the pair. Guilt-ridden images of Augusta wended their way through Richardson's mind, but they were becoming blurry. He willed them into focus, but they would not sharpen. Gillian was an extremely attractive woman but the memory of Augusta was still so fresh, or so he thought. He closed his eyes and Augusta's image returned to sharp focus along with the scent of her hair and the balmy feel of those Sorrento nights. Even the memory was intoxicating. He would fight off the desire of the woman now in his arms.

Richardson's alarm on his phone pulled the couple back into consciousness. It was 4.30 a.m. and the couple were still entwined. And they were still on the sofa. He evaluated the scene in a moment. An empty bottle and two glasses on the coffee table. Nothing had happened. His loyalty to Augusta was still intact. God! How he ached from four hours on the couch. He disengaged himself and laid down a semi-conscious Gillian to spread out along its length.

He found some teabags and made two mugs of strong black tea. She could add her own milk and sugar if desired. As he went to pick up the cups he was smothered by two arms from behind. He gently unwrapped himself and handed her the steaming brew.

8

There were two visitors' chairs positioned in front of the desk in the peculiarly adorned office. Sean Bryant and Sue-Beth Walters were shown to them. Sue-Beth had been here before but it was Bryant's first visit. He looked around, recognising the memorabilia from the descriptions in the Sharpe books he had scanned but not yet read in full. Pride of place went to the replica Baker rifle above where Robert Sharp would normally be seated at his desk – or was it real? A long sword was displayed with the business end pointing to the floor. A green rifleman's jacket was hanging in a glass cabinet next to another that contained a blue coat: French, if his studies had served him correctly. There were musket balls arrayed alongside a cannonball on a shelf. All the walls were adorned with contemporary sketches and prints of battle scenes: cavalry charges against squares of infantry, cannons blazing their deadly load with gouts of smoke ejected from the barrel, and close-quarter fights of steel on steel.

Bryant decided this was a morbid fascination with war bordering on the unhealthy. Perhaps it was a soldier's lust for blood, and war's vicious and unnecessary carnage. Or, the more likely, if Sue-Beth was to be believed, it was a coward's show of power, an image the coward had conjured for himself and, maybe, even believed.

The pair waited fifteen minutes for the man to arrive.

'Here is General Sharp,' announced the secretary who had shown them to their seats.

'You may sit,' said Sharp sarcastically at the sight of both remaining steadfastly on their rear ends. 'Now, Mr Bryant, you are probably wondering why you are here?'

Bryant didn't respond. He had been well briefed by his new friend.

'Yes?' This time the voice took on a more demanding tone, but still the journalist did not react. Sharp turned to Sue-Beth. 'And you, Mrs Walters. I dare say you are wondering about your change in fortune?'

Sue-Beth remained silent but had noted the title of Mrs rather than being addressed by her rank within the Civil Protection Group.

Sharp's face reddened. Sue-Beth knew they were already getting under his skin. Bryant was playing his part well. But he was a journalist. A method they sometimes used was to leave a hole of silence knowing an interviewee under pressure would eventually fill it up.

Sharp indicated he would interview the two separately, in accordance with CPG protocol as laid down by their client. Sue-Beth was escorted from the office, leaving Bryant to face the inquisitor alone. For some reason, he didn't feel intimidated; Sharp carried about as much threat as a new-born puppy. But Bryant convinced himself not to underestimate his adversary. He knew every interview technique in the book and would not be falling for any of those ancient ploys.

Bryant sensed there was someone else in the room and glanced over his left shoulder. It was Ben Morgan. The affable Ben Morgan. Bryant had learned that Morgan and Sue-Beth were an item before the woman's change of fortune within the organisation. He suspected they still were, given the flexible nature of the regime within the guest block. Why on earth hadn't they plotted a way out?

Sharp opened a file and drew out a document of half a dozen or so pages. He slid it across the desk, Bryant catching it before it fell into his lap.

'You'll recognise this, Mr Bryant?' demanded Sharp. Even though the tone was terser than before, it still only carried the threat of a rabbit invalided by myxomatosis.

Bryant did recognise it, but he leafed through it as if he had never set eyes on it before in his life.

'Come now,' heckled Sharp. 'It's not that difficult, surely? If I'm not mistaken, Captain Morgan has already presented you with a copy.'

'The one he stole from my computer. This document is in the ownership of the *Echo and Post*,' Bryant protested.

'Ownership,' Sharp repeated. 'If we looked that one up in the dictionary I'm not quite convinced you could prove title in this instance. There are six persons named in your article who have stronger claims than you do to that piece of libellous junk. In a calculating way you invaded their private space at an invitation-only gathering – a gathering to which you were not invited.'

'You're not in a position to judge. That bitch of yours has already told me your company provided the security. Therefore, if you accept I wasn't invited you must also accept that you're not the most diligent of security companies. True?'

Bryant could see that he'd hit a nerve. The man in front of him was betraying every emotion in his facial and body language. Was it the slight against Sue-Beth or was it the one against the ability of the Civil Protection Group? Sharp balled his fists in a bid to control the anger building up inside.

'You claim that Colin Hunter invited you along?'

Bryant remained impassive.

'Well, I can tell you, Colin Hunter denies having invited you, so how did you get in?'

'I'm not changing my version for one reason...' Bryant paused. 'It's the truth. And another thing,' he continued, waving the document. 'This story is, without doubt, in the public interest.'

'Oh?'

'Your six have been selected by me because the revelation that they're involved in this Europe-wide neo-fascist group will cause them a little discomfort, shall we say? Also, out of loyalty to my source, you'll note that Hunter's name is not betrayed. All six are interesting, but Ms Forbes is of most interest. I'm sure you're aware she's still a paid-up member of the Labour Party.'

Sharp leaned back in his chair and steepling his fingers, continued. 'We'll beg to differ on this matter. I shall move on to the subject of our Colonel Walters. How well did you know her before the event in Dorset?'

'Not at all. Never met her in my life.'

'And you expect me to believe you? The village of Oakshott, I believe, has a population of less than nine hundred. Correct?'

'If you say so.'

'And you don't know one of its residents?'

'I don't,' Bryant confirmed. 'And there are probably another eight hundred and fifty I don't know as well. If you spoke to my wife, however, I'm sure there are only fifty she doesn't know. Anyway, with the limited amount of knowledge your so-called colonel has, she could have looked it up on the internet.'

There was silence, but Bryant was on the attack now.

'And I don't believe for one minute that your ex-colonel is "ex". If you want my opinion, you've planted her with me to get as much info out of me as possible. The thing is, I've nothing to hide. I've told you everything. One thing is for sure, she's extremely fuckable. Ah, but of course, that's one thing we are agreed on.'

Sharp rose and slammed his fist down on the desk. 'How dare you,' he bellowed. 'You're an insolent... Captain Morgan, remove him from this office, but keep him nearby. Show Mrs Walters in please.'

Bryant left the room with Morgan on his tail. As they entered the waiting room, Morgan spun Bryant by the shoulder and aimed a punch at his face. As he turned, Bryant was off balance and tottering. The blow was only glancing, but enough to make him see flashing lights. The next fist caught him low down in the abdomen and bent him over double, driving the wind clear out of his lungs. He sunk to his knees and was defenceless to a boot in the face.

It never came. Instead, he heard Sue-Beth shout, 'Ben! Stop it!'

Bryant dared to look in the direction of his assailant. He was standing, legs apart, fists clenched, ready to land the mortal blow. Slowly the rage fell away from the normally placid eyes and Bryant felt safe again. The blow to the body had been like a sledgehammer and now, feeling the protection of the woman, he slumped to the floor to search out recovery.

'You may leave us, Morgan,' said the general as the captain returned to the room with the former colonel of the Civil Protection Group.

'I don't think we need to be so formal, do we?' Sharp greeted her genially.

He ushered her to a corner sofa positioned in the bay window. To her astonishment, he produced a bottle of red wine and two glasses. He proceeded to fill the glasses, placing one before Sue-Beth. He sat close enough that she could feel the warmth from his body.

'Now, my dear,' he said, sipping his wine. 'A most wonderful claret, wouldn't you agree?'

Sue-Beth took a dainty sip. 'Nice,' she agreed. His glass was half finished.

'Good. Good.' He pulled the last from his glass and refilled it. 'Come, my dear. This will not do. You've hardly touched yours.'

He proffered the bottle to her, but she positioned her hand above the still-full glass.

'Sir, it's only just gone ten in the morning!'

'It doesn't matter, my dear. A good claret is for any time of the day.' This time he smacked his lips and placed the glass on the low table. 'Now,' he continued. 'I wish to know more about your friendship with our latest guest.'

'What? The weatherman chap?'

'Good Lord, no. I had totally forgotten about him.' Sharp waved his hand as if the weatherman was of no consequence. 'No. He was brought in against my better judgment. All he does is keep getting the weather wrong. No, I mean our journalist friend. You know the Knights are sure it was you who passed the information about the six to Mr Bryant.'

'Six?' She knew full well to whom Sharp was referring, but thought it faithful to Ben to find out by other means.

'Ah, I'm sorry, my dear. So remiss of me.' Sharp had now started a third glass and a second bottle stood opened on the table. She observed he was still in control but words ending in 's' were now emphasised by the involuntary addition of a second or even a third 's'. Early indications of slurring were tainting his speech.

Over the next half an hour, he repeated the assertion that she'd passed the information to Bryant. She flatly denied it. His face took on an ever-pinkening complexion. At one stage, he placed his hand on her trouser-clad leg. She didn't attempt a removal. She glared at him, an intent glare that said 'If you go further I will break your hand in two'. He didn't need a second invitation to remove the unwanted attention.

He made her skin crawl. It was all she could do to stop herself from laying him out with one punch. His head lolled and in a few seconds the inquisitor was snoring loudly. She reflected that he was as useless an interrogator as he was a soldier. She had told him nothing, absolutely nothing. Then, with a start, a loud grunt was followed by his eyes opening.

'Sue-Beth. Tell me everything, including how he offered you money for the story, and I'll protect you. I'll write out a full confession. You sign it and I'll make sure you walk out of here. And I'll ensure you return to duty as a colonel again.'

'I'll think on it.'

'One other thing: you surrender yourself to me, let's say a couple of times a month. Then I'll see to it you get everything your heart desires. Yes?'

No, she thought, but it wasn't for his ears just yet, so she agreed to think on it. Passing her still-full glass to him she saw herself out. Sharp lurched over and was fully asleep before Sue-Beth had even closed the door.

Later that day, Sharp prepared the confession. He thought long and hard about how to word it. He thought about embellishing it with flowery legal jargon. In the end, he settled for *I, Susan Elizabeth Walters, do confess that I passed information to Sean Bryant who then attempted to publish it to the detriment of the Knights Tempest and their membership. I also admit that some of the material passed to Bryant was exaggerated in a bid to try to win more favour with the journalist in the way of financial reward. I am truly sorry for causing any offence to the Knights Tempest and the six subjects of the so-called article of news* [he would insert the six names later]. *I also apologise for bringing the good name of the Civil Protection Group into disrepute.* There, that should do.

The following morning, Captain Morgan brought Sue-Beth back to General Sharp's office.

'I will agree to a full confession with a couple of amendments to the reward for so doing.'

'Which are, my dear?'

'One. Mr Bryant will always remain in the guest block and never be transferred to the prison block; two, Ben Morgan is promoted to major and given the salary commensurate with that position; and three, when I give myself to you it is with a meal at a top restaurant and a night at a top hotel.' She had no intention of obliging him but until her freedom was won she'd go along with him.

'Really?' he reacted in a slightly higher voice before calming. Saliva was filling his mouth and his lips started to quiver with excitement. He never believed for one moment she would agree to it. Christ, he was pleased he had drunk that wine to give him the courage to make the suggestion. 'I have already drawn up the confession.'

'One more thing,' Sue-Beth demanded. 'I'll sign now, but no other rights will be granted until such time that the positions of Mr Bryant and Captain Morgan have been confirmed by the boss. Then, and only then, will I take you on an adventure of real filth beyond even your wildest dreams.'

Morgan was standing near the door and even though he had been through the whole plan with Sue-Beth and that bloody journalist, it was all he could do to stop himself from beating Sharp into a pulverised mess. He knew he was more likely to become a high court judge than for Sue-Beth to pleasure Sharp. It still took all the self-control he could muster not to turn him to pulp. He balled his fists and counted to ten repeatedly. Eventually, he was escorting Sue-Beth back to her suite.

General Sharp, pleased with the past few days' work, took a bottle of claret from the credenza and poured a generous portion. Sitting back in his chair, he closed his eyes and dreamed of the first time with Sue-Beth. My God, he felt powerful.

Three days later, and exactly two weeks after lifting Bryant from outside his work, Morgan was summoned to Sharp's office. On entering, he found the man pacing. He was clearly agitated. Morgan could see the blood had drained from his face. Morgan glanced at his watch, 8.15a.m., and Sharp was armed with a glass of red, the half-used bottle perched precariously on the edge of his desk. His eyes were surrounded by the dark rings of a tired and stressed man. He simply stared at the incomer.

'Morgan, sir. You wanted to see me.'

'I know who you are, damn it!' the general snapped and filled the glass to the top. 'I need your help, Morgan.'

'Sir?'

He searched the top of his desk until he found what he was

looking for and handed an envelope to the captain. 'I need you to take this to a man called Hilton in the prison block. An odious character, but as you're my messenger he'll answer everything you wish to know. By the very fact that you're there he'll see you as a confidant. Is that clear?'

'Yes, sir.' It wasn't clear but he would obey the order. He turned to leave.

'Morgan, that way.' Sharp indicated the store door in the corner with his wine-filled hand. 'Here are the keys. You can't go wrong. Just go straight through each door you come to until you're faced with a choice. Take the left. Clear?'

'Sir,' Morgan confirmed but thought 'no'. 'The store, sir?'

Morgan took the keys and, with a tinge of trepidation, entered the store. After the light of the office, he was engulfed by darkness. A tentative step and lights fired into life. It was a good job they did as, no more than a metre and a half in front of him, concrete stairs descended into what felt like the bowels of the earth, even though he was in the second storey. He grabbed a metal handrail to guide his way. No need; as he stepped gingerly to the descent, lights flickered into life to illuminate the path. Down and down he went. After counting twenty treads and not seeing the end, he sensed he was entering a subterranean world he had no idea existed. Down he plunged, lights coming to life in front and dying behind.

Forty-four steps and a steel-plated door barred his way. His heart beat at a ferocious pace. Hands sweating, he leaned into the door. It did not budge a millimetre. He now knew what it was like to be a miner going underground for the first time. He fumbled for the lock and inserted the same key that had opened the store door. It worked.

The door automatically closed, locking him into a tomblike darkness. Tomblike, indeed. The air was stale and he sensed the earth was cradling him to her bosom. Nervously, palms sweating, and memories of potholing while at school flooding through his mind, he carefully moved forward. Once again, lights flickered into life, four or five, illuminating a long sweeping corridor. This time he noticed a PIR sensor perched at the top of the wall. Then there was another, and another. Each sensor turned on five lights. The walls and ceiling were constructed from a crudely finished concrete, whilst the floor was of a polished power float finish.

Onward he went, counting eight banks of lights, each about four paces apart. He reckoned on it being about 160 yards or metres. He tried to picture the ground level image in his head. Maybe it was right, but if the truth be known he didn't really know the distance to be 160 or just 60 metres. He had never given it any thought. He had never needed to. Now, even though he didn't know why, he was trying to take in and cast to his memory as many features as were relevant.

Plantagenet House was full of security cameras but this new underground world had none. As expected, there were two doors, both of steel as before, one straight on and the other to the left. Selecting the latter, Morgan paused. Peering down at the envelope, he noticed the flap was merely inserted inside and not actually stuck down. He knew then he was meant to read it. Something was inside that Sharp couldn't tell him about in the office. Even Sharp must be monitored in his movements. He removed two sheets of A4 paper from the envelope. The first, penned in Sharp's hand, simply read: *You must do something. I cannot offer any suggestions, but I am sure you will think of something. Let me know what your intentions are by personal note, should you require assistance, and I will help. Whatever you do, you must destroy this communication. RS.*

Intrigued, Morgan unfolded the second folio. Intrigue turned to shock and desperate thoughts. The page simply contained two lists of three names. Two names were common to each list. He recognised the two names. He had no idea what the printed lists meant, but the names were known and now it was his duty to discover the purpose of his errand.

He unlocked the door to the left and climbed twenty-six

steps. He was ascending into light and his heart lifted at the thought, but darkness engulfed his mind and blighted his thinking. At the landing, he was faced with another door. Once again, the key worked and he found himself in a room about the size of two squash courts. It was neatly carpeted and decorated with high-level windows to his left facing, he assumed, back to Plantagenet House. In the wall to his front there was another door and a sort of viewing window, except it had black glass through which the view was impossible. A few tables and chairs were scattered about and there was an underlying hint of food as if the room was a restaurant or some sort of café. Once again, the door's lock yielded to the master key.

He entered another room. His heart leapt for this was more of a chamber: a death chamber. It could not be anything else. In front of him there was a mezzanine floor and above that a steel beam with three hooks. A single flight of stairs connected the ground floor with the stage. A lump caught in his throat as he fought to battle retching coming up through his body as realisation struck home. The viewing window, of course, probably hid a selected audience who came here to munch on canapés and maybe, even, quaff wine. The after-dinner entertainment was death.

He mounted the steps and there was the confirmation. Under each hook there was a trap door with a waist-height lever to one side. He was shaking and feeling faint as he stumbled toward the door at the rear of the stage. No key was needed to pass through this door. He was now in a clinical but austere environment. The entire room was finished white. It was some sort of preparation room where poor unfortunates were prepared to meet their maker. He winced and balled his fists at the thought of one of those on the list being brought to this room.

'Who the hell are you?' a squat, thick-set man asked as he entered from the other side of the room.

Morgan tried to stand to attention and hold himself with dignity. 'Captain Morgan. Are you Hilton?'

'I am. Tom Hilton. What can I do for ya, captain?'

'The general has sent me with this envelope.'

Hilton took the proffered paperwork and cast his eye over the contents, the first sheet long banished to Morgan's trouser pocket.

'One of ours, I believe?'

'Yes. Correct,' Morgan confirmed sheepishly.

'I do like it when I get one of ours to dispatch,' Hilton grinned, relishing the prospect. 'Especially when it's like this.' He waved the paper at Morgan.

'The general said you'd fill me in on everything that happens over here. I'm all ears.'

'Yeah. A bit squeamish is our General Sharp. War hero, my arse. He never comes over here. He can't look death in the eye, even when it's not his own.'

Morgan listened intently as Hilton, executioner of the Civil Protection Group, told him everything. No question was stonewalled. Sickened by the harrowing scenes, Morgan made his way back to Plantagenet House. He counted every step and noted every detail. He must not forget; he might not get a chance to come this way again.

9

'You're having a fucking laugh?' Richardson blasted into the mouthpiece of his mobile. 'Please tell me you're pissing me about?'

The caller carried on.

'Jesus Christ! Well, start fucking looking.'

Richardson scanned the field. He spied Gillian watching the beanbag throwing and made his way over, after apologising to astonished parents in his immediate vicinity for his language. He knew they'd find out in due course, but didn't elaborate.

'Gill, I've gotta go. There've been developments. I'll tell you later. But for God's sake don't let any of the kids go home on their own.'

Another light shower swept across the sports day field. Nothing could dampen the enthusiasm of the children as they wound themselves down to the summer holidays. Richardson had agreed to help and now, not even a quarter of an hour in, he had to leave due to a technical glitch with the security ring that encompassed Oakshott. Damn it, not even this was foolproof. In a way, though, he had to acknowledge it had done its job.

He sought out Michael Jones across the gladiatorial field. A half-smile moved his lips when he realised Jones was serving drinks to students and parents alike. What on earth possessed you to do that, Gillian? he thought. The miserable git won't encourage too much in the way of repeat custom! He couldn't make mobile phone connection with the ex-commando. That was something he had learned on this job: mobile communication in rural areas had the reliability of an Italian infantry brigade. He started to stretch out for the drinks table, punching the green send button as he went. On the third attempt a ringtone cranked into life and contact was made. Jonah answered and Richardson instructed him to stay with Amelia and the girls for the rest of the afternoon. He would explain later. He watched Jones leave his serving post and head for Amelia, watching the wellie-wanging in blissful ignorance.

He headed to the police incident room: a Portakabin with police markings standing in the village hall car park.

'Explain,' he demanded of the uniformed officer sitting in front of a computer screen inside.

'There was a break in the link from the camera on the Hadleigh Road to the central computer. Could be climatic conditions. Not sure. Well, it's not so much a break, as a delay. The camera still recorded the information and stored it up before sending it on. In the end, there was a nine minute and twenty-eight second delay. The worst of it is, about four minutes in, an eight year-old, blue Ford Mondeo saloon entered the village. The facial recognition software matched the driver's features to Randolph Soames. And, just to confirm it, the car is registered to a Mrs Eliza Soames of Handsworth in Birmingham.'

'Brains of a goldfish! He hasn't even the intelligence to steal a car. Instead, he uses his mother's.' Richardson chortled. 'Where is he now?'

'Don't know, um, sir?'

'Curt'll do. I don't have a rank. Well, what I mean is has he left the village or is he still here?'

The officer brought an image onto the screen of two men in the front of a car. 'We don't know. We're not monitoring traffic leaving the village.'

'Great. Absolutely great!' muttered Richardson, folding his arms. 'That's them, though. The black one is Randolph Soames and the white one is Stephen Patrick. Older than the images we've been working with, but it's definitely them.'

Richardson pondered his position for a moment. If they were still in the area it shouldn't be difficult to find them. Sure, there were deserted barns and outbuildings, remote copses and thickets aplenty. He didn't believe for one minute that two men brought up in the urban security of Birmingham would be comfortable in the surroundings of the countryside. Nothing could be counted out and nothing could be counted in. If spotted, they would stick out like stranded whales on a beach.

'Send a chopper up,' he ordered, 'and two patrols, armed – look into old barns, buildings, woods – anywhere you could hide a car.'

Bryant was sitting under an oak tree chatting amiably with Sue-Beth. Morgan saw puffs of smoke swirling above each head. He clenched his teeth. It was irritating in the extreme that Sue-Beth had taken up with the journalist, but to have picked up the filthy habit galled him further. He approached the pair, a loathing rising on hearing joyous laughter coming from the table. Both had sweat tops on to protect against an unseasonably cool breeze. He arrived at Bryant's shoulder, Sue-Beth not even noticing his arrival amid a fit of giggling.

'Sue-Beth, Mr Bryant.' The latter introduction lacked the warmth of the first. 'Can I have a word?'

'Sure,' said Bryant, involuntarily caressing the bruise on the side of his face. 'I was just going anyway.'

'No. Please stay. It concerns you as well.'

A pang of guilt came over Bryant for he thought he was about to hear the bleating of a jealous lover. There was nothing to be jealous about. It was true, he enjoyed Sue-Beth's company, they had several years of unknown neighbourliness to catch up on, and all the time in the world to do it. Nothing fazed the woman warrior, though; she was a soldier and without doubt one of the boys. Crude and caustic comments could be exchanged as easily as if he were at a journalists' convention and catching up with old university mates. She would probably make most of those old hacks blush.

Bryant decided to get his defence in first. 'Look, Ben – can I call you Ben?'

The captain nodded.

'You have nothing to worry about from me. I understand you might feel a hint of envy at the time your lovely lady here and I spend together. But we have a lot in common and if I were in the market for a woman –' how crass did that sound? He winced. 'She has told me about her undying love for you and how she wants to spend the rest of her time with you.'

Morgan beamed. Sue-Beth shaded her face like a shy teenager – that wasn't quite what she'd said – and shot Bryant a sideways glance.

'Ah. Or words to that effect... Anyway... Sorta thing.'

An uneasy silence descended. Morgan was floating in another ether at the compliments, which he'd never actually heard direct from Sue-Beth, and at the unease Bryant had brought upon himself. In the end, he broke the silence himself.

'Thank you. But it's not that I want to talk about. So you two know what that building is for?' indicating the prison block with a nod of the head.

'No idea,' said Bryant.

'It's where some of the more unsavoury characters end up,' said Sue-Beth.

'That's true. Have you ever thought we ship a proportionately large amount of these characters over there compared to the size of the building?'

'Not really. I assume they are let go after a while,' she offered lamely.

Morgan shook his head. 'And if they were released, how long would it be before the police were swarming over this place? There's only one way out of there and that's in a wooden box. Or a body bag, anyway.'

Bryant covered his mouth with a hand. Sue-Beth remained impassive.

'What?'

'On two Tuesdays each month they execute prisoners by hanging them. You will be familiar with the Lionheart character from the piece you wrote, Sean?'

Bryant nodded.

'Well, at his behest, and his alone, men and women are sent to the gallows. There is a horrible perverted character over there called Tom Hilton. He's taken on the role of executioner. This Lionheart bloke is equally if not more perverted. Every now and then he selects a woman, normally an attractive one, to be hanged in the nude. She will suffer a long and suffocating death compared to the plunging through a trap door and a broken neck. Hilton and Lionheart sit and watch in splendid isolation.'

Morgan recalled the words of Hilton as he described the spectacle – 'Their titties mirror every dancing kick of their feet as they wobble for our entertainment only. Eventually, they come to rest and they water themselves and I cut them down. I then get time with them on my own. Ha! Ha! Ha!' – but he said only, 'He is honestly the most sickening man I have ever met.'

Bryant was now shocked into silence and with the blood having drained from his face, he felt quite nauseous. Sue-Beth had witnessed all sorts of atrocities in her time as a professional soldier, but the very thought of it happening in her homeland shook her to the core.

'How does that affect us, then?'

'Well, this morning Sharp gave me a job to do, an errand to run. I had to take an envelope across to the prison. There's an underground tunnel linking the two buildings. Did you know? Anyway, the envelope was open, deliberately so. So I read it. There were two lists of three names. One was headed with a P, which Hilton told me stood for new prisoners. The other was

104

headed with an E, those to be hanged. You two were on both lists. And you, Sue-Beth, had an N next to your name on the second list.'

'Oh,' she said matter-of-factly. 'We need to get out of here. But how? Oh and when are we meant to die?'

'Next Tuesday is the answer to the second question. And with regard to the first, that should be easy. On the way back I met Sharp. He was a bit sozzled but he is fully intending to help. Down in the tunnel is the only place in the whole complex that doesn't have cameras; well, apart from out here! He outlined the whole plan...'

'Who's that?' Sue-Beth interrupted with an accompanying nod to a stranger who was lurking nearby.

Morgan turned to look but Bryant, clearly shocked and probably not having heard anything about the escape, was staring resolutely at the centre of the picnic table. Sue-Beth shook him under the table. Eventually, he lifted his gaze and his eyes cleared.

'That's Bartrum Fairweather,' Morgan answered. 'He was brought in yesterday. He's not liked by the Knights. Do you remember that bloke who confessed to murdering those two girls, a taxi driver or a bus driver or something. Even though he confessed to them, he got off on a technicality. Something about not being read his rights before answering questions. Mr Fairweather, there, was his clever lawyer. The Knights don't want people like him in our society. They are a barrier to proper justice. Now I know what I know, I have no doubt he will be fitted with a body bag within the month.'

'Mr Bryant?' the stranger said, taking the looks as an invitation to join. 'You are Sean Bryant, aren't you?'

'I am,' acknowledged Bryant, seemingly recovered from the malaise. 'I don't believe I know you.'

'No. No, you don't. I just recognised you from the news the other night. Night before last. Police decided to go public with your disappearance when they became sure the people they originally thought kidnapped you had not kidnapped you. Quite a story.'

At long last, the story had been made public. No doubt Duncan Cobbold, and the *Echo* for that matter, had kept a lid on it. He hadn't bothered with the news in the last week; it didn't seem relevant any longer. Instead, he had been swatting up on Richard bloody Sharpe and, more interestingly, rereading the outrageous and offensive manifesto of the Knights Tempest and their obnoxious leader.

'What can I do for you?' he asked Fairweather.

'Nothing really. I just want to chat. You must understand that I'm at a loss to understand why I'm here.'

'Can I just finish up here first and then I'll be with you?'

Fairweather agreed and took another table out of earshot. Even so, Morgan outlined the plan in barely more than a whisper. It was agreed, it would be tomorrow. Bryant raised the only objection based on an unmatched belief in the police. The others wanted to do it sooner rather than later. If they were caught, they would be killed. If they didn't try anything, they would be killed.

Lying on a double bed in his room at the Ipswich Holiday Inn, Randolph Soames stared at the ceiling. He had come all this way and had been thwarted by someone else. If the television and newspaper coverage had been three days earlier he and Stephen Patrick would not have made the journey. Still, where was the point in cursing missed opportunities? One door closes and another opens. They had driven right through the middle of Oakshott and hadn't been challenged. It was proof, if proof was ever needed, that whatever the police presence was doing in the village it wasn't on account of him and Patrick.

Now it was time to put a plan into action. Like an unseen eagle, he would swoop on his victims and carry them away to a death as savage as any that could be imagined. He smiled as he relished the looks of horror on the little girls' faces as the pet dog was trussed up and hanged by the back legs with one slash of a sharpened blade pouring out the animal's life in a scarlet torrent onto the timber decking at the back of the family home.

Sure, the mother would try to defend them, but each time she tried she would be cut, just nicked and weakened. Then, as she slipped in and out of consciousness, she would witness the children being drained of their lifeblood to mix with the dog's. It would be cruel to separate them in death. It wasn't her fault she was married to Bryant, or the kids' fault they were spawned by him. Soames would allow them to wait for Bryant together in heaven. He laughed out loud. This scene had played itself out at least a thousand times in his imagination and very soon now he was going to complete his work. It wasn't his fault he couldn't take out the target of his pent-up hatred. He laughed again and clapped his hands as another thought sprung into view. He would film it. Yes, damn it, he would film it. The laugh morphed into a witch-like cackle. There was no need to let Patrick in on the plan just yet.

Then there were the preliminaries, getting to the house. Earlier that day they had driven right past the front door and as far as he could tell, there was no police guard. Why should there be? They were conducting an enquiry into the disappearance of Bryant. Perhaps there was a policeman inside the house, or more likely, a policewoman. No, gut instinct told him the house was empty. Was he to approach the front door as easy as a postman delivering mail? Or was it to be the silent entry of the burglar on the prowl of an evening? Or, the third option, a yomp across the countryside and an incursion under cover of darkness in the early hours. The final option held the appeal of a game of hide and seek. There was adventure to be had, so that is what they would do.

After dinner, and buoyed by a few beers, he and Patrick retired to the room and he went through the plan. Patrick saw flaws in it. Firstly, neither of them had any experience at finding their way around the countryside in the dark. That was easy; they would buy a map in Ipswich the following day. There would be barriers, such as rivers or hedges, so how long was it going to take? Easy, Soames would look at the map and calculate how quickly they would get there. Thirdly, Patrick didn't want anything to do with killing a woman and children, and had recoiled in horror at the thought of harming the dog.

'That's easy,' said Soames, 'because if you don't do it, the police will receive a tip-off about the child porn on your computer.'

'There isn't any,' Patrick protested.

'Just remember. I have powers and contacts far beyond your wildest imagination. That horrible snitch Carter found that out. Remember?'

Patrick conceded that Soames did have some contacts of dubious character, but even he doubted that Carter's death had anything to do with Soames or his brother, Charlton. He never voiced that opinion out loud for fear of incurring the wrath of his partner in crime. How he yearned to break the hold the Soames brothers held over him, but his thoughts were always braver than his actions and he always withdrew when looking into the abyss.

Patrick found a Waterstone's in the town centre and bought the largest scale Ordnance Survey map of the Oakshott area. He didn't want to return to the hotel so wandered around the town. He found a Starbucks and settled down with a coffee and muffin to shelter from another shower. When it stopped raining he went to Christchurch Park and sauntered among the stately oaks and ashes.

He lost all account of time, but school turnout must be roughly the same all over, so he guessed it was about 3.30 p.m. He gazed out on children playing cheerfully while pairs or groups of mothers looked on. He had seen a small school in Oakshott, but that didn't necessarily mean the Bryant children attended it. Oh and there was a golden Labrador chasing a ball for two small girls. That could be the family. And what gave him the right to end their dreams later that night?

He dreamed himself. He dreamed of standing up against the tyrant Soames. He would refuse to have anything to do with it. He sighed as he thought of the reality. Even sitting there he could feel the fury in the monstrous black man. He could run, perhaps somewhere in the wilds of Norfolk, but there was no point; he had no idea about surviving away from his urban homeland. He would be like a lion out of the jungle. He brushed his hand across the table and as it was dry enough, he spread out the map.

There was only one thing for it, Patrick would prove his worth. He would plan the route in. He quickly located the parish church and a few yards toward the village was the Bryant home. As clear as the mole on his neck, there it was. There was a stream behind the house, he reckoned on a quarter of a mile away. The plan was taking shape in his mind.

'Hello, mister,' a young voice broke into his thoughts. 'We've been doing maps at school.'

Patrick turned and was captivated by the innocent face of a seven-, maybe eight-year-old girl. 'Have you?' he asked.

'Yes,' she said with the widest of trusting smiles. 'Can I look?'

He hesitated. 'Um, yes, of course.' He moved along the seat a little to make room.

She pointed out churches and pubs and even telephone boxes. 'Did you know they were where people used to make telephone calls from in the olden days?'

'I did,' he said with a smile. 'Is there one near here?'

'Yes,' she responded excitedly, giving the stranger instructions to where she had seen one.

He didn't want this time to end. It was like an angel had descended from heaven to chat to him. But then the mother came over and took little Rosie away and apologised if she had been a nuisance. A nuisance? Huh, he thought, she had certainly not been that. Now he must take this message from the angels and play his part. He studied the map for a while longer and when content that the plan was fool-proof, he folded it and went in search of the ancient telephone box and the bus back to the hotel.

Plantagenet House was asleep except for one lone figure patrolling the corridors. Doors were checked, lights were extinguished and Ben Morgan found one door open. In the morning, the virtual sentries would not be alarmed at the figure dressed in black entering the suite of Sue-Beth Walters. They had been lovers before Sue-Beth's change of circumstances and so it continued. None of Morgan's colleagues, or mates, would stand in the way of a good man and a good woman breaking the odd rule here and there. Even Sharp could not bring himself to come down hard on his subordinate. The Lionheart was another matter. Like a player with a games console, a press of a button could finish the relationship as gaoler and prisoner and turn it to a prisoner and prisoner friendship. None of the staff of the Civil Protection Group should be tainted by the poison that was a guest of Plantagenet House and therefore a blight to society.

Morgan expected it to be hard. He lay back on the bed, his head swimming with stars. The ceiling was a whirl of lights and even now, as Sue-Beth donned blackened commando gear, his left eye was already closing. She closed the door and Morgan fell into an involuntary sleep. The fist had landed on his right cheek like a hammer landing on an anvil, sparks everywhere! It had been agreed to make the escape appear genuine. Bryant had suggested he assaulted Morgan, but Sue-Beth had doubted the journalist's ability to carry this out. She was trained in unarmed attack and defence so it made sense for her to do it. Morgan had expected some sort of warning, There had been nothing, though. Not even a sorry afterwards. Once Sue-Beth was on a mission she was focused and emotion did not have a place in her armoury.

Bryant was waiting in his suite when the lock gave and Sue-Beth let herself in carrying a plastic kitbag. She threw him similar black commando gear. He picked it up and headed to the bathroom.

'For crying out loud!' she exclaimed. 'Just get changed there. I've been on missions with bands of brothers before and I've seen everything they've got and they've seen everything I've got. Don't be shy.'

Without a word, he changed. Sue-Beth smeared blacking on her face and handed the pot to Bryant.

'Is that truly necessary?'

'Yes. We do this properly or not at all. It's up to you, but I don't fancy a hemp collar.'

He obeyed. Leaving the bag in his suite, they made their way through an unmanned reception and up to the first floor and the office of General Sharp. The officer was compliant with their wishes. It was difficult not to be, lost as he was in two and a bit bottles of claret. The television showed images of two girls cavorting wearing only thongs. Sharp made no attempt to conceal what he was watching. The pair moved the easy chair and tied him up to one of the visitor's chairs and placed him in front of his pornography. Sue-Beth had wondered about bringing out her right fist again but, looking at the lolloping head, decided it wasn't necessary. What a useless excuse for a human being, she thought!

Sue-Beth quickly located a bunch of keys in the top drawer of the pedestal and they were into the store cupboard and quickly descending into the subterranean world beneath Plantagenet. At the foot of the stairs there were two automatic assault weapons, Heckler and Koch AS80A2s, with night sights and ammunition, as favoured by the British Army. At least the drunken fool hadn't messed up on the guns, she mused. She didn't expect to be using them, but there was an outside risk that their abscondment might be noticed earlier than planned. If necessary she would rather perish in a fire-fight than on the end of a rope. At least a small arms battle would attract the attention of locals and, with any luck, would reveal the secretive complex at Plantagenet House for what it really was.

Sue-Beth lingered over the weapon, caressing it like a lover. Bryant looked on and felt a sense of unease. 'An idiot can't miss with these,' she whispered. 'They are so accurate they had to toughen up the tests for them. Let's go. Don't touch the safety catch unless I say so.'

Bryant had no intention of touching any catch, safety or otherwise. They moved deftly along the corridor, lights igniting like flashbulbs as they went, blackness enveloping the space behind them.

At the end of the tunnel they were faced with a choice, to go left or straight on. The key opened the door and straight on they went. It would have been very different a few days later. Now they were on a mission and it had to succeed. This lunacy could not last forever, someone would uncover it sooner or later, but Sue-Beth and Bryant would not have a later if they were captured by a wary guard or suchlike. The next corridor was at least twice as long, metre after metre of the same construction. A cat ladder loomed out of the darkness.

Bryant ascended the ladder first and Sue-Beth guarded the rear, ever alert to the slightest sign of danger, a sixth sense acquired by Special Forces over countless generations of operations in hostile territory and handed down in the barrack room. The sense could not be learned; it was a suppressed instinct reborn. Nothing. Good.

'I can't budge it,' whispered a panting Bryant, battling with the hydraulic hatch above him.

'You're joking,' she countered, not concealing her exasperation. 'Come down, squat here and if anything appears out of the darkness, don't ask questions, just squeeze the trigger. Even the quickest of squeezes will let at least three rounds off.'

'Shit!'

She climbed the ladder. The hatch took some effort but it gave and she was through into a chamber. No lights came on. 'Come on,' she hissed.

'I obviously loosened it up for you,' he remarked as he climbed into the chamber above.

'Of course,' she agreed sarcastically. 'Nothing to be ashamed of; most men don't cut it with me.'

She replaced the steel trap back in its frame and using the night sight on the weapon, scanned the interior of the concrete chamber. She located what she was looking for on the opposite wall – another cat ladder – and if Morgan was correct, this one led to fresh air and freedom.

She started up the ladder as a clattering sound went across the steel trap door above. The two froze and stayed motionless. Bryant's heart was beating so hard and loud that he was frightened of it giving them away. How could she, a mere woman, remain so calm and undaunted by all this?

All quietened and she made for the trap again, edging it up, not daring to make any sudden move, holding her breath so as not to betray her own anxiety. She was aware that any unexpected movement or sound could spook Bryant. She had seen it before with squaddies fresh to the front line. Nerves took over and fear ruled sensible thinking, part of the brain rendering it as good as useless. Bryant was certainly no different to some eighteen-year-old soldiers thrown into mortal combat straight from the training ground.

Peering through the slot, she was struck by the brightness of the night. The vista had taken on a silver hue under the bright half-moon and there, right in front of her, curious at developments from beneath the ground, was the source of the clattering on the manhole cover. Four eyes shone like diamonds from the pair of deer, waiting a moment as the two human forms emerged from the earth. Slowly, they turned their white rear ends to the danger and trotted off into the darkness.

Eyes now fully adjusted, Sue-Beth and Bryant could see the landscape laid before them. Navigation would be easy. Being spotted would also be easy. Sue-Beth motioned for them to cross the unmade lane and stay in the shadow of a hedge. At the end of the hedgerow, she beckoned Bryant to squat.

'Look,' she whispered, barely audible. He moved his ear closer to her mouth, so close he could feel her breath. 'The chances are good that we're safe. I don't think there's any way that our escape will be noticed until the morning, but we still can't be too careful. I reckon it's about six or seven miles to the old fort. Probably a smidgen over three hours in the country-side, and we'll keep to field edges as much as possible. The map shows a small stream to cross and there's a small road that leads to a caravan park or some such. Other than that it will be open country until we get to the main river.'

'Okay. You lead.'

Sue-Beth moved lightly into the next field and waited across the ditch for Bryant. He wasn't quite as dainty and got his feet caught in some brambles causing him to plummet ungracefully to the bottom of the drain. Fortunately, being the middle of summer, it wasn't running ferociously with water, but was only slightly tacky. He clambered up the other bank and took Sue-Beth's outstretched hand. He could feel his face warming with the embarrassment, which was not made any better by the glint of perfect white teeth beaming back from the blackened face above. Even those penetrating eyes caught the moonlight, making no effort to hide their amusement.

'Forgotten something?' she enquired, maintaining the calm whisper of before and holding her weapon in view.

'Ow, shit!' he blurted, shoulders sagging at the thought of more ignominy in crossing the ditch twice under the gaze of a girl.

'Don't worry, I'll go.' With a couple of timed leaps in either direction she was back at his side, gun in hand.

Bryant grimaced at the ease she demonstrated.

114

Sue-Beth led off, looking at one with her equipment. Bryant, on the other hand, found the rucksack a pain and the rifle cumbersome. He was like a useless tail-ender trying to make an impression marching in to bat and tripping over his pads.

The stream was easier to cross than anticipated after they discovered two planks laid side by side. Very soon they were at the road leading to the holiday complex.

Sue-Beth beckoned Bryant to the ground and they lay motionless in a hedge. Then he heard what she heard. No more than 100 yards to their left, two darkened forms were heading their way.

10

When on a mission, fitness is an important factor for any operator in the field. It could be the difference between life and death. Downtime is a commodity normally in short supply because most tasks keep operatives fully employed. So, when opportunity presented itself, Richardson and Jones, like most of their contemporaries, would top up their fitness level. When Amelia and the two girls were safely back after the school sports day, they seized the moment.

Poppy and Daisy both sported rosettes for firsts and seconds. A beaming mother, soaked to the skin from a heavy downpour, headed off to the shower with a promise of dinner to follow. Safely embedded in the house, and with the knowledge that Soames and Patrick had almost definitely driven through the village, Richardson and Jones set up an improvised gym in the back garden of the Bryant home. They set themselves ten repeats of jogging down the hill to the bridge below the church before surging back up like powerful performance cars. Loose weights appeared from the boot of Richardson's Mercedes.

Dumbbells were pumped and very soon blood was pumping also and sweat was pouring. Sunny skies had established themselves as the potent showers had disappeared off into the North Sea. Shirts were very soon discarded and the two muscled bodies flexed and surged like those of gladiators about to do combat in a ring. Jones assumed a sit-up position that saw him lifting up towards the rear gable of the house,

Richardson holding his ankles, with his back to the kitchen and main bedroom windows. One hundred or so in, Jones thought he caught a glimpse of movement in the bedroom. He did. There was a towel-clad Amelia gazing down on the scene. He smiled up at her. Coyly, she retreated into the shadows, but he was sure the smile had been returned.

Amelia had watched for a few moments before she was spotted. God, she missed Sean, and she scolded herself for the lust coursing through her body as she stared down at the defined arms, legs and six-packs. It was cruel; it was like being on a diet and staring at the delicious contents of a chocolate variety box – she could just pluck one out and devour it – but giving in to temptation would come back and haunt her in the future.

She turned away from the window and allowed the towel to drop away, leaving her exposed shoulders and back tantalisingly on view.

Dinner was served on the deck, after which Richardson took the girls in to do the washing up and the tidying of the kitchen. Aware of their bashful exchanges, the two found it difficult to get a conversation going. Not that Jones was the easiest of conversationalists, but there was an electric tension between them.

On returning to join the two men on the deck as darkness descended, Poppy and Daisy wrapped up in their beds, Amelia shared a bottle of chilled white wine with the two men. Richardson eventually made his excuses and sauntered off to see Gillian Francis, leaving the two to chat into the night. But not long after they had made themselves comfortable, Elsa started to get agitated at the back fence, sensing there was a presence on the other side. She stood back and let out a low guttural growl which turned into barking. Jones ushered Amelia into the house before joining the dog at the fence. The hackles were raised along her spine. Something had caught her attention.

He beckoned for her to be quiet and she sat on the spot, alert with ears cocked. Jones was sure he could hear some scrabbling on the other side of the fence. He was sure they were secure; anyone attempting to climb over could not avoid the barbed trap. He decided to leave the dog to guard the fence and crept off to the side gate and into the field. Hugging the side fence, he made his way toward the rear.

Two panels from the end and a scream rang out, sounding as if from inside the garden. He scampered to the corner of the plot and peered around the wooden barrier. Nothing. Gun still in hand, he ran for the gate, not wishing to vault the fence for fear of being foiled by his own trap. Goosebumps rose on his chilled skin for fear of what he might find inside the boundary.

The dark hatchback pulled off the road and glided to a halt, the driver killing the engine and lights. The passenger got out and checked the car was concealed from the road by the wild hedge of blackthorn that seemed to be at least 10-feet tall and at least the same across. The figure walked back along the lane in the direction the car had come. There was no way any car lights would sneak a reflection of the hidden vehicle. Content, the figure joined the driver in front of the car.

'Look, Randy,' the passenger started, 'I'm still not sure the children and their mother need to die because you want to seek revenge on the father. I beg you to think again.'

'No,' the other man stormed. 'You can stay if you wish. But, Mr Stephen "I'm going straight" Patrick, I'll tell you this: the police will soon be informed of your benefit cheating and other misdemeanours, plus a few more I can think up as I go along. Plus, when you're serving your time that little girl of yours won't be comin' to see you in gaol. It won't be that easy for her in a wheelchair. As I say, the choice is yours. Besides, can you imagine the pleasure we'll get when we see Bryant's face when he finds out what we've done? No one crosses Randolph Soames.'

'Okay, I'll come,' a reluctant Patrick agreed. 'One more thing, though, what about all the cops around the place?'

'What cops? For Christ's sake, you've seen the TV coverage of that arsehole being abducted. The ol' bill is sure he's been taken by some group, so they won't even be thinking we're a threat, specially these carrot-crunchers out here. Besides, that's what makes the whole plan so beautiful. The lazy bastard cops sitting in their little building site office drinking tea while blood is flowing like water right under their noses.' He gave a sinister laugh. 'Imagine. How fantastic when they find the three and the dog all trussed up and hanging like sides of beef.'

Patrick cringed. As they trudged through the countryside, and the actuality of the deed loomed closer, he reasoned that even a psychopath like Soames could be talked out of it. His mind wandered back to the park and the children playing with the dog. Could that have been the Bryant family? He doubted it, but he couldn't be sure.

'I'll have the dog,' he offered.

'What?' Soames snapped, then after a slight pause, 'Good idea. We'll both have it. I think it will be really good roasted. Don't you?'

Patrick didn't respond and merely fell in behind Soames as he started out across the first field. Then a sudden screech erupted from the road behind and both men froze. Soames pulled out his rusty old revolver, more akin to a weapon used in an old Western film than the modern accessory of a twenty-first-century villain. He stood motionless. Then, there it was, a shadowy figure stalking along the lane. As it turned into the gateway in which the car was parked, he let off a round in an uncontrolled panic. It had no effect other than to make the animal run for cover.

'A pussy cat,' remarked Patrick. 'If you're going to be like that every time we come across a cat, we're in for a long night.'

'What do you mean?'

'Well, how will you be when you come across a bear or a wolf?'

'There's no such thing.' Soames was uncertain. 'Is there?'

''Course there's such a thing. I've seen loads of programmes about them.'

'I mean in this country, idiot.'

Patrick wasn't sure whether there was or wasn't and clearly neither was Soames. It was not something they encountered in the safe environment of a city, but the country, that was a different matter. He added with confident authority, 'Definitely. There is.'

Soames grunted something and they started across the field again, nerves heightened by the cat experience and doubts in both minds about more challenging beasts ahead.

They marched across the field, soon realising there were tracks interspersed at regular intervals, which made the going easier. The crop was silver in the moonlight and billowed slightly in the soft breeze. Neither knew what it was, perhaps wheat or corn, maybe oats. Who cared, anyway? Doyens of the countryside they were not. Nerves frayed the further they plodded. Scuttling sounds in the field passed them by. Rats, mice, weasels or something.

'Maybe they're snakes,' suggested Patrick, none too sure they weren't.

'Fuck off,' Soames snapped. 'If you think I'm gonna turn back 'cause you're frightening me, you got another thing coming. Snakes, my arse!'

The stoical denials were sounding less convincing with every unidentified sound, every unidentified shadow and even every unidentified smell. Neither would admit it, but each of their hearts was pounding with fear. And one thing becoming more and more apparent to Patrick was that Soames didn't have a clue what he was doing. He was beginning to sense the entire escapade was a charade. If Soames was convinced that the police presence was so low, then why not just march up to the front door and knock? No, as more time passed, Patrick believed Soames didn't really want success. He merely wanted a failure he could blame on others.

At the end of the first field they searched for an opening to cross into the next. It hadn't looked this difficult on the map, thought Soames.

'Get the map out. Let's take a peek,' he demanded.

'I didn't bring no map,' responded Patrick. 'You was in charge of that.'

'No. I wasn't. I told you to sort it.' Soames slammed a fist into the other palm to vent his fury. 'Well, you can fuck off back and get it.'

'What? To the hotel?' Patrick countered as sarcastically as he dare.

'No. The car, you idiot. It's on the back seat.'

'So it was down to you,' Patrick mocked, gaining in confidence at the other's unease.

Without a word, Patrick tramped off through the silver barley toward the car. Soames found a tree to lean against and watched his friend disappear into the silvery abyss. He slid to the ground and rested. A snapping sound in the undergrowth clicked him out of his thoughts of Birmingham nightspots, booze and freely available women. It sounded like someone, or something, of size had stood on a thick plank of wood and broken it clean in two. Was there somebody else at large in the fields? He didn't know whether country folk frequented the fields at night like city folk would spend time in bars or clubs. No, he decided, it was too sinister.

Patrick's attention was taken by an ear-splitting, 'Wait for me!'

On turning, he saw an explosive movement as something reared up from the base of the hedge. The dark background delayed him identifying Soames bolting toward him like a hurdler.

'There's a bear! There's a bear!' Soames yelled. 'Wait! Wait!'

121

Patrick waited as instructed and knew he'd got to Soames. Not sure about bears in the English countryside himself, he suspected not, but that didn't matter. Soames thought there was and that did matter.

'I thought I'd come back to the car with you. I don't want you planning on escaping or anything like that,' said Soames, nerves calmed by the sprint across the field, but breathing heavily.

'Nothing to do with the bears, then?'

'Oh, no. No. That was just to get your attention.'

'Look, Randy. Do we actually need the map? I don't know about you, but I pretty well learned the route off the top o' my head. It's simple: we cross three fields, maybe four. Then, we come to the river that goes behind the church and Bryant's house, turn left –'

'Right,' Soames corrected.

'Left. I'm sure it's left. Then we cross a road and continue on a few hundred yards. It won't be a problem. We'll see the church tower and when we do, we head towards it and then we'll see the house. Hop over the back fence and we'll be there.'

'I'm not sure.' Soames's voice was more conciliatory. Was he broken or did he want to go on?

'Come on,' said Patrick, cajoling. 'It's another ten or fifteen minutes back to the car. Say thirty, thirty-five, back to where we were. We'll lose the darkness if we don't move quickly.'

Soames nodded his head. Agreement reached, they picked up the trail again but their nerves didn't ease. Coming out of a hedge they had to take evasive action as a barn owl swooped down to take off some poor unsuspecting morsel, just missing them as it flew away. The two pioneers, of course, had no idea what it was. Their conclusions ranged from a hovering ghost looking for a lost soul to a seagull, which they eventually settled on. Then there was an animal the size of a large dog, a muntjac deer, silhouetted on a rise of land which they were sure was a wolf prowling their route and waiting for an ideal time to attack. Crossing a ditch, Soames steadied himself on a run of barbed wire and cut his hand. Both men tore their shirts open on brambles. The expedition was unravelling. There was no sign of the church tower cutting the skyline, let alone the targeted home.

In crossing the river, Soames slipped onto his backside and slid down into the water. Surprisingly deep, it engulfed him. On standing in the middle of the stream, he swore and cursed and demanded to be taken back to Birmingham. Patrick, feeling Soames's discomfort, persuaded him they had come so far and they shouldn't give up so easily. And then it was there, looming up like a needle pointing to the heavens – the church tower.

Sue-Beth quickly assessed that there was no threat from the two figures lurching toward them. As the pair closed it was clear that they were a couple of young local lads headed back from a night out at the caravan park. Probably about sixteen or so, it was clear that they felt more grown up than they actually were. The occasional fiery glow showed they were both smoking.

'Just lay still,' she whispered in Bryant's ear. 'Don't move a muscle and they won't even notice us. They're too pissed.'

By now they were close enough to hear every word of the conversation and Bryant sensed Sue-Beth was sniggering at the explicit and intimate insight into the life of a male teenager.

'Did you get a shag tonight, Sam?' enquired the larger figure, lurching from one side of the lane to the other, words influenced by too much alcohol.

'No,' replied Sam. 'Did you then?'

'Oh, yes. Of course. Not only one, I'll have you know, but three. Actually, I think it was four.'

'Who with? You didn't seem to be gone for that long.'

'I was. Each one of those girls on that hen night had the

pleasure of me. And right glad they were too.'

'I don't know how you get so lucky every time, Josh,' said an incredulous Sam. 'You're overweight, totally pissed and you smoke like a chimney. I don't see what they see in you.'

'A cock like a cucumber, that's what. Speaking of which, I need to use it again now. I'm bustin' for a piss.'

'Yeah, me too,' agreed Sam.

They undid their flies and started to urinate to the side of the lane. Bryant, trying to keep still, was now under intense pressure as splashes of urine fell on his head and shoulders. It all became too much when the cigarette end was cast into the hedge and Josh aimed his stream of urine straight at it in a bid to extinguish the smouldering tobacco.

Like a crocodile rising up out of a river to devour an antelope, Bryant was in the lad's face before Sue-Beth could restrain him.

'What the fuck do you think you are doing, you dirty little bastard?' he demanded.

The boys staggered backwards, but said nothing.

'You just pissed all over my head. And if that wasn't enough, threw your fag-end down my neck and pissed on it.'

'Sorry,' Josh managed weakly, having finished pissing down his own jeans. 'We didn't know you were there.'

Josh was now lying on the road, but Sam had kept a bit more decorum by remaining standing, both still holding their cocks in hand. Another crocodile rose from the river. The second crocodile had sharper teeth, in the form of some type of rifle pointing right at them.

They instinctively put their hands above their heads, with their male pride on full display.

'Right, you two. Not a word to anyone, you didn't see us. Right?'

'No,' they replied in unison. 'Whatever you say.'

She lowered the muzzle to point directly at Josh's manhood. 'Good. I'm glad you understand,' she said coldly, 'because if I hear about this from anyone, I'll personally come back and cut that cucumber into thin slices.'

The two tidied themselves up and went on their way, sobered by the experience.

'And, by the way, Josh, tell the truth in future.'

'Huh?'

'However much you might think it, you can never make a pickled gherkin into a cucumber.'

They made it to the old Roman fort without further incident. Now known as Burgh Castle, the old fort at Gariannonum was built in 280 as a defence against increasingly emboldened Saxon raiders keen on taking a little piece of the Roman Empire for themselves. Haunted by the sounds of ancient battles, clashing of Saxon and Roman steel, and figures falling from the almost intact ramparts, the old outpost was now often the haunt of thrill-seekers looking for the paranormal.

Following the river, they came across the south-west corner of the ancient monument. The western wall, long since crumbled, laid the heart of the site open to Breydon Water and then the North Sea. The two entered the old battlements and headed directly for the gate in the eastern wall. A barking dog saw them scuttle to the protection of the south wall. The centre sward, rising like a crown green, was occupied by a tiny cluster of tents, of twenty-first-century vintage rather than Romano Saxon. No chance of ghoulish warriors descending on two modern soldiers. A ghost-weary voice ordered the barking to quietness. No coming out to look for patrolling centurions atop the ramparts, rather a turning over and a search for final deep sleep. The pair skirted the encampment and headed to the gate and the car park.

Three cars occupied the gravel surfaced area and sure enough one was a silver Ford Focus. Dawn was just creeping in and the fort was now blackening against the brightening sky. They were behind schedule, the original plan seeing them back in Oakshott before sunrise; no need to remove the blacking to their faces. Sue-Beth, finding a length of thin branch, fished out the keys from the exhaust pipe and jumped into the driver's seat. Bryant got in beside her.

'Poowr! You stink,' said the soldier as the doors were closed.

'So would you if you'd been pissed on by a drunken Lothario,' objected Bryant. 'Add falling in a ditch and sweating like a pig at times, it's hardly surprising, is it?'

Sue-Beth laughed.

'And another thing, I'm bloody hungry.'

'According to Ben's notes, it's not far back to that caravan park by road, and there's a shower block there. If we get caught, a bit of cash and the manager will be fine, I'm sure.'

'All right. What are you waiting for?'

Bryant emerged from the shower block clean, but scowling.

'What's wrong now?' asked Sue-Beth.

'The shower's freezing.'

'For Christ's sake, man up.'

'You're happy being a soldier. I'm a journalist. Remember, I don't do camping.' He sat in the passenger seat, crossed his arms, rested his chin on his chest and sulked.

Watching Sue-Beth disappear into the showers, a contemplative mood took over. He actually felt exposed and vulnerable without her near, not that he would let on to her. Then he considered his position. Surely they wouldn't really have executed him? What was more puzzling was that Plantagenet House was left alone by the authorities; why and how? Thoughts of how he was in this position flooded in. The kidnapping, the message back to Amelia and the sure knowledge that everyone looking for him knew it wasn't Randolph Soames who was involved. Even the TV coverage alluded to an organisation being behind his disappearance.

Funny how the mind worked. Thoughts of abduction and Soames led to the gangly black teenager in a Ledbury pub;

126

betrayal by the authorities of a forlorn bravery; an unpaid debt that society would never settle for the young lad who had given away everything in the ultimate sacrifice. Even his friend Cobbold, a man well versed in the shadowy workings of the law, could not bring himself to talk about it. The only thing Cobbold ever questioned was his continued role as a police officer. Dwight Carter – rest in peace, my friend.

A knock on the window cut across his thoughts. Shit, he thought, I was meant to be keeping an eye out for our backs. She's going to think me proper useless now.

'Who the bloody hell are you?' It was a voice more akin to Norfolk than Suffolk.

Bryant thought on his feet. 'SAS, mate. We're on a night exercise which we've just completed.'

The man's face showed utter contempt for the answer and Bryant found himself looking at the shower for help. Sue-Beth appeared spotlessly clean and looking every inch an attractive and elegant woman, even in dark jeans and polo shirt.

'She'll tell you.'

'SAS? She's a woman. A pretty one at that. You in the SAS then, lady?'

She fixed the man with her most penetrative gaze. He seemed to wince and look away. 'I'm not; he is,' she smiled. 'Saturdays and Sundays, Territorial Army. I'm regular army. Thank you for the use of the showers. How much do we owe you?'

The stare, although softened by the smile, was still intimidating.

'Nothing at all. My pleasure. Have a good day.'

In the car, she simply said, 'You are a fucking liability.' She turned on the car radio and Adele's 'Set Fire to the Rain' was playing. 'Funny,' she continued. 'Ben reckons this is my song, because I can actually do it.'

You probably bloody well could, thought the irritated journalist, not sure whether he loathed her or admired her.

11

Michael Jones was stirred by the sound of his mobile phone ringing on the bedside table. He was content for he had just woken up with his lover, someone who had, only hours earlier, taken him to the edge of ecstasy and plunged him in. The smile spread as he reached for the device.

'Hey, Curt. What's up, mate?'

'Here as quick as you can, lover boy,' the ex-policeman ordered. 'We found the car in a layby. Engine stone cold. Soames and Patrick have been on the loose for some while. The car was outside the protective ring, so they must be coming across country!'

'What shall we do with Amelia and the kids?'

'We'll move 'em over to Gillian's as soon as possible and we'll sit and wait for our friends to turn up.'

'Right into our trap?'

'You got it. Bang!' Richardson exulted. 'I can't believe they're so predictable.'

'Give me twenty minutes tops.'

Jones looked across at his lover and smiled fondly before taking a whirlwind shower. What a night, he thought, starting with the saving of a small timid cat. The cat had jumped onto the fence surrounding the Bryant home, probably something it had done many times before either to tease or evade Elsa. Never before had the cat caught her paw on barbed wire placed around the top. The resulting injury led to a chilling shriek in the dark. It led in turn to Jones bursting back into the garden, weapon raised, and rolling to the ground to attack. Again, nothing, except the Labrador growling at some invisible prey in the back border and the cat, with a lacerated lower leg, cowering and shaking, hardly able to move.

Amelia dug out the vet's number. An hour or so later, the wound was stitched and bandaged, and Jones was light of a few quid. Should have shot the bloody thing!

And now here he was, gazing down at the lover who'd shared dark hours of passion. He knelt to kiss the lips and whispered, 'I have to go. How about another time?'

The eyes and the teeth said it all. Yes. Yes, I want you again.

Jones allowed his fingers to tenderly caress an exposed arm and the two were locked in mirrored smiles.

'When can we do it again, Michael?' the voice whispered from the bed.

'When we have these two under lock and key, I'll be back,' Jones promised. He moved to the door and with one final look back, said, 'I love you, Peter,' and blew a kiss.

The upper quarter or so of the church tower at Oakshott was shrouded in golden dawn sunshine. Soames and Patrick took refuge in a thick copse and chomped their way through the provisions. Crisps, cake and cans of cola were devoured. Eyes were heavy and before the light had penetrated the thicket, both men were asleep.

A cock crowed in a nearby yard and Soames woke with a start. Wiping the sleep from his eyes, he stood and kicked Patrick into life.

'Christ's sake. What's the time?'

Squinting, Patrick tried to focus on his watch. 'Ten past five.'

Soames became agitated and started to wave the pistol about. 'Come on! Come on! We need to get moving. If we're not finished and out of there by seven it'll be hard to escape. Come on!'

'I'm knackered,' pleaded Patrick. 'Can't we just rest for half an hour?'

'No,' snapped the old gang leader, trying to suppress an anger rising through his body. He started to stomp up and down, cursing the godforsaken countryside and not understanding why anyone would ever want to live so far away from shops. He was hungry, furious and out of control.

'I'm absolutely knackered,' Patrick tried again. 'We've been on the go all night.' He was trying to buy time now as he'd failed in his plan to lead Soames in the wrong direction and get them totally lost. As was always the case, he'd lost his nerve and the images of the family running and playing in Christchurch Park kept playing on the periphery of his mind. Turning Soames over was sharp in planning but, faced with the loathsome creature, he, as usual, failed to deliver. The only hope was to delay the final push toward the Bryant home so the slaughter could be averted. He had no idea whether his plan B would work as when he had made the call the policewoman hadn't seemed to take him seriously.

Soames was clearly agitated, so perhaps the initial plan was working and he was making better progress than he realised. In short, though, Patrick considered himself a man of no worth, no esteem and above all, no balls.

He never felt a thing as the bullet bedded itself in the trunk of the larch he was leaning against. It entered his head just below the left eye and exited with an explosion of brain matter out of the back of his skull, leaving shards of bone and bloody globules on the tree.

Soames looked down in horror at what he had done. He hadn't meant to fire the gun! He knew it was unpredictable. He also knew that was his fault for he never maintained the weapon. Now a surge of regret soared up through his body: Stephen Patrick, despite the threats he made against the white man, was the best friend he had ever had. Was there now a futility in continuing?

'Steve, mate. Are you all right? Please talk to me?'

There was no answer from the corpse.

'Nooo!' Soames bellowed and bent to cradle his dead friend. 'I'm so sorry. I didn't mean to do it.' Blood trickled onto his hand. Soames vomited and crashed to his knees. Then, mustering all his absorbed energy, he pulled himself erect again. Turning to his dead friend, he said, 'I'll finish the job now.'

'That was bloody close,' Richardson commented to Jones on the landing of the Bryant family home. 'Do you know that's the second gunshot I've heard tonight? When the last one went off Gillian convinced me it was a rogue bird-scarer going off. That, though, was the same sound. A lot closer but the same sound. A hell of a lot sharper!'

Jones just nodded and checked his weapons for the umpteenth time since they had taken station on the landing. They were equally as prepared as the last time he had checked them.

The receiver on the floor beside Richardson announced, 'We have a visual: black man climbing up the hill toward the church from woods. Five hundred yards. He's on his own. Repeat that, he's on his own. Over.'

'Copy that. Tell us if you see the white man. Out.' Richardson turned to Jones. 'Take a peek.'

The unmanned camera on top of the church tower of St Peter's and St Paul's afforded the incident room panoramic views over many acres of Suffolk countryside. In periods of boredom during the investigation, officers had even intruded into the private lives of residents of the next village, some four or five miles away. They had watched people eating, playing and resting without a single one of them being aware of prying eyes.

'I see him,' confirmed Jones, standing at the bedroom window from where Amelia had watched him exercising. 'He's now veered across the field heading toward the back fence.

131

This could hurt!' The last comment referred to the barbed wire that waited atop the fence.

'Silver car. Focus. Just pulled into Church Road and heading your way,' the radio receiver announced. 'Woman driving, bloke in the passenger seat.'

'Target now at back fence,' Jones put in calmly.

'Car slowing. Now stopped outside you.'

'Ouch! That hurt,' grinned Jones.

'Man getting out of car and heading to front door.'

'Target recovered and heading down side to front. Holding hand. I think I can see blood.' Jones's commentary continued.

'Shit!' It was Richardson. 'How did he get in the village? Over.'

'All surveillance working. He's not a target. Repeat, he's not a target. Over.'

'ID?' asked Richardson. 'Over.'

'Trying to match now. Nothing found yet.'

'Jonah?' Richardson displayed an outer cool, but his mind was now in turbo mode.

'Trying side gate.'

A knock came at the door. Richardson's view was obscured by the porch roof so the most he could see was a pair of lower legs.

The knock at the door repeated. This time it was accompanied by the snapping sound of the letter-flap opening. 'Amelia, love. Can you hear me? Are you in there?'

Jones was now at the top of the stairs. Richardson had Soames in view. 'That's Bryant. Get him in. Trust a journalist to appear when you least want him!'

Jones was down the three flights in as many strides. Turning the key and opening the door in one smooth move he was out with Bryant in an instant.

'What the –'

'Inside and up the stairs,' Bryant was ordered by the stranger who'd just exploded out of his own front door. 'Police,' the man confirmed, putting himself between Bryant and the front corner of the house. Then backing up to the statued and startled Bryant, he ushered him in.

'I'm Michael Jones and up there is Curtly Richardson.'

Bryant looked up and saw a black man beckoning him up the stairs in haste.

'Quick as you can, sir. There's a tad of trouble out there.'

Jones followed Bryant up the steps and then Elsa the Labrador appeared and charged up the flights, barging past Jones, desperate to get to her master. Tail wagging furiously, she leapt at the man she hadn't seen in over two weeks. Bryant knelt to her and she placed her front paws on his shoulders in an embrace. She whined in delight, the tail nearly causing her to lose balance, it was so vigorous.

Hugs and licking complete, the dog scampered down the stairs and through to her basket in the kitchen. Retrieving a toy that consisted of a tennis ball with a rope passing through the middle, she started back to her long-lost master. As she came into the hallway and made her way to the bottom of the stairs, the front door crashed open and there in the doorway stood a man. Elsa's brain quickly took itself through the recognition process and this man's face did not feature. She dropped her toy to the floor and made for the intruder. About to leap at him, he brought a stick-like thing round and pointed it at her. The crack of the thing was like thunder as it spat a flame toward her.

The sound of the gun being fired was followed by a death-inducing shriek and a series of whining yelps. She looked up at the beast who had brought her down, eyes trying to say sorry. She dragged herself slowly and painfully to her feet, picked up the toy and retired to her basket dragging her shattered leg behind her and whimpering with every ounce of effort.

'No, no, no!' Bryant shouted and made along the landing.

Jones blocked his path and pointed his gun toward the assailant. Richardson had already shouted, 'Police. Put down your weapon.'

133

Soames stood in the hallway, not moving a muscle. He neither dropped his weapon nor threatened with it. It was as if he had been turned to ice. And less than an hour ago, it looked as if his evil plan might be seen through to a bloody yet satisfactory conclusion.

Richardson started slowly down the stairs, the gun sight never leaving the target. One false move and the bastard's lifeblood would be ebbing away. The eyes were glazed over, but Richardson knew that one sudden movement or noise could bring Soames out of shock. A trail of blood led from where Soames had been turned to stone. Moving closer, Richardson saw that the eyes had not actually glazed over, but watered over. He wrested the old rusty weapon from a seemingly lifeless grasp and handed it to Jones coming down the stairs behind him.

'Outside,' Richardson growled. 'And face down on the ground.'

There was no reaction and with what seemed like relieved but pent-up frustration, the policeman slammed his fist into the prisoner's abdomen, bending him over and crashing down a karate-style chop into his neck.

'Outside and down on the fucking ground, I said.'

'Curt!' Jones tried to intervene. In the past few years of working together he had never seen his partner, and friend, lose it like this. 'She's a beautiful and loving dog, but you can't act like this.'

The man fell to his knees and Richardson dragged him to his feet by the collar. Soames was breathing heavily and tried to resist but the other man's strength and determination were immense. The once potential mass murderer allowed himself to be quiescently put in a star-shaped position face down on the gravel drive.

'Cuff the bastard,' Richardson ordered and followed Bryant to the kitchen.

He stood while Bryant knelt by the injured animal. The

shattered look in the once-shining eyes was almost too much for Richardson to bear, but he walked forward and placed his hand on Bryant's shoulder as he comforted the creature.

The dog lifted her proud head. It was as if she was hoisting a lead-weighted collar. The tail wagged involuntarily a couple of times and even a hard old cynic like Curtly Richardson was moved by the pleading eyes. He interpreted them as saying, 'Daddy, I'm so sorry about the mess, but I tried to be brave.' With one final lick of her master's hand, she lowered her head and closed her eyes.

'I think she's going to be okay,' were all the comforting words that Richardson could muster. Turning to Jones, he said, 'Get that scum to his feet. There should be a couple of plods here by now.'

Richardson and Bryant followed Jones and his prisoner outside, Richardson flicking the keys to the family Ford Galaxy sitting on the drive. Pushing the unlock fob, he raced ahead of Bryant to open the tailgate and stood back as the distraught man placed the still form in the back. As two locals were dealing with Soames, Richardson beckoned Jones over. He whispered something in his colleague's ear and slapping him on the back, headed to where the prisoner was being formally cautioned.

'No problems,' agreed Jones. 'I want to see how that bloody cat is anyhow. You sit in the back with Elsa. I know the way to the vet's.' The last bit was addressed to a distraught Bryant who surely had not envisaged a homecoming like this.

Bryant stared after the commanding figure of the policeman as he strode back to the prisoner. There was something about the man. The sincere eyes took Bryant back to another time, but as much as he searched the depths of his mind he could not place the face. He could swear there was a glint of recognition in the other man's eyes as well. He sat with the shallow-breathing dog and coaxed her back.

'Lift him to his feet, please,' Richardson requested. Then,

standing square in front of the prisoner and staring directly into his eyes, he said, 'Seen these before, you bastard?' The captor pointed to his own eyes as if to enforce the point.

'This man assaulted me,' was all Soames could rally while turning himself away from the fiery aggression in Richardson's face.

Moving closer, Richardson tried again. 'So, you shitbag, do you recognise me?'

Soames shook his head this time, trying to avoid the glare of the other.

'Then, allow me to introduce myself. I've been dreaming of this moment for years. My name is… Dwight Carter. Remember now, scum? I'm the one you had killed. Remember?'

There was a released aggression in Richardson's voice and a shaking inside brought on by sheer hatred and loathing of the man standing before him.

Soames's knees buckled under the enormity of what he had just learned and he had to be supported by a policeman from either side. Soames nodded a pathetic recognition.

'Take him away. I think he needs some sugar inside him. It's obviously been a long night. God let your soul rot. One more thing. Where's Patrick? At least he did the right thing and filled us in on the outline plan you'd concocted.'

'Dead,' muttered Soames in barely more than a whisper. 'In the woods.'

Richardson, or was it now to be Carter, turned and walked away. Of all the people he knew in the world only Duncan Cobbold and Michael Jones had known his true identity. In his own mind, he didn't actually mind being Curtly Richardson; not many got to choose their own names. But, for the next few days he would celebrate being Dwight Carter again. There were a few he didn't know who knew his true identity; for a start there was a succession of Prime Ministers and Home Secretaries. Even his mother believed him dead, dying in prison all those years ago. Was he best off staying dead or should the former delinquent puff on the peace pipe? He had, after all, made sure she was well provided for through Cobbold. Perhaps the status quo should be maintained or maybe she would become a proud mother. She had never been a very good parent or him a very good son. There was no hurry; he would think on it.

Sue-Beth didn't turn the car around and go through the village but continued on past the church, the longer route. As she turned left at the end of Church Road to head down the hill toward Ampsley, a police helicopter swooped low overhead moving swiftly from left to right. To her right in the Bildeston direction, a police car could be seen parked in a field gateway. Down into Ampsley she drove before turning left again and heading back up the hill and back toward Oakshott. Yet another police car was in a layby, this time with an officer leaning against it and chatting to someone with a dog. Sue-Beth noted the officer's gaze followed her progress as she passed, much like a hawk would analyse its next meal.

At a sharp left bend and about a mile from the village, she pulled off the road to the right and came to a stop in front of a large pair of gates. Leaving the car, she approached a pillar and punched in a numbered code. The gates started to ease open and she glided through. The scrunching of gravel under the wheels was a reassuring sound. In the rear-view mirror she could see the gates were now swinging shut. Home, sweet home, maybe. Home, safe home definitely.

The nineteenth-century cannon with its blackened mouth pointing over the car roof stood guard on the circular lawn in front of the house, reminding all visitors that this was a military home of distinction. She passed the ancient weapon on its right flank and eased the Ford to a halt in front of the main entrance. Killing the engine, she got out and before she had circled the front of the car, the front door burst open and a small boy charged toward her. The hard training of the soldier dissolved into the instinctive love of a mother. She crouched low and held her arms out wide, and Toby crashed into her tight embrace. She planted a huge motherly kiss on the little boy's cheek.

'God! I've missed you,' she said and began to feel her eyes prick at the emotion of uniting with someone she feared she might never have seen again.

'I've missed you as well. I always miss you when you go away. Why are you crying, Mummy? Are you not happy to see me?'

Sue-Beth found it difficult to muster words and hugged the boy tighter. Through the tears she told him, 'I'm really pleased to see you, more than you can ever know.'

Lady Isobel stood in the doorway. The two women exchanged pecks and moved inside. 'How about you and I go and make some tea for Mummy, Toby?'

With that, the lad ran to the kitchen.

'Slow down,' the boy's mother chided before turning to her mother-in-law. 'There seems to be a lot of police activity in the village. What's up?'

'Well,' Lady Isobel started. 'Since you've been away this time a journalist who lives in the village was kidnapped from outside his office in London. He was quite high up, I think, in the *Echo and Post*. First of all, the police thought it was some odious black man who... Oh, incidentally, one of the leading policemen is a black man, in rather fine fettle, if you know what I mean? Anyway, where was I?'

'He was supposed to have been kidnapped by an odious black man,' Sue-Beth prompted. She decided she wouldn't divulge that she had just dropped Bryant off at his front door. It would be too complicated to explain the link. So she continued to listen to a story she already knew intimately and wondered if the villagers would think it all over with the safe return of the victim, although she knew that it was only the beginning of the next chapter.

'Where's Poppy?' asked Sue-Beth – 'grandpop' (Sir James) now shortened thanks to Toby's inability to conjure the full word.

'He's off with another family who have lost a loved one in Afghanistan,' the older woman answered, her own grief as sore as the day she first heard her son had become the highest ranking British soldier to die in that particular theatre. 'This one is a horrible story. The poor lad was blown up by an Afghan insurgent pretending to be an Afghan soldier. Truly horrible! Anyway,' she continued, 'he can't have got very far. I think it's Lancaster or somewhere that he's going to. I'll call him and let him know you're back. You should have called, Susan, and I'm sure he would have delayed his departure.'

Sue-Beth could see her mother-in-law's eyes glistening as a shaft of sunlight shining through the large drawing-room windows highlighted them like diamonds. Sue-Beth missed Nathan but there was no doubt the burden was greater to the parents. Her grief had been intense but brief. Instead, she valued every living minute with her son. Nate lived on in Toby.

Lady Isobel left Sue-Beth in the drawing room and went off to supervise Toby making tea. Sue-Beth stared at the wheat field beyond the back fence, the breeze playing with the ears and making it look like the swell of a greeny-gold ocean. She sighed at the beauty. She loved this time of year, the few days leading to harvest. Every year there was a competition to be the first tractor boy into the pub who had delivered a trailer of ripened barley to the granary.

She turned inwards and, seeing a newspaper on the coffee table, made her way across to Sir James's favourite chair. Monday's *Daily Telegraph* front page told the story of how rebels had claimed victory in the eastern Libyan city of Brega. Scanning the story, it contained much of the same old, same old, so she moved to the inside. The leaf holding pages five and six had had a cutting taken from it – no doubt the tale of a young squaddie from Lancaster who had met a far too early end fighting this bloody war against terror. She smiled as she wondered if, indeed, it was still called the war on terror. Most people simply referred to it in one word. It needed nothing else. Afghanistan.

Toby appeared, carefully carrying a tray with a cup and saucer on it. Grandma was two paces further back with a teapot in hand. The tragedy of boiling hot tea cascading over the polished oak floor was not worth the risk of Toby delivering the entire service. Sue-Beth peered into the cup to see the slightest of splashes already at home, obviously a negotiated position agreed between Toby and Grandma to make the youngster believe it was all of his making. Isobel filled the cup and the pungency of Earl Grey's concoction caressed her nostrils.

An exaggerated sniffing at the aroma preceded the first sip. Plantagenet House offered only tea or coffee, which was of varying quality depending on whom was entrusted with the shopping on any one day.

Glancing at the clock on the mantel, Sue-Beth said she would deliver young Toby for the last day of school before the summer break. It was still early enough to have a short snooze and set off for a stroll, the return journey being the more enjoyable and free from moaning about walking from her only born. She smiled, finished the tea and slipped into unconsciousness.

'Who's this sitting in my chair said Daddy Bear,' could be heard somewhere in the distance. 'It must be the beautiful Goldilocks,' said Daddy Bear's voice.

Baby Bear laughed. Sue-Beth came too and saw James Daddy Bear and Toby Baby Bear standing over her. Toby clapped his hands and laughed.

'Mummy, you were snoring!'

'I was not,' Sue-Beth feigned indignation and made as if to get up from her father-in-law's favourite chair.

'No. No, my dear. Stay there.' Sir James raised the palm of

his hand. 'I shall sit over here.' He sat himself on the end of the leather sofa closest to Sue-Beth.

'I wasn't expecting you back,' said the old general, then added, 'So soon, I mean.'

Sue-Beth paused, letting the words play in her mind and recognising that there was no importance attached to them, and asked: 'Oh! Why's that? I mean I'm normally away for two or three weeks at a time.' In her role with the Civil Protection Group she was not merely based at Plantagenet House, but could find herself anywhere in the world on personal protection duty for a client. Once she had been away for nearly five weeks guarding a valuable diamond being hawked around the globe for the highest possible bidder. Not a single billionaire had made an offer of interest to the seller, so she had to accompany the thing all the way back to Geneva. Sometime later, she saw a newspaper article saying that the Eye of the Kalahari had sold for nearly ten million dollars.

'That was clumsy, my dear. Do forgive me. What I meant was, you normally call ahead to let us know you're coming.'

'Of course. Sorry about that. I've mislaid my phone. It's in my room somewhere at work. Anyway,' she continued, changing the subject, 'I assume you were on your way to see the parents of that poor lad from Lancaster?' She held up the page from the *Telegraph* with the hole in it.

'I was. Another sad tale to add to all the others. Every death in those lands is only another statistic to the MOD's butcher's bill. But, to a handful of people, sometimes more, it is the ruination of lives. Take this young lad, Gunner Robbie Pryke, aged twenty-one; joined the army as a last resort really. Couldn't find a job doing anything else, you know. His colonel claims he was a damned fine soldier. Not necessarily the brightest, but a damned fine soldier. And, I can tell you, that away from the media, not every soldier gets such an accolade.

'Anyway, Gunner Pryke came from a good and honest

Lancashire working-class family. Mother and father, only in their early-forties themselves, run a taxi business and struggle to make ends meet, and I'm sure they swizzle the taxman out of the odd cash job, but who cares, because they've now made the ultimate sacrifice and many a person in this country of ours would rather the brave gunner could swap places with a faceless, chinless, spineless taxman. And then there are the two little ones and Mrs Pryke. She had the first child when she was only fifteen and now has a boy and a girl, and she's only a babe herself at eighteen.'

The man's furrowed brow betrayed the hurt. He rested his face in his palms. The Walters family might not be on the edge of destitution but they had so much in common with the Pryke family. Brothers in arms brought families from all backgrounds to be united in death. Sue-Beth didn't say anything; she didn't need to. She knew exactly where Sir James's mind had wandered. It was walking hand in hand with hers along a country path with a tall, handsome young soldier.

'Good God!' Sir James muttered. 'This poor lot will barely scrape by while we sit and watch our taxmen taking every last penny from these good folk and handing it to the great unwanted like Hamza the Hook and Qatada, amongst others.'

Sue-Beth stretched across and put her hand in her father-in-law's. 'You must continue what you're doing. It takes a brave man who hasn't yet shaken off his own grief to allow others to unburden theirs on him.'

'I try my best, my dear. I try my best.' He lifted his head and looked at her, the anguish still written across his face. 'But you, my dear, you seem to have shaken off this horrible dark spectre called grief.'

'Oh, no,' she said. 'It follows me with my every waking minute. It's at my shoulder with every single step I take. It lies with me at night and laughs in my face as I still sometimes cry myself to sleep. I can assure you, it will never leave me.'

12

Duncan Cobbold pulled onto the drive of the Bryant home half an hour or so after the incident had been brought to a close. He had received the call earlier from Richardson saying the final scene was about to be played out. Despite expecting a call at any time during the two-hour journey from London, there had been nothing, bar the company of Vanessa Feltz and then Chris Evans on Radio Two.

A uniformed police sentry stood guard over the open front door and a couple more officers appeared to be searching the front garden. Cobbold approached the officer at the door and flashed his warrant card. The officer beckoned for him to present it for further inspection, saying even his excellent vision couldn't work with the speed of a checkout barcode reader.

'Thank you, sir,' he said, handing the identification back to the more senior man. The officer had gleaned that Cobbold was a senior officer from London's Metropolitan force. He did not know that the man was the commander of the Home Security Team. There was a fair chance the young constable would never even get to hear of the existence of the Home Security Team, even if he lived to two hundred.

Cobbold saw the trail of blood leading from the bottom of the stairs through to the kitchen. The constable noticed the concern spread across the senior man's face.

'It was only the dog, sir.'

The stony look from the DCI made him change tack slightly.

'What I mean is, sir, is that no humans were killed.'

A helicopter roared into the air and shot across the sky overhead.

''Cept a bloke in the woods at the back. One of the villains, I'm led to believe, sir.'

Cobbold went inside. Apart from the trail of blood, there was no evidence of a struggle.

'Constable,' he said in a raised voice.

'Yes, sir?'

'The dog? Dead or alive?'

'Not sure, sir, but I don't think it's good. Yer man, Jones, and the owner took him to the vet's.'

'It's a her, actually. I thought Richardson said he'd taken Mrs Bryant to a safe place.'

'Not Mrs Bryant, sir, Mr Bryant.'

'Mr Bryant?' Cobbold was bemused. There must be some mistake. He was convinced the constable was mistaken.

The sound of a car pulling onto the drive and the engine dying caught Cobbold's attention. He returned outside and saw the Galaxy parked behind his own car. Jones got out of the driver's side and, sure enough, the man closing the nearside door was Bryant, his old friend. He made his way over.

'Christ,' he started. 'You've caused some hassle round here, mate.'

Bryant took the proffered hand and the firm, friendly handshake was followed by a hug and complimentary backslapping.

'Good to see you too, Duncan. Sorry about the mess.'

'I was expecting worse. How's Elsa?'

'Not good. Lost a lot of blood and the next twenty-four to forty-eight hours are crucial,' Bryant answered. 'I must say, though, your two men are good. So cool when I was cacking myself. So, Jonah tells me you're in charge of some crack team made up of top cops and the best of the elite soldiers. Him and the black guy, Richardson, I think. Well, they're a credit to you.'

'Indeed they are.' Cobbold glowed at the complimentary tone of his friend. 'Of course, you'll have recognised the black guy.'

Bryant thought on his answer. Despite the glimmer of recognition that had haunted him since the briefest of contact in the kitchen, the truth was that he didn't. Perhaps he'd been involved in a famous case of some sort. Whatever, it must have passed him by. He would be gracious in defeat.

'Vaguely familiar, I think,' he said. 'But I can't put a name to him. Who is he then?'

'Where is he, Jonah?' asked Cobbold of the Special Forces man.

'Should be back soon. Finishing the reconnection process with our Mr Soames.'

'Ah! Here he is now. Good. Let's get the introductions out the way and we'll be on our way. I am sure you and Amelia will want some quality time together before we come and question you. Procedure, you understand.'

'Not so fast,' said Bryant. 'I have a tale that will make your blood curdle.'

'Mr Bryant.' The jovial black man greeted him. 'How's that beautiful dog of yours?'

'Next couple of days are important.' There was something strangely familiar about the guy's smile. His mind quickly scanned every folder and file stored in his own hard drive but could not come up with a match. 'You're a step ahead of me, Mr Richardson. You appear to know about me, probably through swatting up on the case, and possibly info gained from Duncan – we'll discuss which bits are true later.'

'You know me very well indeed, Sean Bryant. I owe everything to you first, and then to Duncan second. But there ain't much in it.'

Bryant was at a loss. No matter how much he searched the archives he couldn't come up with a name. He looked at the other two faces, both betraying huge smiles.

'My name is... Dwight Carter,' the man announced, like a TV results reader. He then bent down as if to pick something from the ground and made to hand the invisible thing to the open-mouthed journalist. 'Your jaw. I hope it's not broken where it dropped so far. You're the second one this morning to have acted as if they've seen a ghost. Come with me,' Richardson continued. 'There are three important people who will be over the moon to see you.'

Sue-Beth had intended to walk her son to the village school but the chat with Sir James had taken more of her time than she thought. This, combined with the thought that she might be vulnerable to recapture so close to home, made her decide to take the car; she was convinced that this would be the first place they would look, despite Sharp's assurances that it would all be covered up until the following week. She pulled up nearer the entrance to the cricket ground than the school gate. Sure, some parents lived further afield, but the majority resided in Oakshott and as with many schools up and down the country, the approaches to the school were cluttered with four-wheel drives, many of which had journeyed less than 500 yards. She still needed to be vigilant and was ever alert trying to scan ahead for anyone or anything that looked out of place as she walked Toby to the school gate. She was comforted by the gun she had concealed in the car, but in the short distance to the gate a feeling of vulnerability came over her. Be alert, she ordered herself.

The usual bunch of mothers was holding court outside the gate. She picked up on some of the comments as she passed, a few even exchanged good mornings or hellos. The hottest gossip seemed to involve the head of the school. Some seemed to think it scandalous that she should be seeing a black man; others said good luck to her and wouldn't mind trying a bit themselves. The same women were critical of their lazy husbands whom, it appeared, would set off for their London offices before six in the morning and not return until after eight in the evening, yet the non-working class that most of these ladies belonged to had to struggle with the gym or spa and hair treatments. Then there were the coffee mornings and the planning of the children's social calendar. Sue-Beth smiled and reflected what a dull life she led herself, whether it was leading a troop of men down an African river to an unlikely rescue, smoking out Taliban insurgents, or guarding a precious diamond on a world tour. Not one of these gate gossipers had any idea what the mysterious woman from the Ampsley Road did, but one thing was for sure: she wouldn't swap her life for any one of the manicured existences of these so-called yummy mummies.

She headed back to the car after seeing Toby safely into the playground for the last day of the academic year.

'Mrs Walters,' a female voice tried to attract her attention from a few yards behind.

She turned to see a woman a few years her junior trying to catch her up. The woman fitted the description she had been given many times over the last couple of weeks.

'Mrs Bryant, I assume?'

'Yes. Please call me Amelia.'

'My name is Susan, but like everyone else, you can call me Sue-Beth,' she smiled.

'Yes. So I understand. Sean explained that one to me,' said Amelia. 'He also explained that we owe you for saving his life.'

'Not really. It was just a by-product of saving my own.'

'Would you come round and have some coffee? I've got a nice big chocolate cake that I've made for the people who've been protecting the children and me. I'm sure they won't mind sharing it.'

You absolute hypocrite, Sue-Beth admonished herself. 'Yes. I'd love to come. Thank you. Here, you might as well get in.' Pointing the key at the car, the locks cranked open.

*

Bryant greeted Sue-Beth enthusiastically with a peck on the cheek and introduced her to the small party, while Amelia went off to perform her home-making duties of tea and coffee. Three other men were present: Cobbold, Richardson and an apparently shy ex-soldier, Michael Jones. Amelia joined them just as Richardson was about to tell the tale of how he started life as Dwight Carter in Birmingham, changed to Curtly Richardson, and was now considering a change back to his given name. She assumed this man of such apparent mystery was also the target of the drooling mums at the school gate.

Teas, coffees and chocolate cake were served up and Richardson – or should it be Carter? – began.

A tall, lanky, black adolescent, he was always bright at school but craved some excitement in life. A couple of brothers about five doors along the street were on hand to provide the answer. They stole cars and sold them, and young Dwight joined in with Charlton and Randolph Soames. They would steal cars and sell them on for a good profit, allowing a fifteen-year-old black kid to see more money than he thought it possible to even dream about. Now, as an older professional, he realised it was less than what the minimum wage would have been, had it existed in those days.

Randolph Soames, after the imprisonment of his older brother, decided to branch the family business out after being given a gun. They would rob rural post offices, much like the one in Oakshott. Easy targets with minimal risk, and the now sixteen-year-old Carter would select a getaway car, steal it, and then drive it to and from the targeted post offices. In the beginning it was exciting and the money earning increased, especially when they worked out that some of the tills would be filled on certain days with pensions and other benefits.

During this time, when he had been sent to the Hereford-shire town of Ledbury to report on some local establishments, he met a newly graduated journalist who needed no introduc-tion to those present. They struck up a friendship. One day, after a robbery that had gone wrong – where some school-children had been frightened out of their skins by Soames discharging his less than reliable pistol – he had told his new friend everything in a tearful confession. Bryant had then introduced him to a young policeman he played football with and over a relatively short period, and after much toing and froing with senior officers, they had a plan which would see Carter testify against the other two gang members in exchange for a non-custodial sentence.

At the end of the trial he stood staring at the judge as a prison sentence was passed down. Expecting to hear words such as 'suspended' for so many years, they never came and he was taken down to the holding cells with the two men he'd just testified against to begin his sentence. Fortunately, the law had the sense to send him to a different gaol to Soames and Patrick. While waiting in the cells beneath the court, Carter lost count of the times and methods that Soames was planning for his end.

After one night in a reception cell, he was separated from other prisoners and taken to a room on the first floor. A couple of blokes were in the room and they imparted an incredible tale of how Dwight Carter was already dead and would assume a new identity. The new identity would offer guaranteed protection from Soames and his family and to a lesser extent, Patrick. The two men apologised to Carter that he'd spent even one night behind bars but a key component of the plan, Duncan Cobbold, had gone on the missing list after the trial. In a bid to keep the plan under wraps not even Cobbold had been informed. He would be needed to perform the official identification of the body.

'I later find out,' Richardson continued, 'that while I was coming to terms with rotting away in prison for the next few years, my old mate here is out on the town getting out of his head with strippers. I believe they call it the caring side of the law.'

Richardson laughed as he remembered the look on Cobbold's face when he walked in the room to find the body of his friend full of breath. The reddened eyes looked like a couple of spilled blood patches in a field of freshly laid snow.

Then there was the name. Could the young man come up with a name he could use for the rest of his life? After a moment's thought it was easy. His favourite West Indian bowler was Curtly Ambrose and his favourite West Indian batsman was Richie Richardson. So, Curtly Richardson was born and for good luck, he threw in the second forename of Vivian to honour the great Sir Viv Richards. Within a few days he had passport, National Insurance identification, birth certificate and bank accounts.

He moved to a new area of the country and settled in Portsmouth. Why would anybody in the old seafaring town ever question the arrival of another incomer when the town was full of transients? He kept himself very much to himself; there was no way he was going to blow this second chance. By the summer in which he was seventeen, he had finished his GCSE courses and taken eleven exams, passing them all with As and Bs, except for one: history was a C. He then studied hard to get four A-levels in a year. That was hard going, but with two As and one B he went to Southampton University where he completed a degree in applied mathematics with a 2:1.

During his exile to Hampshire, Cobbold was a regular visitor. Cobbold, according to Richardson, was like the father he never had, even though there was only about seven years between them. One great shame was that he had to cut his friendship with Bryant, blaming Cobbold, who had always joked that you could never trust a journalist for he would sell members of his own family for a half-decent story. The biggest regret of all was that he had not seen his mother since a week or so before the trial. Dwight's mother was only nineteen when he was born and life had been a struggle.

As Curtly Richardson, Eileen Carter's son had channelled money back to his mother through the conduit of Cobbold who visited her at regular intervals in the intervening years. Now the son needed to make one final use of the conduit. Cobbold would attempt to clear the way and prepare Eileen for the biggest of Lazarean revivals, eleven years after the 'passing'. Richardson could walk away and never ever see his mother again. She had never been a good mother, she had never been a loving mother, but now perhaps she could be a proud mother.

After completing university, Cobbold helped to get Dwight into the police. On completing training, Dwight joined the Hampshire constabulary and after the briefest period in uniform, it was clear the applied mathematical mind would make a useful detective. When Cobbold came calling at the behest of the previous Home Secretary, Detective Inspector Curtly Vivian Richardson didn't need a second invitation to go and join his old friend in the fledgling Home Security Team.

'The rest, as they say, is history,' said a beaming Richardson. 'And that was my weakest subject.'

A warm summer's day greeted the Asian tourists in the centre of Oslo. It was just before lunch and it was Friday, so many Norwegians were planning to finish work early and make for the coast. Boat sheds in the fjords would be opened up and once again this maritime nation would take to the sea. Barbecues would hardly be taken in over the entire weekend as the natives made the best of the occasional warm weather to cover the country in wafts of cooking smoke.

The Asian tourists were beginning to grow impatient. They were all from the Indian sub-continent and a mixture of Muslims, Hindus and Sikhs; they weren't only united by nationality but a love of all things European. There were twenty-four of them and they were touring Scandinavia for the first time. They had now been waiting on the pavement near the Ministry of Justice and Public Affairs for over half an hour. The driver had promised them the tour guide would be along presently and in the meantime, the tourists were to enjoy the facilities on the bus. The contents of the refrigerator were complimentary and if the tour guide appeared before the driver returned from his comfort break, they were to simply leave the bus open. There would be no problems, as crime was so very low in Norway, thanks to the caring and sharing society it had become.

The Indians all agreed that none of them had ever visited such a friendly country before. Some were visiting relatives and on leaving the tour, would be visiting their families scattered around the capital and its environs. Three turbaned Sikhs had wandered away from the group and were admiring a statue, and with the aid of their *Learn Norwegian* books were deciphering the plaque. But they were roused from their reverie by an ear-splitting crescendo of noise filling the capital's streets, as a fierce blast of air knocked them to the ground and debris began to fall around them. Deafened, they lifted themselves clear of the ground and immediately thought to seek the refuge of the tour bus. Turning to head for the bus, the vista that greeted them was of the most grotesque imaginable, even beyond imaginable. The bus had been turned on its roof, what was left of it, and had come to rest some metres from its starting position. Whole corpses and parts of corpses appeared to be strewn as far as the eye could see.

A crater was now where the bus had been and water from a ruptured main was climbing into the sky and falling like a surreal rain from the clouds above. Except, they weren't clouds; it was billowing smoke that had resulted from the carnage.

Passers-by had not escaped the blast. A woman in her thirties lay staring disbelievingly at the roof of a building opposite, blood fountaining from the neck wound that still had the offending shard of glass protruding from it. A man was dazed, bleeding and sobbing over the fallen woman, probably his wife. Another wandered aimlessly, clutching his ears as if some monster was tormenting his very being. A jellied mess of what had seconds before been a smiling baby boy filled the stroller, now abandoned by the parents.

The three Sikhs, mesmerised by the blast, peered into the charnel house that had once been their tour bus. Not a soul was alive. Two women recognised the three men and went to plead their help, but the men could not place the two women purporting to be friends, for these two daughters of Mohammed had lost their veiled modesty to the blast. And, without doubt, they had also lost their husbands.

Sirens sounded and within minutes ambulances, police cars and rescue tenders began to appear. An army of paramedics was bending over crumpled bodies, some administering first aid, others simply moving to the next prostrate figure after realising nothing could be done for the first. The five survivors of the Indian tour group sat in a people carrier commandeered by the authorities to ferry the less seriously injured to hospital. All five entwined their hands and held a silent vigil for their loved ones and the new friends they would never see in this world again. Silent prayers pleaded for all the gods to band together and take the souls to eternity. Trust was put in the hands of all the gods for it was unfair to let one god deal with today on his own. In the land of Odin it would be the World Gods that would take over today.

The policeman stood apart from the other passengers on the train, but his features betrayed the grim news he was carrying to the summer camp. He could taste the salt on the air through the open window as the train rocked across the bridge to the peninsula a few kilometres from the city; the alternative was a car trip of nearly one hundred kilometres. The unmistakable smell of the sea wafted through the door window, but nothing could dampen his resolve. He had to get to the camp.

Thanks to twenty-first-century technology, news had reached the small train, filled with young backpackers heading for a summer conference on the peninsula. Some stood, staring back at the city, some open-mouthed, and others covering their mouths as if they were afraid what may come out of them.

Ingrid Carlsen was nineteen and attending her third summer conference of the Socialist Youth League, this time as a helper. She sat on a slatted wooden bench listening to a running commentary on her mobile phone. There had been some sort of bomb-blast on a tour bus outside the Government building where her father worked. She had tried calling him; she had tried texting him; she had tried emailing him; she had even tried tweeting him. There had been no reply and her mind worked itself to a frenzy of worry.

Initial reports started to lay the blame on a group of Muslim tourists who had clearly selected the friendly nation of Norway to wreak Allah's will. Ingrid realised the policeman had an earpiece. He was clearly not listening to the same broadcast as she was for he was smiling broadly. Glancing in her direction, he caught her staring back and as if turned off by a switch, the smile disappeared.

He turned back to face forward again, this time trying to suppress his smile. He might not have been listening to the same broadcast as Ingrid, but he was listening to the same story and he was enjoying every word. He had no idea the blame would be placed at the gates of Islam, but this would draw any hunter away from the real quarry for hours, maybe even days; hours were all that were needed, though.

The train chugged into the camp's own station and the policeman joined the queue to alight immediately behind Ingrid. She felt a slight unease, but at least there was a policeman coming to the camp at this time of national stress. The pair stepped from the carriage onto a platform before passing through the ticket control and onto a concrete ramp with a steep incline. At the top the policeman spoke.

'Excuse me, miss.'

Ingrid turned to check if it was her being addressed.

'Can I help?' she enquired of the man.

'Indeed you can. I've been sent across from the police department to let people know about the bombing and to act as a sort of liaison. I wonder if you would be kind enough to direct me to reception so I can make myself known?'

'Of course,' said Ingrid. 'My hut is two doors further on. Please come with me.'

'Thank you.'

They strolled along a concrete path, the policeman ever fidgety. He always seemed to be correcting the way his uniform was hanging. Ingrid noticed this and despite the toned face, the officer seemed to be carrying a few extra kilos.

'Have you been at the scene?' Ingrid asked.

'I haven't. No. I have only heard the radio news interspersed with messages from headquarters directing movement of the emergency responders.'

'It's just... No. It doesn't matter.'

'No. Please carry on. If you have any worries it is best to talk about them. I can tell you have concerns. I may be able to help.'

'Okay,' she said. 'Was the Ministry of Justice badly damaged?'

Ah, thought the policeman, she has friends or family who work there. 'Why do you ask?'

'It's... It's my father. He works there.'

From what he had seen, the policeman didn't think many had been injured inside the building, let alone killed.

'It was badly damaged, I am afraid to say.'

'Thank you for your honesty,' she said politely, tears beginning to prick at the corners of her eyes. 'Here is the reception. There should be someone in there. If not, just ring the bell.'

'Thank you, miss. I hope your father is unharmed,' the policeman said. 'If it is any consolation, I think most of the dead were worthless Muslims. I doubt anyone shall miss them.'

The last words stopped her progress to her own cabin for she could not believe what she had heard from an officer of the law. She made her way into the kitchen of the cabin and started to place her provisions in cupboards and the fridge. She found her bed and placed a framed photograph of her mother, father and younger brother on the drawers at the side.

She returned to the kitchen and put the kettle on and poured some Nescafe into a mug. Waiting on the kettle, she tried her father again. No answer to the phone call. She sent a text. Then, tapping out an email, the door to the kitchen opened. The policeman stood in the frame.

'Did you find out what you-' Ingrid started to enquire.

They were the last words she uttered. The policeman had loosed off three rounds from his pistol. The first took Ingrid in the neck, sending a font of scarlet to the wall and ceiling. The second went through her right eye. The third was irrelevant; she was dead. So it was that Ingrid Carlsen joined the queue at the gates of heaven, only a few places behind her father, Sven.

A girl, attracted by the sound, entered the kitchen. Holding her hand to her mouth at the horrendous sight that greeted her, she tried to reverse out but slipped on blood. Because of the slip, the bullet caught her in the arms, knocking her to the ground. The policeman scowled at the fear on the girl's face as he stood over her. Two slugs turned the pretty image to a distorted red mess.

Outside the cabin, five youths were stunned by the sound from within and were tempted to flee. A policeman emerged from within and they relaxed. The one survivor from the group told how he had approached them. They thought he was going to offer an explanation, instead he levelled the gun. And shot a boy. The survivor ran, but the other three were frozen by the trauma and were all dispatched by one round each.

The survivor, a seventeen-year-old named Peter Johansen, turned and ran. He headed for the woods. He shouted warnings for others to lie down, hide or run. He daren't look back.

It sounded as though there was an army behind him, not a single man. He kept running and burst into the woods. Panting and trying to catch his breath and realising that the sound of the gunfire had quietened, he squatted behind a fallen tree to look.

He saw a battleground – no, a slaughterhouse. Bodies were lying everywhere, some displaying the cruel red badge of death, others lying as if they were sleeping or sunbathing on this delightful summer's day. Peter caught sight of the gunman; he was headed towards the wood and Peter was directly in his path. He turned and plunged ever deeper into the trees. His head was smacked by low whipping branches. The shots were growing quieter again, but were relentless as ever. A silver-blue strip reflected through the trees ahead. God, the sea, thought Peter – trapped.

He paused at the small beach, the land ahead he estimated at five kilometres, or even more. The shots grew louder as the shooter progressed through the woods. Peter looked around. A small jetty jutted a few metres from the shore and tied to the end was a small rowing boat. Heart hammering at his chest wall, he sprinted the 30-or-so metres to the small pier. There were no oars. Looking around for a hiding place, the same uniformed man from outside the cabin appeared at the beach. Peter unhooked the rope and, carrying it inboard, he pushed off with every last tired sinew and the boat moved slowly out into the sea. To Peter's horror, the small craft was taken by the ebbing tide and pulled, spinning wildly, toward the open sea. Bullets pounded the hull, splitting lethally sharp splinters from the small boat.

The craft was picking up speed. Peter, now sheltering in the bottom, dared a peek above the bulwark. The gunman was now quite a way behind him and Peter could have sworn the figure raised his gun in salute at a brave escape. He lay back, relief pouring through his veins. Then the pain hit home. With the adrenalin coursing through his terrified body, he hadn't realised one of the splinters forced from the rail had lodged in his shoulder. Blood was oozing out rather than flowing but, even so, he wouldn't keep going all night. Christ, the pain; it must have been lodged there for ten minutes. How on earth had he not felt it when it happened?

He could feel his strength ebbing away with the tide and lay back and wondered what was on the other side. Noises had disappeared the further he got from the shore and he was aware that a blissful and serene peace had descended. He didn't want to die but, now he was fading away, it didn't seem that bad after all. The fear had gone. The fear of those back at the camp would continue. Peter's eyes lost focus, the lids quivered, and then closed.

He awoke, only it wasn't the bright blue sky he last remembered, but the brilliant clinical white of a hospital ceiling. Shortly after he slipped into unconsciousness, a police helicopter passed overhead. A sharp-eyed pilot had spotted a body lying in the bottom of an out-of-control boat and directed a motor launch to its aid. The medical team on board the launch quickly patched up the young lad and within twenty minutes, he was one of the first injured admitted into hospital.

The death toll from the actions of the bus driver-turned-policeman had reached one hundred and sixteen by the time he gave himself up without a fight. Seventy-seven died on the peninsula and thirty-nine at the Ministry of Justice and Public Affairs.

13

'They're both asleep now,' Amelia told her husband. Bryant was in the process of dishing up Indian takeaway food, with the assistance of Sue-Beth, for the guests gathered to celebrate his homecoming. 'They're both in Poppy's room.'

'I'm glad they're asleep. But, I must admit, they seem totally underwhelmed at my return.'

'Don't be so silly,' Amelia chastised her husband. 'Of course they're pleased to see you, but in their minds there was never any doubt you weren't going to come home, mainly because I kept reassuring them. What they can't cope with is Elsa. You must realise the dog is like a sister to them. Anyway, I've promised them you'll take them to see her tomorrow.'

'I'll speak to the vet in the morning. The dog's heavily sedated at the moment.'

Amelia and Sean had set the dining table up in the conservatory and joined the outside table to the end. A makeshift combination of tablecloths adorned the furniture, while a mixture of dining chairs and outdoor plastic chairs would accommodate the guests. In addition to the three in the kitchen, there was Cobbold, Richardson, Gillian, Jones and his partner, Peter Snowling. While Sue-Beth and Sean had been to collect the food, Cobbold headed to the nearest Sainsbury's to select some wines and beers for the occasion. An assortment of beers and wines were being quaffed pre-dinner, and reds and whites offered additional decoration to the table. Cobbold indulged himself with a selection of fruit drinks!

159

It had been a busy day. Richardson and Jones had retired to the cottage rented in the village to keep their faces from the gathering throng of press. News had escaped into the wider world about the sudden reappearance of the kidnapped journalist and the apprehending of a would-be killer, all in the small Suffolk village of Oakshott. The interest had started as a trickle with a couple of journalists from the local newspaper and radio station. As the day progressed, some of the major news organisations attended. Vans were parked at the cricket ground and helicopters circled in the sky above the village. Oakshott would be infamous for a few hours in its history.

Cobbold and Bryant handled the press, to start with in their ones and twos. Eventually, the assembled masses headed for the cricket club bar for an arranged press conference at 6.00 p.m. Bryant felt uneasy at the boot being on the other foot, but Cobbold handled the situation with an exemplary coolness. Both had to be careful what they said, and there was certainly no reference made to Plantagenet House and its grisly secrets. Cobbold cut in with a polite 'It's an ongoing police enquiry and we do not wish to jeopardise it', if a question got too close to the mark. Bryant knew the procedure for he had sat in on many stage-managed press conferences, and he recognised the frustration on the faces of his fellow journos at the stonewalling tactics. But, sitting on the other side of the table, he was relieved at the failsafe back-up.

Dinner finished, Bryant dug out an unopened bottle of port from the previous Christmas and poured generous measures. It was just before 10.00 p.m., and Amelia turned the television to Sky News to watch the coverage of the story. It soon became clear that the story of Oakshott was not going to feature. There had been a series of deadly attacks all around Europe. Thirteen people had been killed and dozens injured in car-bomb attacks in Madrid, Paris and Rome. A lone gunman had been on a shooting spree in Berlin, where the death toll had been held at two, thanks to the quick reactions of a police officer who had shot and killed the attacker. The Balkan cities of Belgrade and Zagreb were hosts to knife and axe attacks with five deaths. Other cities witnessed vandalism to government buildings. The most deadly event of all was in the Norwegian capital of Oslo where a coach, full of Indian tourists, was blown up by remote control, probably by mobile phone, outside a government building. Later, a well-armed man dressed as a policeman arrived at a much-enjoyed nature spot where a socialist summer camp was getting underway. In a torrent of bullets, many more people, all believed to be under twenty-five years old, died. Some had fled into woods where they were hunted down as if it was a turkey shoot at Christmas. Stories were coming through of a young man who escaped the massacre in a rowing boat found drifting in the open sea. When police eventually arrived at the camp, the man gave himself up. He was named as Anders Sven Henriksen.

The news programme took a break and promised to be back with other stories in the news, none of which was from Suffolk. There was a disbelieving silence in the room, eventually broken by Bryant.

'My God. If only the news channels realised they're sitting on a gold mine with our story.'

'What?' asked Cobbold. The others all turning to their host, looking for an explanation.

'I've met that guy Henriksen.' He let the announcement sink in before continuing. 'It was when I went to that Knights Tempest gathering. I met him in the toilet and, to say the least, he was very excited by what he had just heard from this character they call the Lionheart. There were all sorts of characters there. I reckon nearly all of Europe was represented. No wonder they wanted to keep my story out of the public domain.'

A moment's silence followed the revelation. Cobbold picked up his mobile phone from the arm of the chair in which he was sitting.

'Curt. Got a minute?'

Richardson got up and followed his boss out through the conservatory onto the decking. Amelia, with Gillian's assistance, took orders for coffee and went through to the kitchen.

'I can't believe it,' said the schoolteacher. 'Little ol' Oakshott could be at the centre of a world story.'

'Yes,' agreed a teary Amelia. 'And my bloody husband could be right at its heart. It's not enough to be the target of a dozy prat with a gun. Now we have a massive organisation which will probably stop at nothing to silence him. My God, Gill. What am I going to do?'

The question was rhetorical. The only answer Amelia sought from her friend was the arms spread wide. She fell into them and sobbed in the tight embrace. How good a hug from a friend could be.

'Mummy,' a voice said from the kitchen door. 'Why are you crying? Elsa's died, hasn't she?'

Amelia pulled herself free from Gillian's hug, wiped her eyes and dropped down to one knee and beckoned Poppy over.

'No, sweetheart. She hasn't. We've just seen a horrible story on the news and Mummy's just a bit upset. That's all.'

'Daisy and me are both awake again. Will you come and read us another story?'

'I'll make the coffee,' Gillian offered.

Amelia picked up her small daughter, clasped her tightly and took her back up the stairs. 'I love you and Daisy so much, you know.'

'I love you as well, Mummy,' said a smiling Poppy, flinging her arms around her mother's neck and kissing her on the cheek, then giggling as if it were all a big game.

Cobbold and Richardson came back in from the garden.

'I've just spoken to the Home Secretary. He would like to meet you, Sean. He says he doesn't wish to inconvenience you, which actually means he couldn't give a toss, but would like to meet you at eight in the morning.'

162

'You're joking! Where?'

'He'll come here. He would also like to speak to you as well, Mrs Walters.'

'No problem.'

'Oh. And another thing; this has got to stay quiet. I firmly believe Sean's and Mrs Walters' lives are under real threat. The Home Secretary will be ordering the chief constable to send armed officers to Oakshott.'

The following morning saw a black Jaguar arrive in Oakshott with a couple of police outriders. Cobbold met the Home Secretary at the front door. The government minister was not dressed formally, choosing an open-necked shirt with grey slacks. Douglas Cochrane was courteous and appeared amiable to Sean and Amelia.

'Please call me Doug,' he said.

Cobbold introduced the Bryants and Sue-Beth and reintroduced Richardson and Jones.

'Will you be re-adopting your old name, Mr Richardson, uh, Carter?'

'It all seems too complicated, sir. I think not. I doubt whether Carter is my proper name in any case as I surely must come from slave stock.'

'Quite so,' Cochrane said before addressing Bryant and Sue-Beth. 'Now. I understand you two have quite a tale for us?'

'We do,' said Bryant. 'First of all, I'll let you have these.'

'Oh! What are they?'

'The pages of A4 are an article I wrote about a group of six well-known public figures and their link with a right-wing group with fairly extreme views. Now, as you have seen, those views have turned to rather extreme right-wing action with yesterday's slaughter in Europe.'

'Quite so,' said the Home Secretary. 'And the other?'

'As you can see, that's a document called *Knights Tempest: A Path to Government*. Basically, it will be their manifesto for an election sometime in the future. And I can assure you that, if they ever get in, life will never be the same again. They believe there are people all across Europe waiting to rise up and take the once-great continent back for the people. There will be no more benefit scroungers and no more illegal immigration. The events of yesterday demonstrate they mean business.'

'If they are linked,' said the Home Secretary.

'Oh, they're linked. I'm sure of it,' Bryant countered forcefully.

'How so? After all, your little group of people are well-renowned and if we make a connection with them and the violence around Europe yesterday and we're wrong...' Cochrane paused to let his words sink in. 'Well, Mr Bryant, I'm sure I don't need to spell out the repercussions to you. As a journalist, I'm sure you're used to flirting with the laws of libel and slander. Well, I can tell you that in government we cannot take the same risks.'

'That character, Henriksen, the one who killed all those people in Norway, he was at Beardstock Manor where I saw the Lionheart deliver his rousing speech to his fellow crusaders.'

'And you say that all of these others were there as well?' Cochrane flourished the report Bryant had compiled. 'Curious bedfellows. Let's see: a minor royal in the Duke of Woodbridge and, setting aside political correctness, a tad eccentric, some might say bonkers; a wealthy former porn star in Isabella de... whats-her-name; an old sixties rocker in Munro; a newspaper tycoon. They're all fine. But, then, you're asking me to believe that Jonathan Smithson, a Conservative Member of Parliament, albeit pretty much on the right, and Shona Forbes, belong to this party as well?'

'That is the case, I assure you.' Bryant tried to sound authoritative, but Doug was getting under his skin.

'Do you know who Shona Forbes is?'

That's condescending, thought Bryant, but he did his level

best to maintain a decorum. 'Yes, of course I do. She's the former Labour Party Parliamentary chair and the lesbian lover of Willow, now known as Isabella de Montmartre.'

'Evidence is what I need, Mr Bryant. If I'm going to take this to the Prime Minister, I need evidence. Perhaps a guest list or something for Beardstock Manor?'

Bryant's shoulders drooped.

'There is nothing,' he conceded. 'Only what I saw with my own eyes and heard with my own ears.'

'Umm!' muttered Cochrane, steepling his fingers. 'I need more. Get it and I will take it further.'

Bryant could feel the fury rising and exploded.

'You lot! All you want to do is lie back in your ivory towers and like Nero, fiddle while Rome burns. Courtiers told him Rome was burning, but still he fiddled. Now, Mr Douglas Cochrane, I'm one of those courtiers and all you can do is carry on plucking your violin, or whatever you do! Now, I suggest you grow a pair of bollocks and do what you're paid for, and make a bloody decision.'

'There will be a guest list,' Sue-Beth put in assuredly.

'Mrs Walters?' the minister enquired, raising his eyebrows and turning to face the penetrating gaze of the blue eyes he'd failed to note at introduction.

'Not exactly a guest list. We were assigned to provide personal protection at Beardstock and Sharp will undoubtedly have a list of protectees in his office.'

'Cobbold tells me you work for the Civil Protection Group. Who is Sharp?'

'*Did* work for them,' Sue-Beth responded tersely. 'Sharp is in charge at Plantagenet House.'

'The research and development facility for the CPG?'

'Indeed, sir. In fact, it is nothing more than a prison where executions take place by the bucket load.'

Cochrane sniggered. 'This tale gets more fanciful by the minute. You're telling me that executions take place by the bucket load and nobody suspects anything. Frankly, I'm staggered by your tale.'

'It's true. Sean and I were due to be hanged next Tuesday when the great and the good of the Knights Tempest gather for the entertainment. There's an insider I can trust. I also believe we could get Sharp on side.'

'Why? And who is this insider?'

'I think Sharp has always liked me and when the order came through I was to be added to the death list, he took a man named Ben Morgan into his trust. He is the one that got me and Sean out. And he's the one who'll come up with your list.'

'Rupert,' Cochrane snapped. One of his assistants stepped forward and Cochrane handed the documents to him. 'Take these to the car and send them direct to the Prime Minister by secure link. And when you've done that, I'll have them back to read myself.'

'Yes. No problem,' said the flunky.

'Mrs Walters, get me the list and I do believe we may proceed.' As an afterthought, Cochrane added, 'Cobbold tells me you're an ex-army officer. Are you the same woman who led the rescue of one of ours down a crocodile-infested river in Africa?'

'The very same,' she confirmed. 'But, I am afraid to say, rumours of crocodiles were much exaggerated!'

'Quite so,' allowed the Home Secretary. 'Anyway, it's good to have you on our side.'

Just before noon, a helicopter swooped in from the south and came to rest in a wheat field opposite. The crushed wheat, caused by the aircraft and the several pairs of security men, plus the polished brogues of the Prime Minister, didn't meet with the wholehearted approval of the farmer who passed by half an hour later. The pilot was sitting on the road verge talking to a couple of armed police when a beaten-up four-wheel drive pulled up.

'What the hell do you think you're playing at?' The farmer

ranted at the pilot who slurped some coffee before answering.

The pilot turned to look at the helicopter before turning the table.

'What do you think I'm doing? I thought that might be a bit of a clue.' He nodded in the direction of the chopper, its rotors drooping like branches laden with fruit.

'Who's going to damn well pay for this?' The farmer wasn't intimidated by the bristling weapons within a pace or two.

'If you'd care to wait, sir,' said the pilot. 'The Prime Minister will be out when he's concluded his meeting inside.'

'The Prime Minister?' the farmer managed a squeak. He skulked back to his dust-covered vehicle. An hour later, he was back with a piece of paper in his hand. 'This is my address. Ask him to pop by when he's done. I need a word!'

The Prime Minister sat in the single armchair near the fireplace. He introduced his chief security adviser, James Bland, and acknowledged all the reciprocations made by Cochrane.

'Splendid,' the PM acknowledged. 'Right, Mr Bryant. Would you be kind enough to start at the very beginning and for the benefit of the recording equipment, we won't make assumptions that we know some of the information. Led by you, Mr Bryant, we shall have a full and frank discussion about the Knights Tempest.'

The Prime Minister let the instructions sink in before continuing.

'I'll announce your name for the sake of the recording and then you can begin.'

'If you're ready,' said Bryant, 'then I'll begin.' He described events at the meeting at Beardstock Manor, who was there and what was said. He went on to explain that the cornerstone of the campaign would be to hand Great Britain back to its people and this would be done in six key areas, all of which would win over the popular vote in some numbers: economy, crime, housing, education, health and immigration.

The first speaker, on the economy, was the one who

interested Bryant the most. At the beginning of the nineteenth century, there was no income tax in the country; what you earned remained yours. This was a state to which they aspired to return. Income tax would be abandoned and consigned to history. It would be based on a purchase or sales tax, loosely based on VAT with four or maybe five bands. The lowest band would be set at 0% and would be for essentials such as heating and lighting, water and unprepared food; the second band would be for goods and services such as telephones, computers, televisions, takeaway meals and restaurant eating; the third and fourth levels would be luxury items and maybe set at on-cost percentages of up to 50 or 60%. Everyone accepted a car was fairly essential; therefore, a small environ-mentally friendly vehicle would be in the lower 5% range whereas a luxury car could be in the highest level. The same would go for all other services and goods. Also, there would be a burden of proof placed on a purchaser in regard to some items; for example, a boat in an area where it was needed to get around as part of everyday life would be treated differently to one that was used for pleasure.

The backbone to the economic policy would be the intro-duction of the eight-day week. The normal working week would remain unchanged at Monday to Friday, but there would be a three-day weekend, perhaps the eighth day could be called Lionday. This would mean the year would change from fifty-two to forty-five weeks. There would still be twelve months and three hundred and sixty-five days to each year, leap years remaining unaffected. Salaries and wages would be recalibrated so people got the same for working less. It was realised that international agreement would need to be sought to progress this idea.

Benefits would be cut out altogether. Charities would be set up to cover the requirements of the very needy and there would be no restriction on anyone from applying for assistance if they thought it required. There would be no national insurance, but it would be made a criminal offence not to carry minimum standards of pension, salary protection and health insurance. If someone couldn't afford basic cover, but could find a way of paying for subscription TV or smoked or drank, there would be a banding of fines which would lead ultimately to imprisonment for persistent offenders.

'They're the main headline parts of the economy,' Bryant concluded. 'There are other things in there relating to duties on fuel, alcohol, drugs and other things.'

'Drugs?' asked the PM, forgetting his own rules.

'Yes, Prime Minister. Under the crime section they propose to legalise the availability and taking of recreational drugs. And, of course, they'll then be subject to duty, Prime Minister.'

'Sounds interesting. I think we shall have to have a word with the Chancellor and get her to crunch the numbers. I like the income tax one. All that fuss about avoidance or evasion will be out of the window. Perhaps that idea would attract inward investment as well. Please continue, Mr Bryant.'

'Crime is the next mainstream target for the KT. Tough on crime, tough on the causers of crime. That's what they preach. Be aware that if I didn't pronounce it correctly; that was causers, spelled c-a-u-s-e-r-s. In the opinion of the leadership of the KT, and who knows, possibly the Lionheart himself, people are the cause of crime, not economy or environment. So if you happen to be involved in a crime there will be no sympathy. "Beyond all reasonable doubt" will be replaced by "beyond absolute doubt".

'Prison will remain the main form of punishment. Punishment and retribution are the strengths of the KT policy. All convicted felons will forego their rights in their entirety. One of the more interesting punishments of old they wish to reintroduce is the stocks for first-time offenders, except for the more serious. Stocks will be placed on village greens and in shopping centres, and sentences will depend on the crime, anything from one hour to five days at eight hours per day. Minor offences will result in further visits to the stocks. It's believed by the KT that once stocked, most will refrain from further crime.

'As I'm sure you can imagine, the ultimate penalty will be death by hanging. While at Beardstock, I did hear chatter about hanging, drawing and quartering being quite a crowd-puller. The movement is very keen to see that justice is carried out. Executions will be held in public, ideally during intervals at football matches and the like. Convicted defendants may save themselves the ignominy of a public execution, which in turn is meant to save the embarrassment of their families, by pleading guilty. Blood money could save someone from the rope if the family of the murder victim should choose to accept it. The sentence will then be commuted to life imprisonment or an unconditional pardon from the head of state. There will be no mercy for child-killers.

'The most curious of all punishments will be for those who've committed the most heinous of crimes, paedophilia or murdering a policeman, and others to be specified. They will be the subject of SROs, scientific research orders. Before their penalty is carried out, they will be subjected to unrestricted scientific experiments to assist the future of mankind. As they'll have foregone all human rights they'll be subjected to whatever the researchers deem fit. This will preclude the need for animal experimentation. If an experiment needs to take twenty years or more, so be it! Whatever happens, criminals will wish they'd never carried out such a crime. The experiments would be covered on television news programmes, and the KT is sure the images would have a detrimental effect on potential criminals and act as a warning that crime will not be tolerated.

'Homosexuality will become a crime. If convicted, prisoners may opt to be cured of the ailment and if they can satisfy a management committee that they're free of the condition, they'll be granted a conditional discharge. Homosexual acts will be permitted for the entertainment of the opposite sex.'

Sue-Beth raised her hand.

'Walters,' said Bryant, thus inviting her to speak.

'I've read this document fully and it's never occurred to me, until now that is, and I would like you all to consider this; I think the Lionheart is Colin Hunter.'

'Do you have evidence for this, Mrs Walters?' asked the Prime Minister.

'Not concrete, I must admit, but he's on the scene an awful lot. My first experience of him was when he put his hand down my shirt and grabbed me. I can assure you, he came off worse. And, if you want my opinion, he has just the sort of perverted mind that would have an attractive woman dangling on a rope, gagging for air, solely for his entertainment.'

The Prime Minister raised his eyebrows. 'I don't under-stand.'

'Mrs Walters and Mr Bryant were due to be executed next Tuesday,' said Cochrane. 'And the perverted Lionheart gets a perverted joy from watching attractive females stripped naked and seeing their bits… Well, I'm sure you can picture it.'

'Then he's one of the main protagonists at Beardstock,' Sue-Beth continued. 'And now this. The man's a disgusting bigot.'

'As an ex-lawyer, I would consider that evidence as circum-stantial, at best. I wouldn't prosecute on that basis. Catching him red-handed would be useful. Please continue, Mr Bryant.'

'That's pretty much the end of crime. There are sub-sections that cover the cost of new prisons, and families of prisoners will be expected to contribute to their upkeep. The government will provide only the bare minimum. If families cannot afford it, the KT is sure charities will spring up with do-gooders at their head to visit the prisons. Oh, and there's one interesting subtext to all this: lawyers who continually waste the state's money and defend lost causes will have their licences revoked and could face a prison sentence themselves, or at the very least, a few hours in the stocks. Oh, and another thing,' he said, running his finger down the page. 'The KT will introduce a law that a dead person cannot be challenged in a court of law unless the action was started prior to their death. The reason, they say, is to stop weak people jumping on band-wagons.'

There were no questions at the end of the crime section, just shocked looks on all the faces, except for Sue-Beth who'd seen it before and was still seething at the put-down from the leader of the country. Bryant moved smoothly on to the next title: Housing. This one was radical and it was one of the policies he thought had legs. He wasn't sure of the financial implications, but he thought it was a goer. The KT believed that house prices were a barrier to the movement and flexibility of the work-force. Their proposal would eliminate the need for traditional house sales. The government would take possession of the entire housing stock in the country; no individual would ever own property again. Renting would be the way forward and through the creation of arms-length management companies, various types of leases would be made available from the traditional short-term to longer lifetime leases if required, where the entire lease could be paid off much like a mortgage and the property may be occupied unencumbered until the tenant's death. Once any tenant had paid off a tenancy, they would have the freedom to move to any property of a similar value or less. If they chose a more valuable property they could take on a further lease.

On death, all property would pass to a spouse or other legal partner. Children would not have any inheritance rights. As far as inheritance was concerned, and it was mentioned in the housing section only as property normally formed the largest portion of any will, it would be limited to one £150,000 per beneficiary up to a maximum of five. The balance of the proceeds from an estate would automatically pass to the Exchequer.

The biggest advance in housing would be a lack of choice for the 'can't be bothereds'. Those who were not willing to work would have to live in institutional communes. There was no way these divisive sorts would be put in houses next to hardworking families, so their pernicious ways would spread like some virulent cancer of society. That accommodation would be the equivalent of twenty-first century hovels. There would be no luxuries. Entertainment such as subscription television would have to be earned. Charitable hand-outs would cover only the minimum to allow survival. No one would get comfortable without contributing to society by working.

Pros of this area were discussed in brief, Bryant clarifying some of the points, not because he had a superior political mind than two of the foremost exponents of the art, but simply that he had studied the document many times, quite often to the point of exhaustion and like a small compendium, he could open his memory at any point and pronounce on some point in the manifesto. Overall, it was agreed that housing wasn't a challenge to the accepted norm of running a government.

'Right, guys,' Bryant restarted after a sip of water. His mouth was dry. He always wondered at the reaction of the human body to differing challenges: why was his mouth so dry? And why was there a knot in his stomach? He'd interviewed politicians before; he'd interviewed Prime Ministers before. He was always comfortable in their company. This, for some reason, was a change and the body was taking over despite the brain challenging it to stay composed. 'We shall move onto education.'

School is for learning. It's not there for mending social breakdowns such as poor parenting. After the election of the Knights Tempest, education would be returned to the educators. Every child would be given a fair crack of the whip. If the parents did not support the child it would never be the educators' fault. Schools would return to the tradition of teaching academic subjects: English language, maths, the sciences, geography, history, English literature and art. Subjects beyond these, such as physical, religious and sex education, would become the responsibility of parents.

League tables would be maintained. Parents needed to know if the local school could cut the mustard. They also needed to know that teachers were up to it as well, so tables would be increased to list the best teachers in each subject, as well as the best head teachers, whose job title would change to educational chief executive officers. There would be cash awards for schools with the best results. Teachers would negotiate their own remuneration, good teachers commanding the highest salaries and poor teachers the lowest. It would, therefore, be acceptable for good teachers to agree longer contracts while poorer teachers would not be rewarded for their failures.

League tables would sort the wheat from the chaff. Schools in less motivated areas would remain at the foot because of the poor material that fed into them. If a good school, or any school for that matter, identified a student with extra special abilities at another school it would be enabled to offer financial inducement for the child to move, much like head-hunting in industry. Eventually, the better students would end up at the better institutions and they would encourage one another to succeed. Poor schools would continue to babysit the children with less ability. The economy would always produce menial positions for those who lacked motivation or those with a genuine lack of ability.

This system would make England the highest achieving country in the world. Competition would be encouraged from a very early stage. As with all KT policies the ethos was 'survival of the fittest'; the rest don't matter. The main benefit, according to the manifesto, was that every child in the nation would have the opportunity to succeed if they wanted to, but if they did not they could live a menial life where a caring government would not be around to bail them out.

Bryant guided the Prime Minister and his entourage through the rest of the *Path to Government*. At the end, the Prime Minister put down his glass of water, sat back in the armchair, let out a huge breath and said, 'My word, that's certainly food for thought. The manifesto, the goings-on at Plantagenet House and now the link with yesterday's attacks across Europe are a clear sign of wrongdoing on an industrial scale under our noses. I need to do something. I actually think it's so serious a threat that I need to convene a meeting of COBRA. First, though, I understand I've the more pressing matter of an irate farmer to pacify for parking our helicopter in his field. The obligations of this office never cease to amaze me.'

14

In a flat in the Suffolk coastal village of Southwold, overlooking Gun Hill, and with a view out over Sole Bay, Ben Morgan was relaxing in the living room. He was nursing a swollen black eye. Never had he thought a woman would be capable of inflicting such an injury on a man without the use of a weapon. Sue-Beth had hit him so hard he'd seen stars. He should have known her fists would have hit like a kicking horse. This Saturday morning, all he wanted to do was relax. Maybe Sunday he would call Sue-Beth and see how she was. It had been a struggle to get through the day of work at Plantagenet House for the headache had been all-invading and no over-the-counter drug could alleviate the pain, let alone his restricted sight.

The door entry phone rang. Morgan cursed and lifted himself off the couch and staggered to the front door. He picked up the handset.

'Hello?'

'Ben? Ben, is that you?' asked a tentative voice.

Morgan thought the voice was familiar, but it was out of context, so it didn't immediately register.

'Yeah. Yes, it is. Who's that?'

'It's Robert Sharp. Can I come in, Ben? We need to talk.'

'Are you alone?'

'Yes. Yes, I am. And I must admit, quite desperate. I need your help.'

Morgan wasn't sure whether he really wanted Sharp in his

flat. Looking out of the panoramic window, the day looked welcoming.

'Hold on. I'll be down in a minute. We'll walk some.'

Sharp sat down on the brick-capped wall that shadowed the path from the roadside to the main entrance of the complex and waited. Alone with his thoughts, he reflected on how he'd made a mess of his life. His father had been an officer in the army and so had he. The difference between the two was that Sharp didn't want to have anything to do with the army. He'd been keen on becoming a Church of England vicar. Then, his father had taken a stick to him one day and at the end of the beating, he decided he'd follow his father's wishes and become an army officer. After scraping through Sandhurst, he started to rise up the ranks. Not that he wanted to rise up the ranks. Within a short time of a career development meeting, he found himself dragged into a commanding officer's office or study and handed his new commission.

God was never far away. Every time he committed a sin to avoid military duties he would visit a church to beg forgiveness. He faked illness, something he could get away with as he'd always been a sickly child. He even made out once that he was required at a court martial, an action that got him out of a tour of duty in Afghanistan. Worst of all was the time he sent his charges over a wall into the face of ferocious fire from insurgents in Iraq. He rose up in line with his men, but immediately fell back as if shot by the enemy. Watching the others disappear over the wall, he shot himself in the leg. The sound of the shot attracted the attention of one man, he knew not who, for tears were in his eyes and the man's face was blurred. The pain was instant. What on earth was it with soldiers who came back from firefights with half a limb missing only to claim they hadn't realised as they couldn't feel a thing? Cowardice and guilt were surely the answer; perhaps adrenalin didn't flow in the same way for a self-inflicted wound?

Sharp had felt secure in his position behind the wall knowing that, after the exchange, the insurgents would flee the scene as soon as possible to avoid capture by reinforcements that had surely been summoned. Then Sharp had heard a rumour that a soldier, obviously the one who had glanced back, had survived and told a medic of how he had seen his officer shoot himself in the leg. Within hours, the soldier had died of his injuries and the testimony never got to a court martial or enquiry. That death had cost him £5,000 and probably a place in heaven. It was at this time he sought the solace of Christ's blood and now couldn't go for more than a few hours without supping from his grail.

Now, in the quaint little Suffolk village, he rubbed his thigh. It shouldn't really be hurting today. It was normally in cold weather that it played up. Psychological pain took over whenever he gave those horrible events any in-depth thought. Post-traumatic stress was the obvious next route and this time it worked. With the help of some convincing hamming, he was able to persuade the medical board he was suffering badly and he was soon discharged out of the army. Of course, he was an utter disgrace to his father, who believed there were only two ways out: retirement with distinction or in a wooden box. In a telephone conversation with his father, there was no doubt the older man would have preferred the latter to some modern leftist condition that hadn't existed in his day. He hadn't seen his father since but had tried to keep up contact with the Holy Father, and now the sins were building against him as well. Soon, there would be no alternative than to butter up the devil. This was his last chance to do something of worth, but there would be a price.

Morgan joined him at the front door.

'Lunch?' he offered.

'Why not,' answered Sharp.

'It's a nice day. We'll walk across to Walberswick, if the old war wound can take it?'

Sharp noted the slight from his inferior but chose to ignore it.

'That'll do fine,' he said. 'I understand they do fine fish 'n' chips at the pub.'

'They do,' said Morgan. They turned out of the flats and headed along the road, before cutting down onto the dunes for a bit more privacy. A camping and caravanning site came and went before they turned along an unmade road heading to a footbridge that crossed the River Blyth.

'What can I do you for?' Morgan had asked as they stepped down into the dunes.

'Well, you probably have learned more about the true pur-pose of the Civil Protection Group's research and development facility at Plantagenet House than anyone else except for me.'

'That information is now shared with the outside world, and I think that could be my insurance policy.'

Sharp shot a sideways glance.

Morgan was sure he saw desperation in Sharp's look.

'And yours, I suppose.'

'Maybe. It's true I've received a call from the odious Lion-heart chap, who's not best pleased at the escape. The annoying thing is, I haven't even reported it yet. I have no idea how it leaked out.'

Morgan laughed. Probably while you were cradling a bottle of claret, he thought. 'Was Bryant's face not all over the news last night?'

'No. No, I wasn't aware... Oh, shit! Actually, thinking about it, I don't think it was. The stories from Europe were just about the only items on the main news. I never saw the local news.'

'You wanted it to happen. Did you not?'

Sharp had wanted it to happen and even thought that one day Sue-Beth would jump into his arms and thank him for what he'd done. He glanced nervously around him as he'd done ever since leaving the security of his flat at Plantagenet

House and making his way to Southwold. Hiding behind the barrier of drink, he'd concocted the plan for the two absconders to get out. The shield slipped away as the wine lost its effect and doubt crept in to fill the void. In between, the claret had intervened again and convinced him he'd done the right thing. He was now stone-cold sober and the doubt had come back. After the Lionheart's call, doubt had been replaced with paranoia. Slowly, though, even the sober mind had aligned with the intoxicated one and agreed he was on the right course. The only problem was that the sober mind was not as strategic as the one befuddled by a good French red.

They walked on in silence. Morgan was growing frustrated at the lack of continuity from his superior. Once he'd got some ale into him perhaps the inhibitions would disappear and the decisive Sharp would return.

On the other side of the bridge, the pair followed the seawall path past some extravagantly appointed beach huts and into the village of Walberswick. At the Bell Inn, cod and chips was ordered for each of them, accompanied by an Adnams Ale.

Sharp and Morgan collected their drinks from the bar. The tables on the outdoor terrace were about a quarter occupied, leaving plenty of space for them to select a table isolated from the rest. Sharp poured the ale down his neck and Morgan took his glass back for recharging. On return, he had two pints in his hands. The sooner he could get Sharp to alcoholic satisfaction, the quicker he would start to talk.

The second beer joined the first in quick succession, but then the third started to slow. This was painful, thought Morgan. Still the food hadn't yet arrived and Sharp was halfway down his third pint while Morgan had barely taken the top off his.

The food came and was devoured in relative silence. Odd comments were exchanged about the atrocities in Europe and would the England cricket side become the number one test-playing side in the world? But, despite the occasional prod, there was nothing about the Civil Protection Group, the

Knights Tempest or Sue-Beth Walters and Sean Bryant. There was nothing for it. Morgan would have to invite Sharp into his flat. He was fairly sure there were two bottles of red in the buffet hutch in the lounge.

Pouring two generous glasses of Australian red and after suffering a lecture about the merits of French wine versus colonial brands, they sat down. Morgan's sip was more than matched by Sharp's huge gulp. Sharp smacked his lips together and even conceded the Aussie grape was not actually that bad. It wasn't long before Morgan was refilling his guest's glass and soon after that the screw top was being removed from the second bottle. Morgan had taken three sips.

Finally, suitably doused in alcohol, constructive words were beginning to spill from Sharp's mouth. By the end of the second bottle and with Morgan's first glass not even half empty, they had formed a plan. As Morgan was not due back to Plantagenet House until Monday afternoon, it was agreed that they would meet back at the Southwold flat earlier that day.

The Prime Minister paced the cabinet room at Number Ten. It was unusual for him to be in the room before any of his ministers attended, but this was different. Murder had been committed on an unprecedented scale across Europe and there was a more than evens chance the terror had been exported from England. This was no Muslim plot, this was no republican Irish plot, nor was it a Basque separatist plot. This plot had been hatched in England, not Britain, for Scotland, Wales or Northern Ireland were clearly not involved if that journalist was to be believed. What a time to put your trust in the press, when they were at their most unpopular, possibly in all time: phone hacking of murder victims and their families was a step too far, the Rubicon had been crossed.

Now, at a time when journalists were increasingly being put in the spotlight for the wrong reasons, he had to convince his cabinet that he was going to authorise the biggest military security operation undertaken in these islands since, since... well, he didn't know when, nor did he really care. The link with the Norwegian gunman was tenuous, even with the guest list, if it existed; it was circumstantial to say the least. After briefing the cabinet he would convene a meeting of COBRA, short for Cabinet Office Briefing Room A, where a selected group of government ministers would meet with senior members of the armed forces and security institutions to form a strategy to respond to grave issues of national security. This time it would be a matter of rubber stamping Duncan Cobbold's plan.

The PM stopped pacing and looked around. He'd never aspired to be Prime Minister, he'd never even planned to enter parliament; it had just happened. Now, thanks to natural leadership qualities and a big slice of the luck cake, here he was: Number Ten Downing Street. What would his predecessors have thought of him? He remembered climbing the stairs for the first time under the gaze of their portraits and he swore that every set of eyes followed each step he took. He soon realised they weren't casting loathing toward the upstart, but were wishing him luck with each tread, for it was only they who knew how he was feeling at that time. Relatively, there had been only a handful of Prime Ministers measured against the whole population and, no doubt, each one of them had stood or sat in this room and wondered what they were doing. Great historical names had walked this floor before him and wrestled with their consciences over decisions that could change the direction of a nation if they went right. For that matter, they could change the direction of a nation if they went wrong.

A deep intake of breath cut him from his daydreaming. The grand polished table was the centrepiece guarded by chair sentinels. The only untidiness was his own papers unceremoniously tossed in front of his own place at the fat midriff of the table. What would those faces on the stairs have thought of him? Surely they would have been more decisive. He reflected on events that had taken place because the man, or woman, who'd sat in that chair had decreed it. Prime Ministers would be judged by their leadership and in a few days, maybe he would be celebrating with the best of them. Or maybe he would be taking the short drive to see the Queen to tender his resignation.

It was Sunday morning and the summer recess from parliament was well underway, but this was important. When he'd called the meeting yesterday afternoon, the cabinet was as far flung as it could be: Europe, North America and, of all people, the Chancellor of the Exchequer was visiting relatives in New Zealand. If the vote to send the British Army into action against an English domestic foe was close, the Chancellor's was one he could count on.

The Home Secretary was the first to join him, quickly followed by the Foreign Secretary, William Walker. The rest were all gathered within the next ten minutes. Some looked as if they'd travelled all night to get there, which they probably had.

'Ladies and gentlemen,' started the Prime Minister. 'Thank you all for attending at such short notice. I shan't detain you long, but this is a matter of the utmost urgency.

'You will all know by now there was a series of barbaric attacks on many of our European neighbours' capital cities yesterday. I have already spoken to each head of state offering our sincerest condolences and, of course, offering any assistance they wish to call upon.'

Sipping from his glass and glancing at his notes, he continued, 'I have to tell you there was one piece of information I didn't share with the other leaders.' Pausing, he risked a look around the table; every pair of eyes was on him, except for the Minister for Education, whose unsighted pupils were staring intently, but about 3 feet to his left. 'It is with much regret that

I have to inform you the attacks are linked to a right-wing neo-Nazi organisation based in this country known as the Knights Tempest, and they are led by a self-titled character, the Lionheart.'

He sipped more water and interlocked his fingers. 'We only have the word of a journalist, Sean Bryant, of the London *Echo and Post*, on this, but I must tell you I found him to be an extremely creditable young man. I know many of you are familiar with his work and unlike many of his contemporaries, he is not given to sensational writing.'

There was unanimous agreement around the great table which, when combined, sounded like a series of approving grunts.

'The Home and Foreign Secretaries have tried to corroborate the story but to no avail. This group was below the radar of both MI5 and MI6. Somehow, I can tell you, there are strong links with the international security company, Civil Protection Group, CPG. Maybe they are funded by the CPG; too early to tell for sure.

'You all have a fuller report in front of you, which I asked Mr Bryant to compile, together with an investigative report he worked on for a number of weeks before he was abducted from outside his office and transported to a place that I can only describe as a modern-day concentration camp. The third document is what I can only describe as a preliminary manifesto, *Knights Tempest: A Path to Government*.' To illustrate his last remark, he held up a copy in his left hand. 'You will find many of their grisly promises in full in here, but I shall apprise you of some of the pertinent points.' He went on to share the salient points of the manifesto, as Bryant had relayed them to him, and then moved on to the contentious issue of immigration.

'England will not be part of the EU any longer. There will be no automatic right to the general dross of the world through that channel who see us as an easy touch; no one will

184

be allowed in unless they achieve minimum standards including answering questions on English history and culture; the other nations of the British Isles will be able to secure leave to travel without limit back and forth providing they meet minimum requirements, thus keeping out the dross – their words not mine. Any criminal of less than three generations will be deported to their nation of origin together with all their relatives; in short, there will be no messing with immigration. Reality will dull aspirations there as we all know.'

'A minefield, I agree.' Cochrane supported the Premier with his experience.

The PM took advantage of the interlude to refill his glass and take a few refreshing sips.

'Finally, health: the cornerstone of the United Kingdom, our pride and joy in full view of the world, would be torn apart by the Knights; there would be two levels of treatment, private and charity; all treatment can be purchased as it is used, or insurance policies can be purchased, everyone paying the same flat rate; people with special medical needs will have their contributions topped up to meet their requirements as long as they are contributors themselves and are in full-time employment; those who couldn't afford it would be forced to knock on the charity hospital's doors. All low-lives would be sterilised to keep the lower class at bay, which would include low-IQ people and benefit scroungers; people, unless they could afford to live by their own means, would be euthanised at eighty; indeed, predictability tests would be carried out so that residents would know their expected time of death and pensions would be matched to their personal needs. Should this date be envisaged to be earlier than eighty, they would be humanely dispatched six months after the date predicted; no one will be a burden in the Knights Tempest's brave new world; a cure will be sought for homosexuality, this vile disease will be treated by drugs and punished by law. A little different to our own views, I believe.

'The euthanasia policy is interesting, and apart from the statutory ending of life, the Knights will introduce what they call a pathway to death, which will prepare people for the inevitable end so it can be spent in the surroundings of family and friends and final goodbyes can be said. Death will become like marriage; it will be a celebration of life, and people will be free to choose where they take their final breath. The population of the planet is of grave concern as we move further into the twenty-first century, so what is the point in striving to extend life beyond what nature intended? Why are we always seeking cures for this and that when our small island nation is bursting at the seams? Why try to encourage the end of smoking and drinking? Let the people have the choice; the pathway to death is available to all, at whatever age. An abused body will not be given help to overcome its addiction, not at the expense of the state, anyway. News programmes are full of the paradox of obesity curtailing life and then, within a few minutes, an item about the human toll being taken on an ever-shrinking planet. Let them eat, drink and smoke themselves to death. It is their choice.'

The leader threw the floor open for questions and other views to be put forward. He was not surprised by the reticence for military action.

'They are just another wannabe right-wing political party who won't get anywhere,' was a common perception. Another was: 'And that's what I gave up a fortnight's holiday in the sun to listen to!'

However, the PM had only set out the political aspirations of the Knights Tempest. He now took up the report that Bryant had written. All six celebrities were well known to the gathered. There was no surprise at the batty old Duke of Woodbridge being involved; he was known as a big fan of almost anything to the right of Margaret Thatcher. Many thought him to be one of several royals who craved a return to absolute power. There was the time he attacked parliament for failing to deal with the creeping underclass, after which cartoonists had portrayed him as the head held aloft while King Charles I's body lay slumped on the block spurting blood. It was his view that God put female servants on the planet to pleasure the well-born and he could do as he wished, many a victim withdrawing claims of rape shortly before being seen in an expensive sports car or on a luxury holiday. The newspapers quickly branded him 'the Teflon duke' as nothing ever stuck.

Then there was the ageing rocker Alan Munro. He was still embittered by the murder of his son by an illegal immigrant in the seventies and was well known to harbour a hatred of anyone with a darker skin, refusing treatment at hospitals from black doctors and nurses, leaving restaurants if there were Asian waiters, and so on. He had once started to campaign as a prospective Conservative candidate in a by-election in the eighties, but had dropped out when the secretary he had been allocated was of Oriental persuasion, giving him the name of 'the Chinese fade-away'!

Isabella de Montmartre was an interesting case. She was not known for her right leanings during her career as a porn star under her acting name of Willow. Party girl? Yes. Political party girl? No. While filming a nude volleyball game on a private beach in Montenegro, a Serbian billionaire nationalist Dusan Costavic had been watching from his private yacht in the fjord and had invited her on board for drinks. Within six months they were married, Willow herself bringing a not insignificant fortune to the partnership. A change of name and with a little Balkan indoctrination, she started to lean to the right and was a major influence on young men and women who wanted to bathe in her glamorous shadow, given a perverse respectability by her nuptials. After her later divorce she became one of the richest women in Europe – a long journey from the South London council estate where Clare Willis had grown up, before a boob job and creative marketing made Willow. Popularity having sagged with her breasts, here she was again as a senior member of the KT.

Just as he commenced a résumé of the fourth member, the PM's mobile phone let out a shrill ring.

'Mr Bryant. Good morning. How's Elsa...? Tell the girls I'm thinking of her... You have? That's great... Ah! I was going to suggest that... Many thanks... If we need anything, we'll call... Goodbye.' He pressed the end-call button and stared at the screen as if willing it to life. His apparent thoughts did their work as a ping signified the arrival of an email. Holding the gadget in his left hand, a series of taps with his right index finger brought a smile to his face. 'My God!' he uttered.

He stood, quickly followed by chair legs scraping back to allow the occupants out, except for the Education Minister, who remained impassive. The Prime Minister beckoned for them all to remain seated, just as the blind minister had tuned into what was happening and began to rise, a friendly hand patting her forearm, indicating she should remain seated. The PM felt his face warm; he had always promised himself he would never embarrass this very able of ministers by making sure that any visual instruction was accompanied by a clear audible one. Every now and again, like now, he lapsed, instantly reddening. A secretary met him at the end of the table and after an exchange of whispers and another series of taps on the screen of the phone, he returned to his chair.

'I'm sure you're wondering what that was about? Well, it was a guest list of the event Bryant refers to in his article. Once it has been printed, it will be circulated. I copied it to you as well, Judith.' This to the Education Secretary knowing her phone would have the ability to read the document to her. 'It should be in your inbox now. There are some very interesting names on there, I can assure you.

'For the time being, I will stick to the main table.'

He continued with the press mogul, Barrington, or Barry, Swift, an American who loved all things English except for paying tax, income or corporation. No government would dare take him on for he had too much hold. He knew every skeleton in every cupboard and if the cupboard was bare, he had the ability to make up his own contents.

'Bryant believes him to be one of the money men behind the organisation. I believe that in his dream of ruling the world he's gone a little too far. It's true; if his papers swung in behind the Knights they would stand a good chance of getting a sizeable slice of the popular vote.'

'Christ!' said Walker. 'We'd better be right. If we cock up and implicate Swift, can you imagine the pasting we'll get in the majority of the papers, let alone his television and radio outlets?'

The Prime Minster stared Walker down. 'Let me make one thing clear, to you all. It is true, internally, I will seek your support; after all, we rule by cabinet, but it will go down as my decision. If I'm wrong, and I have dialled a wrong number, I will resign and make it clear that none of you was implicated.' He clasped his hands in front, knowing that his hand movements usually betrayed an insecurity. 'I shall also tell you that I firmly believe this is the one single group to have threatened domestic security since the Civil War. I will cont... Ah. Wait a minute.'

The secretary reappeared with the printed paper.

'Thank you,' said the Prime Minister. 'Pass them around, if you would.'

The Prime Minister took his copy and studied it intently. The list was in alphabetical order and, sure enough, all the names being discussed were present, plus a number of others he recognised. There was one missing. He would not say anything; as far as he was concerned, it changed nothing.

'Of course, I need not go through the history of the other two in the article. I'm sure you're all familiar with Jonathan Smithson and Shona Forbes.'

Heads nodded and grunted acknowledgements came forth as

well as gasps of total disbelief, not so much at the Conservative Member of Parliament, for his right-leaning was well known, but the former Labour Parliamentary chair was another matter altogether.

'Good. As you can see from the list there was also a character present by the name Anders Henriksen. This is the man now in custody in Norway who stands accused of the terrorist attacks the day before yesterday. You can also see that there are representatives from other nations around Europe who were also caught up in the co-ordinated attacks on Friday.'

'I notice your Mr Bryant is not on the list.' It was bloody Walker again in a challenging tone.

'That's true enough. I have his word he was there and I believe him. We're dealing with a secret meeting and if he wasn't there, there's no way he could have knowledge of this information.'

Walker kept up eye contact with his leader. 'How do we know he didn't concoct this story over Friday night?'

'Allow me to answer, if you would Prime Minister?' It was the Home Secretary, Cochrane.

'Please do.'

'These details have been authenticated in their chronology by a number of witnesses of the highest reputation. I am with the Prime Minister. I have no doubt Mr Bryant's tale is genuine. I cannot divulge any names at this juncture as the case is active and advanced.'

'Umm!' was all that Walker could utter.

'Now,' said the Premier, 'we know there's a place on the Norfolk-Suffolk border named Plantagenet House, which purports to be the R and D facility of the Civil Protection Group. After his abduction, Mr Bryant was held at this facility for just over two weeks, along with others. Three of the prisoners – that is all they can be described as, and I have met two of them – were due to be executed the day after tomorrow.'

There were gasps around the table as the Prime Minister let the words hang.

'They have been holding regular hangings at this facility for a number of years now. It appears hundreds have met their end on the end of a rope.'

'This is getting more and more far-fetched – what the hell do they do with the bodies?' snapped an irritated Walker.

'They are cut up and cremated in with other funerals. Dear old granny might have been burned with an extra leg or a favourite uncle with two heads. Gruesome in the extreme and we must stop it.'

The Prime Minister slurped more water.

'I propose we use Special Forces to take this place out and I can tell you that plans are well advanced for such an assault. All I need is your support.'

Hands were slowly raised around the table until there was only one dissenter.

'What of the others?' Walker snarled.

'I briefed the leader of the opposition last evening and he has given me his full support.'

The two men were locked in a stare combat. Neither yielded. A cough from an unseen minister cut the building atmosphere in two. Walker glanced up and down the table. Like a classroom of naughty pupils, the ministers' hands were held to the affirmative. All eyes were now locked on the renegade Foreign Secretary, daring him to reject the plan. He acquiesced and slowly brought his palm from the table top to join the others.

'Thank you,' said the Prime Minister and turned to his Home Secretary. 'Mr Cochrane, please proceed.'

Cochrane rose and made to leave the room.

'And... Good luck!'

15

Richardson sat on the decking at the Bryant home and stared at images of Augusta posing in front of the ruined brothel of Pompeii, another one peering into the giant and gaping crater of Vesuvius, and a video clip of her lying on a sunbed floating on the sea below magical Sorrento. Why on earth wasn't she replying to his calls or his texts or his emails? There had been nothing. He promised himself that he'd get this business out of the way over the next few days and then be on the next plane to Naples. He closed his eyes and conjured up an image of a pretty dancing girl on the deck of the *Legend*.

'All systems go.' It was Cobbold, who had just received the green light from the Home Secretary. Morgan was expected at any time and the final plans would be cast into the concrete.

Arms and armour were checked, cleaned and loaded into the boot of Richardson's Mercedes. Cobbold had already arranged for a rural holiday home to be booked within two or three miles of Plantagenet House. A young couple would be arriving there later on Sunday afternoon, giving the impression that it was to be used for a late holiday booking rather than a temporary headquarters for the assault. The house had only two bedrooms and was detached. It wasn't ideal for a large group of people, but sleep was not the most important human condition over the next few days, even though cat-napping would be encouraged.

Morgan arrived and introductions were made. The dining room was commandeered as a meeting room. Sue-Beth brought Toby, who was taken in hand by Poppy and Daisy, and taken into the garden with his tennis ball and cricket bat. The girls weren't interested and after a few minutes of tough negotiation, settlement was made for a game of hide and seek. Toby's face reflected the thundery nature of the weather.

Cobbold chaired an impromptu meeting, sitting in the carving chair in the bay window, Bryant at the other end. Richardson and Jones took one side and Sue-Beth was joined by Ben Morgan on the other side. Cobbold invited Morgan to offer up his report following his lunch with Robert Sharp.

'He has no problem in assisting us,' said Morgan.

'But?' Cobbold put in.

'Well. Umm. He wants to secure a better position for himself.'

'Understandable. What?'

'He wants a guarantee of immunity from prosecution. Second, he wants to give evidence from behind a screen or by an audio link. And finally, he wants a new identity to start a new life in a country of his choice.'

'Okay,' Cobbold acknowledged. 'I'll speak to the Home Secretary as soon as we have gone through everything.'

'He says I'm to obtain the concessions before I offer his assistance,' Morgan said doggedly. 'Oh, and one other thing: all the concessions must be in the Prime Minister's hand.'

'Mr Morgan,' Cobbold rounded on the former soldier. 'May I remind you, Robert Sharp is a criminal with a lot of blood on his hands. May I also remind you, you are an accessory to murder and in the frame for the kidnapping of Mr Bryant. I will also point out that I can call on whatever forces I wish to turn... umm' – Cobbold consulted his notes – 'Plantagenet House to ashes. Your bargaining power is toward the bottom of the league. I'll hear the plan first then I'll decide whether to obtain these concessions. Is that clear?'

Morgan saw a resolution in the other man's eye, but countered anyway. 'I'm aware of that. But that would lead to many innocents being killed and injured. I think you'll approve of this plan.' Morgan tapped the few sheets of A4 in front of him. 'If successful, it will deliver all the main suspects into your hands with no loss to government agents.'

'That may be true. I will, however, have your report first. Look at it this way, Operation Sledgehammer is already formed. I will consider Operation... ah... Precision Surgery. But, Mr Morgan, *I* will decide.'

Morgan moved uneasily in his chair before conceding. 'Very well.'

'Thank you,' Cobbold smiled. 'Please proceed.'

Using his notes, which had been written as soon as Sharp had left the flat, Morgan went through the plan. Cobbold, Richardson and Jones listened intently. Sue-Beth was ambivalent until her name cropped up. Negotiations continued for a couple of hours. A few amendments here, the odd tweak there, and the final blueprint was formed.

'Okay,' said Cobbold leaning back in his chair, holding his pencil in both hands. 'We are agreed?'

All nodded except for Bryant, who was the only one not in the firing line. 'As long as you guys are happy, that's fine by me.'

'One thing, though,' Cobbold said as he saw a slight flaw in the plan. 'How well do you know Hunter?'

'Never met him,' responded Bryant. 'Well, that's not strictly true. Obviously I set eyes on him at Beardstock Manor.'

'He must have seen you as well? Surely, if he had invited you he would have been looking out for you?'

'Never got close enough. And, in any case, it was a long time ago.'

'Did you not meet to discuss thing before you went? I mean, how did you get the invite?'

'Arrived by post. Out of the blue,' the journalist recalled.

'A bit peculiar. Are you sure it was him?'

'I've never actually questioned it before.' Bryant pondered for a moment. 'Who else could it be?'

'Just a theory,' answered the policeman. 'But our Mr Sharp is being very helpful now. You don't think we are all bit players in his own big plan?'

Cobbold excused himself and went off to report to his superior. In less than five minutes, he was back in the dining room. The others looked on reverentially like a gathering about to be read a will, none knowing who was going to get what.

'Mr Morgan,' Cobbold started. 'Third demand first: all agreements will be the decision of the Home Secretary and, if required, will be in writing. He cannot guarantee any evidence can be delivered anonymously; that will be the decision of the trial judge, but pressure will be brought to bear. Finally, the pair of you will be guaranteed immunity from prosecution. When Sharp indicates his satisfaction with the generous deal, I'll get an electronic version forwarded to me.'

'I'll consult,' said Morgan. He picked up his mobile phone and sent a text. *X deal.* It simply meant counter-offer and Sharp should ring as soon as it was convenient to do so.

The telephone was barely back on the table when it burst into life.

'Morgan.'

Silence fell. Indecipherable words could be heard by those around the table, but all could work out the gist of what was being said.

The scent of lovemaking hung in the air. Jonathan Smithson stood at the window and gazed at the setting sun over the golf course. Wearing a hotel dressing gown, he admired the sun as its reflection dazzled from the lake just beyond the eighteenth green. He watched as a couple of players sent their shots skywards, the first becoming a bright white dot on the green; the second had either got stuck in the sky or had missed its target. He turned back to the luxury bedroom and couldn't believe the sight on the gloriously large double bed. He'd just had the experience that most men around the world could only dream of: one of the highest paid models in the world was stretched out in front of him, a dressing gown to match his own worn in such a way that it hardly concealed her charms. To him, she was a model. To the rest of the world, Isabella de Montmartre was Willow the porn star.

Aware that she was being watched, a feeling that still thrilled her, she turned to look at the man silhouetted by the setting sun. Rippling light played on the ceiling from the lake's reflection. In his white robe, she thought, Smithson exuded angelic qualities.

'He's runnin' scared,' said Isabella in a matter-of-fact manner.

'Who is?'

'Sharp. Did you see the look on his face when I told him two of the condemned had escaped from his care? Useless! Nearly soiled his pants there and then.' She laughed at the image of the man's discomfort. 'The man is a first-class twit. Calls himself a commander? To be brutally honest, Jonathan, the man couldn't run a bath.'

'I understood him to be an officer of some distinction. Is that not so, my lovely?'

Her face hardened. Smithson felt an unease about what would come next.

'Don't call me my lovely. I'm nobody's lovely. Don't think you're special because you've fucked me. You, my lovely, have just been added to a very long list, which I can assure you hasn't been exhausted yet.'

Smithson pulled the robe tight around him like a shield. His face warmed as the onslaught continued.

'I've been with each and every one of the management, including, if you're wondering, Shona Forbes. It's amazing how this friendly pussy can control all you married boys and girls. One man, the despicable Hunter, thought he held power over me and because of that believed he could have his will with me when he wished. He raped me, or so he thought. I swallowed him whole before spitting him out in tiny pieces. The video cooled his ardour.' Her smile turned to a sinister giggle at Smithson's dumb look.

'Video?' he croaked, glancing around the room.

'Up there,' she said pointing to the top of the wardrobe. 'Trust me, I didn't turn you round to make sure you were evenly done on both sides. It was so that our faces were clearly linked to the same scene.'

Smithson's face turned crimson as he rushed to the wardrobe and snatched the miniature device from its perch looking down on the bed. He dropped it to the floor and, crawling around, located one of his expensive Italian shoes. Reputed to be the best made shoes in the world, they needed to be, as one of them was turned into a hammer to thrash repeatedly the micro-camera into oblivion, much like a blacksmith wrought iron on the anvil. He collected the pieces together and, panting heavily, deposited them on the bed.

Isabella shook her head contemptuously and with a couple of taps on her phone, said, 'Oh, my word. I've just received a message. Shall I play it?'

Smithson's look was of a defeated man. The video images were disgusting. The image of his own hairy backside pumping away for all it was worth nauseated him. Then the animal noises. It was all too much to bear and he collapsed into an armchair, a quivering wreck. Images of his wife's face filled his tearful and guilt-ridden mind's view.

'Man up for Christ's sake,' demanded Isabella. 'I hate crying men, even though I've seen a fair number. My security team now have these images and I will keep them as insurance for as long as I need them.'

She moved to the edge of the bed, allowing the gown to rise up to her hip on one side. Leaning over, she teased, 'I don't suppose you fancy another shag. Sex is so empowering. Don't you agree?'

Smithson didn't answer, burying his face in his hands, wishing the scene would dissolve and the power-crazed bitch would disappear with it. He stood and straightened the dishevelled robe. He then headed for the bathroom and locked the door.

'Umm,' sighed Isabella. 'Thought not! Must be camera shy.' She lay back on the bed, picked her cigarettes from the bedside table and lit one. She was a powerful woman and if she wanted to smoke, no one would stop her. She could do whatever she pleased. What a load of tripe the feminist movement spoke when condemning the porn industry as demeaning to women. The first time she'd taken her kit off for a camera had been nerve-racking and a pang of guilt had played on her mind as she thought of her mother's shame and embarrassment. A smile brightened her face as she remembered the day she appeared topless in a national newspaper and the tittle-tattling women at the office where her mother worked offered her support and sympathy, mixed with utter condemnation. She turned on them and said, 'At least my daughter has the looks and figure to carry it off, unlike all of your perfect little sprogs!' If shame had ever been a part of her mother's life she'd never shared it with her. God, Isabella thought, sex is so empowering!

Smithson dumped his clothes on the bathroom floor. He lowered the pan seat and cover and sat down, resting his elbows on his knees, cupping his head in his hands. He was furious. Why on earth had he been so stupid? Others had warned him away from Isabella, saying she was dangerous and manipulative. He would be different, though, he'd kidded himself. Twenty-five years her senior, sure, but his place in government was waxing, not waning like others who'd fallen into her honey trap. Now he was with the others, no doubt to be held to whatever ransom she wished.

He got up, picked up his tailor-made suit and straightened it as best he could before hanging it on the towel rail. Something bulky thudded against the metal of the heater. He'd totally forgotten about the small Magnum he'd bought now holstered in an inside pocket. He fingered the toy. One squeeze of the trigger was all it would take. He'd never killed before, nor even shot anything for sport. He wondered what it felt like. Now would be as good a time as any to find out. He replaced the weapon and showered. He scrubbed and scrubbed. He scrubbed the filthy bitch from every pore.

Dressed, except for his shoes, and aware of the killing weight inside his jacket, he toyed with the bolt before sliding it back. In front of him, Isabella stood naked, glaring at him in an intimidating manner that made him avert his gaze. Go on, he dared himself, just pull it out, point it and squeeze; easy, it would be all over.

'You were a while. Why lock the door? Come on. Get yer kit off and soap my back.'

He didn't say a word as he sat in the small armchair and pulled on his shoes. Isabella disappeared into the shower room. The door was not bolted. Smithson pulled the gun from his pocket. Would it really muffle the sound if he fired through a pillow? The shower would contain the blood. By the time she was discovered he could be in America or Brazil. Yes, Brazil. He thought he'd heard there was no extradition agreement between Britain and Brazil. Taking a pillow from the bed, he pressed the muzzle against it.

'Right,' said Cobbold as he came into the room brandishing a piece of paper. 'Here you are, Mr Morgan. Here's the guarantee that Mr Sharp will not be prosecuted for any action related to the Knights Tempest and its associates. And, in his own words, the Home Secretary has promised Mr Sharp will never be required to give evidence in a court of law. The signature is only a facsimile at this stage; the original is on its way by bike as we speak. Will you read it, please?'

Morgan accepted the proffered document and read. It was there. Everything Sharp had asked for was there. It hadn't been signed by the Prime Minister, but what the heck; the Home Secretary was high enough.

'This is most acceptable, sir.'

'Good. You must be on your way then.'

Morgan left and Sue-Beth arrived soon afterwards, sorry to learn she'd missed her man. The next time she saw him they would be as actors playing a role in the downfall of the Knights. She would now travel back to Plantagenet House, or at least to the property nearby, with Richardson and Jones. Cobbold accompanied them to the driveway. Jones took a seat in the back of the Mercedes and Richardson opened the near-side door for Sue-Beth.

'Be bloody careful of Morgan,' warned Cobbold. 'I don't believe we can trust him as far as we can throw him.'

'Umm. I beg to differ. I think he's okay. He's on side. He's smitten with Sue-Beth in any case.'

'Oh, and another thing: don't forget, you must separate Sharp from the rest. We can't allow the local plods to get hold of him. He's clearly yellow in the belly and will submit to the lightest of pressure from anyone.'

'Don't worry. I'll take care of him,' Richardson assured his old friend. 'We'll see you and Sean at the house.'

Just after crossing the Orwell Bridge and taking the turning where the A12 separates from the A14, Sue-Beth allowed her inner thoughts to slip out in the form of a chuckle.

Richardson glanced to the side, a quizzical look on his face.

'How ironic!' she said.

'I'm not with you.'

'Well, just think about it. A white supremacist male-dominated neo-Nazi organisation is just about to be taken out by a small army led by a black man with two of its lieutenants being a gay and a woman.'

They all joined in the chuckle.

A police car cruised past in the outside lane, two officers

assuming the interest of a lion seeing a herd of gazelles moving across its territory. The car sped away to their front and a *Police Stop* sign was displayed as it pulled into a layby.

'A bit of sport, Jonah, me thinks,' a mischievous Richardson suggested.

'Why not?'

A policeman got out of the passenger side door and headed toward the Mercedes. Richardson could see the driver was on a mobile phone or radio, no doubt waiting for confirmation of the vehicle owner.

'They think we've nicked the car and I'm a drugs dealer,' Richardson said.

'Why?' asked Sue-Beth incredulously. 'Because you're black?'

'You got it. Racism is alive and well throughout every force in the land,' Richardson answered. 'Jonah and me've got a little game, 'cause this happens far too regularly. You'll need to get out of the car to enjoy it, though.'

Richardson got out first, followed simultaneously by Jones and Sue-Beth. The policeman hesitated, faltering slightly in his step. Not the usual black drug dealer, he thought, all three were dressed identically in some corporate livery. The officer came to a halt about six feet away from the muscled black man. Biceps bulged under the short sleeves and the shaven head glinted in the sun like a black diamond – an impressive and confident figure. Glancing at the other two, the policeman realised these were two impressive individuals as well – even the woman had high muscle definition. The policeman thought to tread carefully.

'It appeared you went slightly over the speed limit back there a little,' he said in as accusatory a manner as he could muster. To emphasise the location of the crime, he pointed back down the road.

Richardson's gaze followed the pointing finger. 'Oh, I'm sorry, officer; it must have been a lapse of concentration. I won't let it happen again. Is your colleague coming to join us? He must know who I am by now.'

The policeman swapped from one foot to another nervously.

'Know who you are?' He collected his thoughts for a moment before continuing. 'Who are you then?'

'Might as well come clean,' sighed Richardson. 'We're gun smugglers.'

The policeman stared, an incoherent look on his face. Here was a man confessing to a serious crime. He looked nervously over his shoulder. His colleague was just getting out of the car.

'Ah, I see,' said Richardson. 'You thought we were drug dealers.'

'No! No! We only pulled you over 'cause you were speeding,' the officer spluttered.

'I don't think so,' said Richardson. 'I was three miles an hour inside the limit. I'm black and driving a smart car and in your carrot-crunching way, you assume I can only have made it by selling drugs. Yes?'

The officer shook his head in a less than convincing way and wished his mate would join him quickly.

'That was peculiar,' the second officer announced as he joined the group. 'When I gave them the index number I was told to wait a moment and got put straight through to a DCI's mobile who says that Mr Richardson is known to the police. Are you Curtly Vivian Richardson?'

'I am.'

'Would you open the boot of your car, sir?'

'Of course. Jonah do the honours, would you?'

Jones walked to the rear of the vehicle, closely followed by Sue-Beth who had already worked out that Cobbold was involved in the ruse as well. The two policemen joined them at the boot as Jones released the lid. The cops were mesmerised by the contents. Not only guns, assault rifles at that, but body armour, night vision goggles, clips of ammunition and so on.

'There's enough stuff for a small army,' said the police driver.

'That's right,' agreed Jones, offering both hands as if inviting handcuffs to be applied.

A car honked its horn as it passed. The occupants, a group of young men, windows already down, cheered and jeered as they passed, offering up racist chants, audible and all too common. Both policemen, clearly nervous and certainly suspicious, jumped at the sound of the horn. One reached for the cuffs.

'Enough's enough,' said Richardson.

'What?' said the other policeman turning to face him, aware of the big man's hand moving up to what he assumed to be a firing position. Instinctively, the policeman flinched, but soon recovered his composure when he saw Richardson was flashing nothing more than an identity card, a warrant card even.

'You're one of us,' the policeman with the cuffs said with relief, hooking the unused restraints back on his belt.

'Not exactly. Was one time, but we're on secondment to a special unit that fights terrorism,' said Richardson. 'Now, not a word to anyone. After tomorrow you can tell who you like. But I wouldn't do that if I were you. Our existence will be denied at very high levels. Enjoy the rest of your day, gentlemen. Oh, and by the way, you can watch the TV news tomorrow night. That'll give you a clue. And one more thing: try not to judge a book by its cover, guys.'

The three gun smugglers got back into the Mercedes and headed off towards Lowestoft, leaving the two policemen to saunter back to their patrol car not knowing what to make of their encounter. Part of them said they should report it. But the sensible part said they should keep silent. They would hand over the recording of their patrol. It would be marked up and stored to library and probably wouldn't ever see the light of day again.

*

It was dark when Smithson entered the reception of the hotel. All seemed normal; the receptionist greeted him politely. The clock behind her showed it to be just after midnight. He got in the lift and made his way to the top floor. He was slightly sweaty from about two hours of walking around the golf course, trying to get things straight in his head. He swiped the key-card three times before the lock yielded and let him in.

He'd left the room in a mess, tossing his suit jacket and trousers on the floor as he changed into casual attire for his night-time stroll. The corridor lighting was brighter than the room interior, but slowly Smithson's eyes adjusted to the dark orangey hue cast from the hotel's exterior illumination. The room had been tidied and made ready for sleep. He felt uneasily for the small pistol; it was still in his pocket. He'd intended throwing it in the lake below the eighteenth tee but thought better of it when he realised he was under the gaze of the terrace bar, well-populated on such a mild evening.

'You took your time,' came the voice from the armchair in the window, which was turned to face the same green as Smithson had been staring at a couple of hours earlier. Smithson hadn't noticed Isabella concealed by the chair's high back. She got up to face the man who earlier had thought he was making love to her.

'What were you doing down by the lake?'

Smithson didn't answer, keeping his head bowed.

'Were you contemplating suicide? You wouldn't be the first weak-hearted man I've sent to an early grave. Is it such a sin to have fucked me that you thought about ending it all?' The last question was asked in a mocking tone.

Still, Smithson didn't respond. All he could feel within was the utter shame of his earlier irredeemable action. It was only his loyalty to the Knights' cause that kept him here, otherwise he would have slipped away into the night.

'I now have all the members of the KT council under my complete control. As I said, I find sex to be so empowering.

Many see it as an abuse of women. But me, I only use it for power. Power is seductive and I fall for it every time. I now have vivid recorded images of you all under me, and under my power.' She giggled at what she'd just revealed to the Tory politician.

Smithson remained silent. He refused to believe it; surely this slut from the South London council estate was not the leader of the Knights Tempest? No one knew who it was. The assumption was that it was a man. But why?

'When the Knights Tempest come to power, which we surely will, I need a firm hand on the tiller. I now have that hand. You will all do as I say. You all have far too much to lose.'

Smithson took in what had been said. He'd always assumed the leader of the Knights was a hitherto unknown, an anonymous leading light of the right. True, he thought, no one had ever seen the Lionheart. They had all seen someone dressed as the Lionheart. It was now clearer in his mind; the suit of armour contained only a puppet with a voice synthesiser!

'You didn't need to do it,' he said. 'There was me flattered by your advances. There was no need. I'm one hundred per cent behind the Knights and the dream of driving the weak from our society.'

'You are now further devoted. I can make you and – understand this – I can also break you whenever I wish.'

Smithson held the woman's eye with as steely a look as he could muster. 'Are you the Lionheart?'

It was going to be a long night. Richardson and Jones were holed up in the underground concrete chamber Sue-Beth had taken them to earlier. They'd walked with her along the first subterranean tunnel as far as a door where Morgan had met them. Together, they sauntered along the second tunnel, Morgan whispering the layout above as they went. At the final doorway they went through the plan meticulously before bidding their farewells. Richardson gave them both the opportunity of withdrawing, assuring them the organisation could still be busted without them, although it might take a bit longer.

As the two Home Security teamsters made their way back to the chamber, they blocked off all the movement sensors with black tape. Next time they travelled this way it would be with the aid of night-vision goggles. The corridor between the two buildings was left with PIR protection, but the one from the chamber would remain in darkness.

Resting against the walls in the chamber, the two ate supermarket sandwiches and drank coffee. Richardson used one of the plastic bottles to urinate into before sealing the rubber sealed cap and setting it down within easy reach.

'Cobbold doesn't trust Morgan,' Richardson whispered after a prolonged period of silence.

'I know,' replied his colleague. 'What do you think?'

'I actually think he's all right. It worries me, though. Cobbold normally has a good instinct to judge character after the briefest of meetings.'

'But sometimes he can get it wrong.'

'Name such an occasion.'

Jones smiled.

'Go on then, smart arse?'

'Well, I think it came from your mouth. You said Cobbold thought that feller Dwight Carter was the most intelligent person he knew. We know different, don't we?'

'Ha! Ha! Ha!' Richardson smiled. Jones had earned the right to say things like that. He looked at his watch; just after midnight. 'I'll take the first watch. You try and get a couple of hours' kip.'

16

Isabella and Smithson were the first to arrive at Plantagenet House. After making their way through security they immediately made for General Sharp's office. He was not to be found, his secretary offering up his apologies, but they were offered wine anyway. The pair was soon joined by Munro and Hunter. Shona entered on her own and shot a knowing glance in Isabella's direction. Smithson shifted uneasily in a chair in the corner of the office. Soon after, the Duke of Woodbridge's bulky figure filled the doorframe and on spotting Smithson, made his way across to join the MP, sitting in a chair vacated by Isabella who was now caught in conversation with Shona.

Sharp entered the office from a door behind his desk, wringing his hands as if coming in from a cold garden to greet old friends in a warm drawing room. Rather than accept a glass of wine or champagne, he helped himself to a cup of steaming black coffee from the credenza under the window. He took one deep breath and turned to face the company. He could feel his heart pulverising his ribcage. He didn't feel very brave, but he knew he must see this through.

Replacing the cup on the saucer, he coughed into his spare hand. Quiet descended.

'Ah, good,' he started. 'We're all here.'

'Where's Swift?' asked Shona.

'He sends his apologies,' said Sharp. 'He's detained on business in the States. Please help yourself to these marvellous canapés. I spent all night preparing them!'

'What a shame,' said Hunter. 'He'll miss the unveiling of the Lionheart. Apparently, we've been summoned for a couple of high-prestige executions. Then, after the scum have gasped their last breath, the Lionheart will reveal himself.'

'Or herself.' Smithson spoke for the first time.

Shona spluttered into her wine as she sensed the Tory MP looking in her direction. She knew it wasn't her. She also knew it couldn't be Isabella. The South London slapper could manipulate by sex, and even Shona had fallen into her trap, but her time with Willow, latterly Isabella, had proved rewarding and lit a path previously hidden by darkness. Bisexuality satisfied her carnal hunger far more than a monogamous relationship with a loony-left trade union leader whose ardour was saved for stirring speeches rather than passion in the bedroom. Leaving her husband had destroyed him, the right-wing press led by Barry Swift's publications having been the most salacious. Shona had not given a backward glance as she shook herself free of the double-buckled chastity belt of politics and a Scottish Presbyterian father. But the girl from South London's brain was between her legs and there was no way she could even dream up the Knights, let alone lead them successfully.

'Maybe it's Swift,' Woodbridge guessed.

Conjecture flew around the room as wild as pheasants beaten from their roosts. Sharp called for order.

'It's true. After this morning's proceedings, the Lionheart has expressed a wish to make him or *her*self known to us. Rest assured, I'm no wiser than the rest of you. However, he believes the time is now right for our great nation to make its mark. As you all now know, the war, which I pray has already reached its zenith as far as spilled blood is concerned, has started in Europe. Today is the day we start to march. Today is the day the silent majority of this country will thank us for putting their concerns ahead of all the minorities who take too much time from our elected members at Westminster. It's the majority who have won elections in the past, then followed by the minority who drive the agenda. From today, this will change.'

'General Sharp,' Isabella stepped in with a sneering challenge, 'we're meant to be hanging the journalist who brought all this to a head, along with the woman who betrayed us to him. Yet you've lost them, allowed them to escape, haven't you?'

Sharp remained silent. The speech had calmed his nerves, but now the flood began to flow again. He'd seen Smithson shoot her an accusing glance earlier. Maybe this woman was the Lionheart; as far as Sharp was concerned, it was only the Lionheart who was aware of the escape. And God only knew how that was leaked. Like everyone else in the room, he'd only ever heard the Lionheart speak through a computerised device of some sort. Sharp turned to the credenza and placed the cup and saucer down. As he turned to face the nail-spitting Isabella, he held his hands together in front of him in a bid to hide the broiling within.

'Well?' Isabella demanded with venom.

'They're still here,' said Sharp, the words almost tripping over his tonsils on the way out. 'I can have them brought here, if you wish.'

'I do wish,' she snarled, eyes trying to lock with Sharp's dancing pupils.

Sharp could sense a fluttering in his intestines and his legs felt weak as they propelled him toward his desk. He took the phone from its cradle and hit a button. After the shortest of pauses he pushed two more in quick succession. He coughed to clear his throat then said, 'Ah, Captain Morgan. Bring Sean Bryant and Sue-Beth Walters to my office… No, now… I don't care if it's lunchtime… Good.' He replaced the receiver and slumped into his chair behind the desk. God, he needed a drink. But the plan was that he would remain sober. He had promised.

After a moment's silence, Woodbridge engaged Smithson in a conversation about the test series between England and

India. The others either joined in or chatted inanely. Sharp felt easier when not the focus of attention. Time moved slowly for the general who felt abandoned like a lamb amid a pack of wolves. His heart started to pound again as he tried to trace the steps of Morgan and the other two in his head. The moment of reckoning was almost upon him.

A knock on the door. A man and a woman entered followed by another man who sported a holstered gun at his side.

'Thank you, Morgan,' Sharp said to the armed man, who turned on his heel and left.

Isabella stood and took the few paces to stand in front of the two incomers.

'Allow me to intro –' said Sharp before being interrupted.

'No need,' said Isabella. 'I know the bitch – without a doubt the same woman who used to front up the corporate stuff.'

Sue-Beth's eyes locked onto Isabella's. The latter, even though in the position of power, buckled slightly at the penetration of the laser-like gaze.

Isabella unlocked herself from the hypnotic glare and turned to the man.

'I haven't had the pleasure,' she said to him. 'Who are you?'

'Sean Bryant, Miss, umm, Willow.'

'De Montmartre,' she snapped. 'Ms de Montmartre to you.'

'Many apologies. I thought you were someone else.'

Don't push your luck, thought Sharp. He surveyed the rest of the faces in the room. My God, he reflected, feeling an inner glow, we've got away with it! He turned his attention back to Isabella. Despite Bryant being a nationally famous journalist his pieces had never carried a picture of him. Sure, there was a photo on the paper's website and there was scant coverage of his return to Oakshott on the local news the previous Friday but, due to events around Europe, it had barely got a mention. Sharp believed the deception to be working, and it was his part of the plan. Nobody in the room could distinguish Bryant from Morgan. There was a similarity, but Sharp thought the two tall dark-haired men were far too different to allow the plan to succeed. But, succeed it had. The young member of Cobbold's team, who had earlier played a young husband collecting the keys for his and his wife's stay in a country cottage, had played the part of Ben Morgan convincingly.

Richardson gazed into the eyes of Augusta, flirting with him from the screen of his mobile phone.

'Still not got hold of her?' Jones asked. He hoped it would work out for his colleague whom he now counted as one of his best friends. He could even feel the pain himself.

'Not a thing,' said Richardson. 'Get this out the way and I'm headed straight for Sorrento.'

'Listen, mate,' Jones said, gulping in a mouthful of air and treading on eggshells for fear of hurting his friend's feelings. 'Have you thought there might be someone else and if she leaves it, well, you'll just go away.'

'Course I have. I've thought all sortsa fuckin' things.' Richardson betrayed anger, but managed it within a whisper, knowing he and Jones were active. He turned off the sunny image, noting the time as he did so. 'Bloody hell; it's ten forty-nine. You don't think we might not have heard the signal?'

'No chance. It would be loud and clear. Nearly damage our eardrums in these enclosed spaces. Let's give it until just after eleven. Then we'll go. Agreed?'

Hunter was the only one who noticed it. It must have been a soldier's instinct. A man used to entering dangerous situations had brought the military awareness with him into Civvy Street. The rifle propped in the corner at the bottom of the stairs had been missed by all. Both Morgan and Sue-Beth had expected it to be found where it was. Neither thought they'd given anything away. Sue-Beth caught a glimpse from the corner of her eye but was adamant she'd not peeked in the weapon's direction and given the game away.

Now the success of the mission was in the hands of Sharp, a man renowned for breaking up and giving things away under pressure. How would he handle it? A gunshot of any type would at least save the two condemned from a neck-stretching.

Sharp didn't move. Fear had frozen him to the spot.

'He used to bring it down here to clean it – didn't like the smell of oil in his office.' It sounded lame, even to Sue-Beth, but something had to be said.

Hunter picked up the weapon and ran his nose along the length of it. 'Smells good, Sharp. Nice and clean. Is it loaded?'

Sharp longed for a glug of red wine. It was a source of strength. Nonetheless, he mustered a response.

'No, Mr Hunter. It's not loaded, but it is primed.'

'What would happen if I pulled the trigger?' asked Hunter.

Don't mess it up now, thought Sue-Beth. Show him how to fire the damn thing. Not the greatest of timing, but it wouldn't be far out. Everything depended on Sharp's words.

'You'll have to cock the weapon first, Mr Hunter. Allow me.'

Hunter handed the weapon over to Sharp who pulled back the hammer to the fully cocked position before letting Hunter have it back.

He's done it, Sue-Beth realised, fighting back a smile of victory.

Hunter made as if to aim the musket along the underground tunnel into the darkness and squeezed the trigger. The crack of the explosive powder was loud and echoed in the concrete walled surroundings. A gout of fire blasted from the muzzle and was quite blinding in the relative darkness of the underground world below Plantagenet House. None of the former soldiers reacted to the sound. Hunter, Sue-Beth, Morgan and even Sharp were unperturbed by the crack of small arms fire. The others, including the Duke of Woodbridge, who was not averse to a spot of pheasant shooting, flinched at the small explosion and grabbed for their ears. The sound seemed to take seconds as it ricocheted along the corridor. The warning shot had been loosed, even though it was not Sharp who had fired it: he was meant to have remembered the weapon at the last minute and made to take it back to his office, and before he had realised it, the rifle had gone off by accident. Hunter hadn't realised it, but his interest in the old gun had started a chain of events that was irreversible.

In the chamber beyond the second tunnel there was no mistaking the sound. Jones threw open the manhole cover to the outside world, speaking into a two-way radio to Cobbold at the rented home.

'Signal received. Making move. Confirm? Over.'

'Affirmative. Out.'

Simple. The plan conceived in a Southwold flat was now in the birth canal. The two comrades scrambled down the steel cat ladder to the floor of the tunnel. Both had foam lagging around their boots to dull the noise. Darkness shrouded them, but they made swift progress along the corridor with the aid of night vision. As they rounded the bend, Richardson beckoned Jones to a walk. Light was escaping from the other tunnel under the door. They crept along noiselessly. The prey inside were unaware of the hawk circling, talons armed and ready to strike.

The light creeping under the door eventually turned to black, indicating the area beyond the door to be uninhabited. The night goggles were discarded. Both men listened intently. Nothing. Jones pulled open the door and Richardson slid in. Lights responded from all directions as he slid 7 or 8 yards along the polished floor. Richardson covered the length of the corridor from the prone position while Jones held a kneeling position in front of the door leading to the execution chamber. Nothing. They were on their own. No guards had been posted. Why would there have been? They were in a secret link that no one, apart from the two government agents and the small party that had recently passed this way, knew about.

Jones slid a haversack containing spare weapons and body

armour into the corner and made for the door. Both discarded their sound-absorbing footwear. Noise didn't matter anymore. Soon, there would be lots of it, the more the better now. Noise would confuse the enemy, no matter how big or small.

The pair took the steps in twos and threes, bringing them to the entrance of the prison block. Richardson spotted a helicopter racing in from his right as he crossed the landing.

'I don't know what your game is,' Tom Hilton whispered in Morgan's ear, 'but I will hang whatever is put in front of me.'

Morgan felt a twinge of fear as Hilton, the executioner, finished pinioning his arms. His legs would be tied together as he stood atop the trap-door waiting for the final plunge to eternal darkness.

The man to die first had not known of his fate as he'd breakfasted that morning. When he was found in the library and told to collect his belongings from his cell, his heart leapt at the thought he was going home. He now stood sobbing and shaking as the hardness of the situation hammered home. He'd been shown the rope to be used and taunted by Hilton to such an extent he had pissed himself. The only crime he had been convicted of was to have objected to a massive corporation wanting to build a new retail park on the edge of the town where he lived. The next thing he knew, he was bundled into the back of a van and brought to Plantagenet House where he had been found guilty of being a do-gooder and holding up the creation of hundreds of jobs. No one here seemed to care about his job as a shopkeeper in the town centre.

Morgan could hear muttering between the sobs. He recognised girls' names, wife and daughters perhaps? He heard the words 'mum' and 'dad'. Then he heard something else, faint at first, but the sound grew quickly. Rotors were churning the air around them as helicopters roared through the sky, heading toward Plantagenet House.

'You'll be all right, mate.' The words sounded hollow as

214

they formed in Morgan's mouth, but he was now sure. Any moment there would be short bursts of fire and Richardson or Jones would burst through the door followed by paratroopers.

The man looked at Morgan, the colour long since drained from his face, with a mortal disbelief in what the calmer man was telling him.

'Take him,' ordered Hilton to one of his assistants. 'Tell the bigwigs to ready themselves for the first one,' he ordered another.

'Struggle and resist as much as you can,' Morgan told the man. 'Delay it for as long as possible. Salvation is on its way.'

The man did not react to Morgan's words. An execution assistant took the blabbering man under the arm. The man stayed in his chair, so the assistant used more force and urged the condemned to make it easy for himself. Hilton could make the death long and painful. The pinioned man kicked out at the assistant, catching him in the shin. Another uniformed man came over to assist. Both men lifted the condemned to his feet but, just when they thought they had control, he slipped to the floor. Every second was vital.

'Get her smock,' ordered Hilton then turned to a bound Sue-Beth. Sneering, he continued, 'When Mr Morgan has died, I'll cut your clothing off. I'll then have a good look, 'cause I like to. You'll then be covered with the smock and taken out, where you'll piss yourself at the sight of these two dangling on the ends of ropes. The rope will be tied around your neck and I'll lift you up until you are on tippy-toes. I'll then cut your smock free so you'll return to your maker in the same way you were delivered by him – naked!' He scoffed at the thought. 'Then I'll hoist you in the air and you'll dance for the audience's entertainment. You'll take about twenty minutes to gasp your last. Then I'll cut you down and you'll entertain me out the back.'

A sinister laugh accompanied the last statement. It was intended to frighten the poor defenceless beauty. It didn't work. Sue-Beth's eyes penetrated deep into Hilton's soul. His knees nearly gave way at the piercing resoluteness.

'I won't be dying here today,' Sue-Beth smiled, wanting to turn from the reeking tobacco breath. 'But you might.'

Hilton continued the sneering laugh, but this time it was more of a nervous reaction to the considered threat from the woman warrior.

Jones and Richardson flung the door open and threw in a thunderflash. The noise was deafening in the confined space of the viewing chamber. Smoke filled the room where only seconds earlier friends with a common cause had been chatting amiably, even planning their final march into Downing Street. Victory speeches were being rehearsed. Richardson saw a tall slender man in an exquisitely cut suit delve into his pocket. Metal reflected in the light as the smoke dispersed. The man levelled a pistol in Richardson's direction, but two bullets from Richardson's weapon found their targets with unerring accuracy. The first caught the man in the wrist, causing a shriek of pain to erupt, immediately snuffed out by the second catching the man's throat. A jet of crimson fountained toward the ceiling, the victim's already lifeless eyes fixing Richardson with a look of disbelief. The body toppled to the floor, and not a person in the man's company escaped the scarlet rain as it fell to earth. The woman screamed.

'Jonah,' shouted Richardson. 'Round 'em up.'

The group didn't need any rounding up. They huddled in a corner as far away from the dead man as they could get, as if distancing themselves from the body would distance themselves from the heinous crimes committed at this place.

Thunderflashes were going off all around now. Paratroopers were crashing in through every conceivable door into both buildings. A pair of squaddies took over the rounding up of the hierarchy of the Knights Tempest.

Richardson shouldered his way through the door into the

execution chamber. Up on the mezzanine, a tied-up man was being manhandled toward a noose suspended from a steel beam. The two uniformed handlers let go their charge and headed for the door at the rear of the stage. The condemned man fell to the floor and rolled against the wall where he took the foetal position and started to thank God for his deliverance.

Richardson and Jones ploughed on, leaping up the stairs to the gallows floor and through the door at the back. Inside, Morgan was trussed up like a turkey at Christmas and Sue-Beth was sitting with only her hands tied, fully clothed and with the execution smock in a pile at her feet. Jones took his knife and cut Morgan free while Richardson did the same for Sue-Beth.

'You two, go and isolate Sharp,' Richardson ordered Morgan and Sue-Beth.

'No,' said Morgan. 'I know the layout of this place better than any of you.' That was partly true, but if he stepped through the next door he was venturing into foreign territory. The only advantage he had over the others was he'd studied the layout plans Sharp had dug out for him.

'Okay,' agreed Richardson. 'Jonah, let him have your weapon and then go with Sue-Beth and find Sharp.'

Morgan took on Jones's gun and followed Richardson into the next area, a corridor with doors along its length on either side. Morgan inferred this was one side of the building, there was a mirror image on the other and the layout was replicated on the ground floor below.

They continued through another steel-plated door and onto a deserted staircase. At the bottom, three paratroopers had five guards as prisoners under their muzzles.

'Saladdin,' shouted Richardson as he descended the stairs. The men recognised the password as their own.

'Are you Richardson?' asked one of the soldiers.

'Yeah.'

'Three men are holed up in the library.'

'Is one of them Hilton?' demanded Morgan of the captives.

'It is,' one of them said. 'Just let him be, Ben. There's no way out.'

Morgan was taken aback. He didn't recognise the man who clearly knew him. He turned to Richardson.

'The bastard's mine. We're going in.'

The library door was closed but not locked. Standing to one side of the door, Richardson tested it with the butt of his gun. Taking out his final thunderflash, he ordered Morgan not to follow him in as he wasn't wearing body armour.

'I want Hilton,' Morgan snapped.

'No.' Richardson emphasised his order.

Ducking low, Richardson shouldered the door open and tossed in the thunderflash. Following the bomb into the library, he lay prostrate on the floor. The flash cracked into life and the smoke very soon filled the room. Richardson peered over the top of a table and recognised a muzzle flash in the smog. Within the split of a second he felt the passage of the projectile over his left shoulder. Richardson instantly loosed off a response in the direction of the muzzle flash and was sure he hit a target. The echoing sound of the gunfire subsided as the smoke began to lift.

'Man down! We give up!' came a voice from behind the shelves.

'Throw out your weapons,' Richardson bellowed.

A clatter of metal on the floor told him two weapons had been surrendered. The smoke had now virtually disappeared between him and the former prison guards.

'Hands on your heads and present yourselves one at a time. Any sudden movement and I will drill one right between your eyes.'

The first man wandered out slowly, hands clasped behind his head.

'Good. Stay there. Ben, go and bring him over.'

There was no answer from behind.

'Ben,' repeated Richardson.

'Man down behind you, sir,' a voice he didn't recognise came from the doorway.

Richardson turned to look. 'Shit!' It was Morgan. Flat out on his back, he let out a low groan.

'I'm a medic,' the first captive said. 'I'll help. We're finished anyway.'

'Okay. No funny business, though. Shoot him if he does anything underhand.' The last order was addressed to the paratrooper who filled the door opening.

Richardson rose and made his way across to where the fallen man lay and the uninjured man still stood with his hands upon his head. 'Go and report to the squaddie over there,' he ordered the prison guard, nodding toward the soldier at the entrance. He knelt beside the wounded man, a quick examination revealing a superficial shoulder wound.

'You'll survive. Get up.'

'It hurts bad,' the man said. 'I need a doctor.'

Richardson frisked the man for hidden weapons. Nothing found, he said, 'Stay there then. I'll get someone over to you.'

'Thank you,' the man said and lay back with his eyes closed.

'How is he?' asked Richardson of the medic attending to Morgan.

'I must admit, he's not good. He's losing a lot of blood.'

Richardson patted the medic on the head like a master rewarding a dog that was trying its best, and walked out into the lobby. Sue-Beth appeared, concern etched into her face.

'How is he?' she asked.

Richardson collected his thoughts and tried his best to avoid eye contact. The word stuck before coming out through a dry mouth.

'Struggling.'

She brushed past him and kneeled beside the medic.

'Will he make it?' she asked.

The man's blank look said it all.

She ushered the man aside and supported her lover's head in her lap. The breathing was becoming shallower, barely audible above the background noise. Morgan opened his eyes and saw Sue-Beth cradling him. He tried to mouth words, but was too weak.

'Just save your strength, Ben. You need every ounce.'

The shallow breaths were now ejecting faint mists of blood into the air. Morgan closed his eyes again and breathed his last.

'No,' whispered Sue-Beth in his ear. 'Come on! Wake up! We're gonna get through this.'

She felt a hand on her shoulder. A glance at the hand showed it belonged to Richardson. She bent to Morgan's face and kissed his lips.

'Rest in peace, hun. You were the one who could set fire to the rain.'

She rested his head on the floor and stood to receive a hug from the big man. After a few muffled sobs, she opened her eyes and saw another injured man across the room. She released herself from the man's grasp and bent to pick up Morgan's gun.

'I promised you I wouldn't die today, you bastard. But you might as well've killed me. You've taken away one of my beating hearts.'

'Spare me the melodrama,' the executioner sneered. 'No – you can't do that!'

The last four words were a reaction to Sue-Beth raising the muzzle to point at his face. It was doubtful whether his eyes even had time to register the flash from the gun as three slugs turned his face into an unrecognisable, jellied mess. She uttered three words of revenge as she fired.

'But you will!'

17

Richardson found Cobbold and Bryant in Sharp's office sifting through paper folders and scrolling through electronic files. Bryant was taking advantage of Cobbold's generous offer to be in the vanguard of the investigation, having given an undertaking that nothing would be published until Cobbold said it was okay.

'Rather successful, I would say, wouldn't you?' Cobbold commented.

'Except Ben Morgan is dead, killed by Hilton the hangman. Sue-Beth went for him without body armour and took him out. I reckon we could find a spot for her in the Home Security Team, if she wants it.'

Cobbold didn't really react, but felt a pang of guilt for questioning Morgan's loyalty to the cause. He pushed a button on the keyboard and the nearby printer roared into life.

'How's Sue-Beth?' asked Bryant.

'She's a tough nut; she'll get over it,' said Richardson.

'Why is life like that? First of all her husband is killed and then the very next bloke she really had a thing for perishes. Why?' Bryant wasn't expecting an answer. He realised he was thinking out loud.

'Wouldn't want to get into a relationship with her, would you?' Cobbold joked. 'Given things happen in threes.' Realising the other two were not seeing the funny side, he changed the subject. 'Here, look at this.' He handed some paper to Richardson.

'What is it?'

'I believe it's a list of people who've had the misfortune of meeting the executioner. It even presumes a successful outcome to today's events. It's a full list containing dates and names. The last group includes Susan Walters and Sean Bryant.'

Richardson studied the list.

'Two questions. What are the names in the third column? They seem to repeat themselves quite often. And Rameez ul Shafiq, the first one on the list; wasn't he the guy who went missing a few years ago after that foul-mouthed rant on the radio? Came from up north somewhere?'

'Burnley, I believe,' said Cobbold. 'And yes, I think it is. I think you'll find we can solve a number of missing person cases from this list. If you look back four groups there's that banker who got that massive pay-off even though he took the bank to the brink of failure. Then there's the bloke who fiddled the government out of millions, maybe billions, by setting up an offshore trust scheme to avoid tax. I must admit, there are some you think good riddance to. Others, though, like the woman who blew the whistle on industrial scale corruption on security deals... no.'

'Nice to see they had some sort of moral compass, then,' Richardson smiled.

'The names in the third column,' Cobbold continued. 'I reckon that if you check the local Yellow Pages under funeral directors, they'll be the ones who disposed of the bodies. We'll certainly follow it up. Sharp?'

'Already gone.'

'And I understand we lost one of Sean's six?' Cobbold turned to face his subordinate.

'No, two, I'm afraid,' said Richardson.

'Two?'

'Yeah. You already know the Tory MP is dead. Yes?'

Cobbold nodded.

'Well, Isabella the porn star is on the missing list.'

'How come? She was here, wasn't she?' Cobbold asked, without any particular concern in his voice.

'Yeah, she was here. It appears she had the good fortune of being off powdering her nose when we burst in. Now we can't find her.'

'Not to worry. She won't get far.'

Four or five hours after Plantagenet House was secured, the media were thronging at the gates. It was like vultures gathering above an Indian plain to pick at the carcass of a mortally wounded wild beast breathing its last.

There had been no official word about what had happened. A couple of walkers had heard explosions from within, but there were no fires visible. A delivery man had been stopped from making his daily delivery of bread and pastries and had seen helicopters hovering above and armed soldiers everywhere.

The earlier activity of the day had caught the attention of a local newspaper and BBC Radio Suffolk, and a local BBC television news reporter had joined them later. A press conference was now scheduled for 5.00 p.m. outside the main gate to catch the teatime news broadcasts. The arrival of police officers and army officers with all sorts of glorious shoulder markings only served to deepen the rumours. Leaks had persisted over the weekend that a British organisation was behind the brutal terrorist attacks in Europe. Was this something to do with it? Some believed they'd caught a sight of the abducted journalist being driven into the compound. Was this the cause? One sharp-eyed local reporter had recognised the unmarked van of a local undertaker driving away. Had there been an American-style shooting within?

As the afternoon wore on, the local news outlets and BBC were joined by some international household names: Sky, CNN, ABC Australia and Al Jazeera among them. The bakery delivery man didn't miss a trick and was selling goods intended

223

for the office blocks to the hungry news city population that had sprung up. He was doing a roaring trade in pre-made sandwiches, pastries, rolls and cakes, and even unsliced loaves were shifting.

Cameras and television reporters jostled for the best view of the compound's interior, but the best they could get was a view of the entrance with its guarded barrier and, further on, the impressive double gates. A sign read:

Welcome to Plantagenet House.
The Research and Development Facility of the Civil
Protection Group.
Strictly No Admittance Unless by Appointment.
Please have your identification and authorisation papers
ready for inspection.
Vehicles may be subject to a search.

The first news briefing would be vague and cover only the use of the buildings and the operation in general terms. When the abhorrent truth was eventually out, the world would be shocked at the type of research and development carried out at this facility.

The military had enforced a no-fly zone over the complex. News helicopters would be shot down if necessary. What the crew of a helicopter gunship could see below were vehicles coming and going in all directions, like bees flying to and from their hives. Why, therefore, should anyone pay any attention to a burgundy Range Rover picking its way through the crowds? Small consternation arose when a towed trailer clipped the rear nearside wing of the car as it gingerly made its progress. A quick glance from the news team and they decided not to pursue the issue any further. The driver of the trailer's truck signalled to the driver of the four-wheel drive that there was nothing to worry about. The driver acknowledged with a thumb in the air and continued on his way. There was no way the car was going to stop; its cargo was far more important than a scratch to the paintwork.

A mile or so down the road, in a secluded layby, the Range Rover pulled over. A figure that had been crouching under some old horse blankets got out of the back, stretched a bit and got into the front passenger seat.

The Lionheart cupped the black hooded head in hands and thanked God for the close escape. The leader of the Knights Tempest had held back as the party made its way along the subterranean highway to the execution chamber. Pulling on the full war-dress of a twelfth-century Crusader, the thought of the death of infidels in the air made the blood course through the veins at an excited rate – especially the woman. However, the Lionheart was shocked to hear the sound of helicopter rotors whirring in the sky above. Looking down at the spent musket, there was a realisation that betrayal was afoot. Sharp, the bastard, had sent some sort of warning shot.

The escape route was now the only door the Lionheart would be taking. Moving as quickly as the chain mail would allow, the second tunnel was reached with heavy breathing and a pounding heart. Lungs were working overtime with the burden of the additional weight. A backpack lay near the door, which raised the question of whether the escape route might be already guarded. There was no way out the front so it was necessary to plough on regardless.

Into the second tunnel and total darkness – the lights always came on; perhaps a fuse had gone or something? The Lionheart found the wall and clawed along until eventually the end of the tunnel was found. Feeling along the end wall, the cat ladder blocked the way with a solid thud to the shoulder. Ignoring the pain, the Lionheart located the rungs, clambered up and forced open the hydraulic manhole cover that served as a doorway between the upper chamber and the tunnel. The chamber was illuminated as if by magic, temporarily blinding the Lionheart. The room had clearly been occupied. Empty sandwich and energy-bar wrappers were strewn over the floor, indicating the occupants must have been confident they wouldn't be discovered. Once again, thought the Lionheart, the whiff of a Sharp betrayal filled the air. Two large plastic bottles, one about half full and the other three quarters, were sitting near the wall. They were a welcome sight, for the Lionheart's throat was parched due to the anxiety of flight. Bending down and unscrewing the cap of the fuller bottle, the Lionheart recoiled as the pungent aroma of urine almost destroyed the sense of smell. The slaking of thirst would have to wait. Perhaps drinking your own urine to survive might be an option – but someone else's! The line was drawn well before that.

Scampering up the final cat ladder and through into the fresh air of the late afternoon, the Lionheart swallowed gallons of air to rid the nostrils and throat of the filthy odour. The Range Rover was already parked in the camouflaged shelter, just in case such an emergency should arise. Flinging open the tail-gate, the Lionheart dived in, the driver arranging the dirty horse blankets over the hunched figure. The smell of stale horse sweat somehow felt more comforting than the nauseating pong of human urine. The car pulled away. Within yards it had stopped again. The Lionheart, not daring to breathe, heard one of the back doors open and then close with a slam. Heavy breathing could be heard through the back seat. After a few minutes the car shook as if it had been struck by something fairly light. The driver could be heard saying, 'Don't worry about it... Thanks.'

A Chinook helicopter, used to transport paratroopers to the complex, now rose into the sky from the prison block yard, soldiers having cut down pre-stressed cables designed to deter the machines from landing. On board were Cobbold, Richardson and Jones, and the latest prospective member of the Home Security Team, Sue-Beth Walters. The Home Secretary would sanction her acceptance into the elite squad, subject to a few aptitude and medical tests, entirely at the behest of Cobbold. She would be only the second female member of this fledgling group.

Following a short briefing in Sharp's old office between Cobbold, Richardson, Jones, the Chief Constable of Suffolk and a staff general from the Ministry of Defence, it was agreed that, to allay any unwarranted fears, the Chief Constable would make a statement to the press. All agreed it would be less suspicious left in the hands of the civil authorities rather than revealing that a military operation had taken place.

The senior policeman waited patiently as the various media engineers rigged their microphones to a lectern produced from within Plantagenet House, the CPG logo having being covered over. As he stepped forward to speak, the double rotors of the Chinook appeared above Plantagenet House.

'My name is Aubrey Spendlove and I'm the Chief Constable in the county of Suffolk. At this time, I shall be reading a brief statement agreed by all the services involved in this operation today. I shall not be taking questions during or after today's briefing, but I promise you there will be opportunity to cover more ground in the future.

'Following the receipt and evaluation of intelligence, we have today launched a joint operation, led by the police but involving the army as well, at this location known to be the research and development facility of the Civil Protection Group. Having now completed the first phase of the operation, we are convinced that this facility was harbouring some serious criminal activity.

'You will understand this is the early stage of an ongoing criminal investigation and that I'm unable to divulge any further information at this stage. We can say that, as a consequence of this operation, we will be seeking to interview the senior management team of the Civil Protection Group. We can confirm that we have taken into custody members of a political movement known as the Knights Tempest. They will be answering questions over the next few days. That is all I can let you have at the moment. Thank you.'

With that, Spendlove turned on his heels and marched smartly back into the confines of Plantagenet House. Despite reiterating that he wouldn't be answering questions, he could hear a torrent of indecipherable babble coming from the direction of the gathered press of the world. Over the hubbub he could make out a few of the individual queries. 'What was Sean Bryant's role?' 'Is it true this was a place of execution?' 'Is this linked with the terrorist attacks in Europe last Friday?' 'Is it true the PM cut his holiday short to personally authorise this?'

'Jesus Christ!' said Spendlove as he sat down at the coffee table in the corner of the office. 'I've never ever seen so many journalists in one place. Where do they come from so bloody quickly?'

Bryant was tapping away at his laptop on Sharp's desk. He didn't even look up as he answered. 'Word spreads like a fire in a dry forest when a big story hits town. And, Chief Constable, I can assure you there will not be many bigger this year.'

'I suppose this is true,' said Spendlove, resignedly. 'Right, we'd better get on with getting everyone out and into police stations. God knows where we're going to accommodate them all.'

'What about here?' suggested Bryant. 'After all, it's what the place is designed for.'

'By Jove, you're absolutely right. Now we need someone who can look after so many prisoners. Ah! Not that they're prisoners, of course.'

'Are there any prisons round here that can spare some staff for a few days?' asked Bryant.

'No. I've got the idea. Some of these squaddie chaps will have processed large numbers of prisoners in Iraq and Afghanistan.' He turned to the diminutive general from the MOD. 'Russell, can you spare some of your chaps from the Colchester glasshouse?'

228

The general said he'd make the necessary enquiries. Bryant grinned to himself as he thought of this so-called general as being a pen-pushing civil servant rather than a frontline soldier.

'So, Bryant, this place strikes me as being a small-scale concentration camp.'

Bryant sat back in Sharp's chair and for a moment, considered his reply to Spendlove. 'Yes. I think you're right. And, having read their manifesto, I think it would be the first of many. Not on the same industrial level as Hitler's, but despicable nonetheless. This lot certainly mean the strong, or at least the financially strong, to survive and the weak to perish.'

It was hot as Richardson alighted from the local rattler of a suburban train that had brought him once again to Sorrento. He'd find out once and for all why Augusta hadn't been returning his calls and messages. There must be someone else. If there was, he'd retire gracefully and head back to England to conclude his role in the Knights Tempest case. There was always Gillian Francis, the teacher from Oakshott. Indeed, he cared for Gillian. But fate had thrown him in Augusta's direction first. And he couldn't get the dancer's twinkling eyes under the Vesuvian sky out of his mind.

He travelled light: just a few summer clothes. The room would have toiletries enough for his short stay. He skipped down the steps from the platform level to the concourse, took his life in his hands as he crossed the road in front of the station and wandered off along the Corso Italia. The familiar scents lingered in the hot afternoon air. Lemon and leather wafted in to bombard the nasal passages with a Continental thrill that Richardson felt only in Italy. Even the wafting cigarette plumes pouring out from the roadside bars and cafes took on a more magical form in the Sorrentine paradise.

Through the square he strolled, only one decision to make: to call on Augusta first or book in at the hotel and clean up?

Even if seeing Augusta was to prove a fruitless exercise he'd see the stunning beauty with the thick wavy hair falling down her back like a torrential waterfall; he'd see those brilliant white teeth smile again, framed by the lips of a temptress. Butterflies played in his belly yet, as a bullet had passed within a hair's breadth of taking his life and had seen for a very good man behind him, nothing made butterflies flutter like love.

He went in through the open door into a bright coolness within. The door seemed to contain a hidden message Richardson saw as a promising omen. It was the beginning of a path to an open heart: Augusta's heart.

'Hello,' he called as he found no one on duty at reception. He called again, his voice bouncing back from the cold stone walls. 'Hello.'

A pounding heart added to the anxious cacophony within his torso, but now was not the time to turn around and flee. He needed an answer.

'Ciao, señor,' a woman's voice greeted from behind, startling him into turning around. 'Ah! It is you Señor Curtlio.'

Pleasant memories flooded in as he recognised Augusta's name for him, memories of discussing the virtues of each language. Richardson had playfully argued that all Italian words were English ones with an 'o' added on the end. Augusta, of course, had argued the opposite, that English ones were Italian with the 'o' missing.

The girl was familiar, but he couldn't recall her name.

'Ah, ciao,' he returned uneasily. 'Is Augusta here?'

The girl's face betrayed an uncertainty before she answered. 'I will go find.'

She was here. Richardson's heart rose and it felt as if he was walking on air. A man appeared from along the corridor. It was Marco, the director of dance. At first, Richardson merely thought he was headed outside and moved over to let him pass. Marco's eyes followed Richardson's movement.

'Señor Curtlio.' He offered an outstretched hand. 'I am

Marco Albertini. I am the director of dance – Augusta's boss, if you like.'

Richardson instinctively took the proffered hand at the same time his flying heart crashed to land.

'I remember,' he said. 'Augusta spoke fondly of you.'

Why couldn't she come herself to give him the news? What sort of person sent a messenger?

Albertini offered Richardson a side office. 'Please? Go in.'

Richardson took a chair nearest the door and Albertini took the chair on the other side of the desk. He had a grave look, as if trying to work out what to say. He hadn't expected the big man to make the journey back to southern Italy and hadn't even rehearsed this situation in his mind. He had assumed Augusta's Englishman had boarded the ship and forgotten about the tall slender dancer. The entire troupe had tried to persuade Augusta to put the man out of her mind; some had suggested she find someone more appropriate.

'Augusta is not here,' said the director of dance.

'When will she be back?'

'She won't be coming back.' Albertini averted his gaze.

'She's left?'

'No. No, she has not left.' Albertini swallowed as if battling to find the correct words. 'Friday last week, she go to Rome for weekend off. When she was leaving the railway terminus a car goes boom.'

Richardson looked at the ceiling. He looked at the floor. The image misted as he looked at the wall lights. 'Dead? No!'

'She died straightaway. We are all saddened. Did you know she was planning to come to England to see you?'

'No. No, I didn't,' was as much as the big man could muster. He leaned forward, resting his elbows on the edge of the desk and supported his head. Tears pricked at his eyes before cascading down his cheeks. Albertini stood and walked around to stand behind Richardson. He rested his palms on the broad quivering shoulders. He was taken aback by the hardness of

231

the muscles, but soon banished those thoughts from his mind as he realised even the strongest and bravest of men could be brought to their knees by grieving love.

'Knights Tempest – the bastards.' He lifted his head and turning to Albertini, said through gritted teeth, 'I didn't know it, but I've already avenged her death.'

'I don't understand.'

Richardson stayed in Sorrento for the evening's show as Albertini's guest of honour. He sat in the front row and applauded as loudly as he'd ever done before. The show must go on. It was followed by a short memorial service, where members of the cast talked about the fun-loving dancer who'd been stolen from them. A soprano managed an unaccompanied version of Ava Maria. There wasn't a dry eye in the house, including a giant of a man in the front row.

Albertini beckoned for Richardson to join the cast on the stage. The last time he'd got out of his seat towards the end of a performance in Tasso's Theatre was to say hello to a girl who'd change his life forever. This time it was to say goodbye to the same girl.

18

The Lionheart? Who is the Lionheart? Bryant was back in the newsroom of the London *Echo and Post* and that was the question he was pondering. He had been in only a few hours and it was already as if he hadn't been away, like coming back from a holiday. This was different, though. He had walked in with a head full of a story that would rock the world. It was true that many news organisations from around the globe had covered the events at Plantagenet House three days before. All had speculated about the goings-on at the place and the people behind it, but there was only one journalist in the world who had the full story, and that was Sean Bryant.

He had exclusive interviews in the bag from many involved and despite being pursued vigorously for the past few days, he wasn't about to sell his story to another media outlet. The *Echo and Post* had promised him a huge bonus payment for the story as they knew offers were on the table from around the world. He had a loyalty to the paper that had stood by him and even if they hadn't offered the inducement, there was no other publication or channel that was going to get the story. The additional money would help to make it up to Amelia for missing the anniversary celebrations. The whole family would go to New York and Amelia would have the best seats in the house for the final of the US Open Tennis Championship. But pay day didn't seem to be getting any nearer. Who is the Lionheart?

Two large television screens were tuned into twenty-four-hour news channels and there'd been a couple of mentions of the police incident in Suffolk. It was underplaying what had gone on and when driving back to Oakshott late on Tuesday night, he'd heard a traffic report on local radio that had described it thus. His laptop was full of reports from around the world that had covered the police incident and not a single one of them had yielded a clue to the possible identity of the Lionheart. In the last few days he'd watched hours of coverage and read yards of news columns. Nothing.

The general consensus, including Duncan Cobbold, was that the ring leader was Isabella de Montmartre. When this theory had been put to the other prisoners, there was a shared disbelief at the suggestion. But they were all divided about the person they were following. Colin Hunter was another suggestion. Even Bryant was coming round to the theory that it had to be one of those two, but he was convinced there would be a twist. The immaculately kept records of Robert Sharp suggested it was the yellow-bellied former army officer; no one else would have that one, though. All of the KT members had laughed off that suggestion. Sharp had been the only one not interviewed and, when Bryant had asked for access, it had been denied by Cobbold – a denial accompanied by a knowing and warning look from Michael Jones intimating that the former head of the CPG R and D facility was no longer able to talk. It certainly meant he would never be prosecuted, nor would he have to give evidence in a court of law, behind or in front of a screen.

Bryant's laptop was still trawling its way through the coverage and he was sitting back in his chair chewing the end of a biro. He was losing concentration with the tedium. He lurched forward, tossing the pen onto the desk, and closed some programmes before turning off the computer. He headed for the door to the street and fought his way through the posse of film crews gathered on the pavement outside. He'd never experienced it from this side before and felt like a fox hounded from its lair for the final kill by a thousand bites. He hailed a black cab, which he never normally did, but sometimes the hunted had to jump in water to throw the dogs of the scent. He boarded a train at Liverpool Street and instead of going all the way to Ipswich, alighted at Manningtree. He took a cab from the railway station through to Hadleigh. He then got out in the High Street, paid his fare with a generous tip, crossed the road and entered Crabtrees, a well-established coffee shop of many years. Passing through the shop, into the garden, no one gave him a second look and that was the way he preferred it. Seated at a table with a huge pot of tea and four cups were Cobbold, Jones and Richardson. Bryant still could not believe this bulked-out muscle machine was the tall and gangly Dwight Carter of all those years ago. There was no doubt it was, for no imposter could have retained a memory of all the things they'd done together. Nonetheless, Bryant was still awed by the transition from shy teenager to super-confident government agent.

Richardson had toyed with changing his name back to Dwight Carter but had grown to like Curtly Vivian Richardson and claimed the documentation was too hard to complete. Bryant thought the Dwight Carter identity carried around too many ghosts in its haversack.

'Sean, come and join us,' said Cobbold. 'Tea?'

'Please.' Bryant turned to Richardson. 'Sorry about Augusta, Curt.'

Richardson acknowledged the concern.

'I know it's a, well, you know – what's the word? – indelicate of me. I don't know, doesn't sound right, but you know what I mean.'

'Spit it out,' said Cobbold. 'We've got business to get on with.'

'Well, Amelia reckons Gillian Francis has a flame burning for you and I'll vouch for her; she's a real nice girl.'

'Thank you. She is somebody I care for. Maybe too early, though.'

235

A waitress brought a tray of mixed sandwiches to the table with four plates and some paper serviettes. She moved the tea to one side and placed the tray in the middle of the table. 'Is there anything else I can get you?'

'No, that'll be fine, thank you,' said Cobbold.

'Enjoy,' said the waitress and departed.

Richardson rolled his eyes and balled his right fist, playfully slamming it on the table. Cobbold laughed.

'I'm obviously missing something.' Bryant was puzzled.

Jones simply shook his head.

'It's one thing I hate with a passion,' said Richardson. 'Waiters or waitresses who order me to enjoy my meal. It always sounds like a threat rather than an invitation.'

'Are we quite finished?' asked Cobbold. 'Sean, how's my bet coming on that the Home Security Team will solve the issue of who the Lionheart is before the journalists?'

'Can't say. I'm doing crap, but I don't know how you're doing?'

'Crap as well. Out of the five remaining who were in your article, none of them reckon they know who the Lionheart is. I know they weren't all at Plantagenet, but they are all in custody now. Swift was arrested at Heathrow on Wednesday lunchtime. Unfortunately for him, the story didn't break until he was airborne from America, so there was no turning back.'

'Are you going to charge them?' asked Bryant.

'Oh yes. Questioning will continue, but we've got a minimum of conspiracy to murder on all of them. They should be charged about now and in magistrates' court tomorrow morning. That'll give us quite a time to press home for all three points.

'Let's run through them. Smithson; he's dead and none of them speak very highly of him. Without exception, they think he's lily-livered and couldn't organise a bunk-up in a brothel. Then there's the dear old Duke of Woodbridge: frankly, a bottle short of a case; no chance it's him. Munro, well, in short, as bright as a Toc H lamp, thick as shit. Forbes certainly has the ability to lead, but chronologically joined too late. Swift, not sure on him; the only thing is, it was anticipated that the Lionheart was due to be at P House on Tuesday and without doubt, it was impossible for him to have been there.'

'Could've sent a puppet?' Richardson put in.

'Yes, could've done, except that each and every one of them was convinced the Lionheart was going to reveal his or her identity at the gathering. Then there was the stripper...'

'Porn star,' Bryant corrected.

'Same difference in my mind. Sinks and basins are different, but you can wash your hands in either.'

Childish giggling subsided.

'Montmartre, or whatever she's called; you can't make a silk purse out of a pig's ear is the general favourite from all of the assembled. In my opinion, a possible and not a probable; in it right from the start, recruits by whatever means necessary, demands loyalty by a library of sordid videos, which will make interesting viewing at her trial should we ever get hold of her and, above all, and notwithstanding the other stuff, she's popular. However, she's always denied it when challenged by the others and for what it's worth, I believe that to be true.'

'Umm,' murmured Richardson.

'Don't even go there,' Cobbold warned. 'Last of all there's Hunter, an odious cunt if ever I've met one. Not a word I like to use, but he is just horrible. Personally, I think he's our man. He is unbelievably right-wing, despite his public sympathies with socialist movements and good causes, which would all suffer if the Knights came to power – a tarantula dressed as a money spider if ever there was one.'

'That's not the Colin Hunter I know,' said Bryant.

'Come on, please,' snorted Cobbold. 'He masquerades as a patron and even benefactor of all those worthy causes, yet invites you along to a right-wing, neo-Nazi, whatever you wanna call it, do in the country. You didn't get to that party unless you were, or were thought to be, over one hundred per cent for the cause.'

'No one owned up to it, then?' asked Jones.

'I never get that sort of luck. At the moment, if I fell into a barrel of tits I'd come up sucking my thumb.'

'Now, I want you two' – Cobbold was addressing Jones and Richardson – 'to fly to Oslo and have a word with this Henriksen bloke. Sean reckons he was at Beardstock, and Henriksen claims he had connections with the Knights and met the Lionheart. We've arranged two hours with him through the Norwegian police. I also understand they'll give you fifteen minutes unsupervised and untaped while they forget themselves for a while. They feel hamstrung by their polite society. If they can pin a good beating on to a foreign agent, that'll be allowed. Our government, of course, will deny knowledge and to be fair to them, they won't actually know the finer details. Your tickets, instructions and contact details are in this envelope.'

Richardson took the envelope. Cobbold now turned to Bryant.

'Sean, I can't ask you any more than to keep trawling through, time and time again if necessary, all the media stuff. Boring, I know, but welcome to our world.'

Jones and Richardson were driven to a facility that didn't resemble a prison in the British perception. There was no doubt that it was secure, but it was far more welcoming than the high walls of a gaol in the home sense. The interview room was sparse and functional. A table with four chairs and video and audio recording equipment were highly visible. There were no bars at the window.

Having being briefed on the security present at the entrance to such Norwegian facilities, the two British agents had left their weapons in a safe at the hotel. The risk was low and neither had any reason to believe the weapons would be needed. Jones had recently purchased a new pair of tan cowboy-style boots which proved the only barrier to gaining access when they set off the metal detector. A cursory inspection by the guard satisfied him that there was nothing more sinister than an array of metal zips, and he let the agents pass.

A squat man, about 5 feet 8 inches tall, was brought in, a healthy crop of fair to strawberry hair atop a rugged tanned face that demonstrated an outdoor life, even in these colder climes. The escort was a man in his mid-forties, 3 or 4 inches taller than the prisoner and with the erect stature of a man drilled in the military.

'I'm Robert Torstvig, a deputy governor of the Norwegian prison service. This is Anders Sven Henriksen, the man who, by his own admission, committed the most heinous crime in modern Norwegian history.'

'There were worse in earlier history?' asked Jones.

'Of course. We were a nation who liked to rape and pillage and we did that on an industrial scale.' A smile spread across Torstvig's face. Even in the presence of one of the worst mass murderers alive, the black humour lifted the gloom and broke the Scandinavian ice between three hardened men of conflict. It later transpired that Torstvig had been on UN peace missions around the globe and was no stranger to the butchers of Bosnia or the slaughterers of Serbia.

'The rules are that I can allow you thirty minutes to talk to Mr Henriksen then we will have a fifteen-minute break, maybe for some coffee or something, and so on, until one hundred and twenty minutes have been completed. Then, if you are not satisfied, you may apply to have another two hours tomorrow. Okay?'

'Plenty of time, thank you,' said Richardson.

Torstvig got up and held his finger over a button. 'When I press this button, it will start the recording and the timer at the same time. Ready?'

The two Englishmen nodded their assent.

Torstvig started the ball in motion by introducing all concerned for the purposes of the recording and then Henriksen addressed the camera in perfect, but slightly accented English.

'My name is Anders Sven Henriksen and I have been brought here to be interrogated by a British agent and his inferior being.'

Richardson balled his fists under the table. They'd been warned this might be Henriksen's reaction, but declined the invitation to send for another agent as time was too tight.

'My interrogation is taking place without my lawyer being present,' the mass murderer continued. 'I will not allow any evidence that I give in these conditions to be used in my trial, except with my lawyer's permission. I will not answer questions from the black heart of an African immigrant. Your Enoch Powell warned of the rivers of blood years ago. Nobody listened. They should have. He was a prophet. Thank you.'

Richardson was about to speak but Torstvig held up his hand.

'For the record, this interview is connected with a separate incident under investigation by the British authorities and is for their use only. It will not be used in court. Point two: Mr Henriksen freely gave his permission to partake in this interview and agreed there was no need for a lawyer. Mr Richardson.'

'Thank you,' said Richardson, turning to face the prisoner, who immediately looked down at the desk. 'In a blog you posted prior to the bombing and the shootings, which you uploaded to go live at the time of the attacks, you claimed you had been influenced by a political group in the United Kingdom known as the Knights Tempest, whose leader is a charismatic character known as the Lionheart. Can you give us more information?'

Henriksen continued to look down at the table and did not respond.

240

'Please?' added Richardson, as if he were a young child forgetting his manners.

Still no reply.

Richardson sighed and tried another question. 'Is the Lionheart male or female... please?'

Henriksen remained motionless and silent until Jones repeated the opening gambit of the interview.

'Yes, Mr Jones, that is true. I have attended a number of rallies organised by the Knights, and the Lionheart is indeed a brilliant leader. My only problem, as is the same for many of my colleagues around Europe as you saw last Friday, is that the Lionheart wishes to carry out his reforms through the ballot box. This is slow, so a group of us got together to blast our way into the minds of the people. God has now willed us on to take Europe back from the left-wing thinkers that have scarred our continent and the immigrants who have fouled our way of life. You must join us, Mr Jones.'

'Thank you,' Jones said graciously. 'But I'm as far away from the ethos of your organisation as it is possible to be. I take male lovers, my best friend is black and finally, but not necessarily least, I favour socialist parties.'

Henriksen remained calm, without raising his voice in counter argument as he said, 'That is no problem, Mr Jones. Scientific breakthroughs have now proved that all three conditions can be cured. There is a place for you but not for this scum. It, and others like it, will be rounded up and put in cages and dumped back in their jungle world where they belong. In twenty years or so, Europe will be returned to the Europeans and I will be spoken of as one of the greatest figures in history. The majority will take the governance back from the bleating minorities. The dog will begin to wag the tail again. Is that how you say it?'

The first half an hour continued much along the same line. Richardson would ask a question, Henriksen would not answer, Jones would repeat it and Henriksen would repeat the spiel with more and more vigour, as if lurching to an unpredictable climax. At the end of the first session, the Lionheart's identity was still a mystery. Coffee was brought in and Henriksen remained silent while the others talked among themselves. The second half-hour followed the same pattern as the first. At the end, Torstvig again asked for coffee, but there was no response. This looked like the fifteen-minute slot they had been promised, as Torstvig had manufactured a reason to leave the room.

'I will find some cookies as well,' he said as he closed the door behind him.

Richardson put an ear to the door and tested the handle. 'Locked. Good.'

At the same time, Jones had fiddled with his new boots. 'These bloody boots – the new leather is nipping a bit.' He undid zips and fiddled with the heels and as Richardson passed around his outside, slipped what looked like a length of cord to him. In a blur of movement, Richardson was behind Henriksen with the cord wrapped loosely around the other man's neck, the cord turning out to be a length of stainless steel cheese wire. Henriksen resisted to start but, as the razor sharp wire tightened and dug into his neck, he realised that resistance was futile.

From the heel of his other boot, Jones produced a short blade, an improvised weapon made from a razor blade and a length of rubber to hold it. Jones brought the blade up in front of Henriksen's face and tested the sharpness with his own thumb, allowing the mass murderer to see the short scarlet line on the tip of the digit. Henriksen grappled with the cheese wire, but it only got tighter.

'I can twist this, you bastard, until your head drops on the floor. Bit messy, but the choice is yours.'

Richardson hoisted the petrified man to his feet.

'I do believe you're shaking, Mr Henriksen. I do hope you take a long time to answer our questions and depending how well you do will depend on whether your head is still attached at the end. I hope those girls and boys you slaughtered are looking down on you now. The fear you're feeling now was the same as they felt. But, despite what you've said, I'm a civilised human being and might let you live.'

'Who is the Lionheart?' asked Jones, holding the blade in Henriksen's full view.

'I do not know,' came the weak reply.

'Not good enough,' said Jones and put his hand on the zip of Henriksen's trousers. 'You'll still be able to live without one of your testicles.'

The terrified slaughterer, who could now feel his own quivering, lashed out with a kick. Richardson soon rendered both legs impotent with a well-aimed knee into the outside of the hamstring on each leg. Jones undid the button and Henriksen started to talk, so fast it sounded like babbling. After it was all done, Jones packed away the instruments of confession and Richardson allowed the sobbing wreck to collapse back into his chair.

Seconds after they resumed their own seats, the door swung open and in walked Torstvig with coffee and cookies.

'Oh dear, Mr Henriksen. What is the matter?'

'So sorry, Mr Torstvig,' Richardson started. 'But Mr Jones told him a sad story. One good thing, though, is that we won't need to bother you any longer.'

Torstvig placed the tray on the edge of the table and clapped his hands together. 'Ah. That is good. Coffee, gentlemen?'

'Thank you, no. We must be going.'

'I'll see you out.'

Torstvig followed the two Englishman into the corridor.

'Got what you needed?'

'The truth, Mr Torstvig. The truth. Now, may we have the tapes?'

'What tapes?' the Norwegian smiled. 'There are no recordings. I did not want to waste money if it was not necessary. I do, however, have the press release.' He handed over a sheet of A4.

Richardson scanned it. 'Yep. That will do fine.'

'Let us hope we do not have to use it,' Torstvig retorted.

'I'm sure we'll have to. Henriksen is not going to let an opportunity like this slip by. Interviewed by two British agents? At least that press release from the Norwegian government will mirror the one put out by us. Most acceptable.'

'Your fellows caused a bit of a stir, Cobbold,' said the Home Secretary as he poured tea for his guest. 'The press briefing by that blighter's lawyer has caused a bit of an incident at news level. Two English agents torturing a self-confessed mass murderer into divulging the true identity of this Lionheart chap. Have you ever heard of anything so preposterous? Both governments agree it won't do and have released joint statements saying no such incident took place.'

'That's good, sir,' said Cobbold, sipping his green tea with lemon. 'Very good, sir.'

'Now you have the blighter's name I suggest you get him under lock and key as soon as possible.'

'Ah, that's just the thing, sir. We don't actually have a name. My men, as you know, are very well experienced and it was the opinion of both that, despite every effort, Henriksen, despite his claim to the contrary, hasn't a clue who the Lionheart is. I'll spare you the details, but you cannot get blood out of a stone.'

Douglas Cochrane slumped into his chair.

'This won't do,' he mumbled. 'The Prime Minister was relying on us.'

'Leave it with me, sir. He, or she, must be rattled now. We've taken out the UK HQ and, thanks to Henriksen, we know there is a definite link. I'm sure we'll have him within the week.'

'Or her,' added the Home Secretary. 'Is there any chance you already have the blighter?'

19

'How about I drop you at the Walters' house and then go on to get the stuff for the barbecue tonight?' Amelia suggested. 'Then I can get you on the way back?'

'Good idea. But we'll walk back,' said Bryant.

'Don't wanna walk,' Daisy put in from the kitchen table where she was drawing another picture of Elsa, which she showed to her father. 'She will come home, won't she, Daddy?'

'Are you still saying your prayers?'

'Every night and every morning.'

'That's good. Keep the prayers up. And you need practice at walking so you can walk Elsa. When Mummy goes to see her, she'll want to know you're practising your walking.'

'Okay. We'll walk back.'

'Gillian feels a little awkward after what happened with the Italian girl. She sort of wants to know if it's a road worth driving,' Amelia said as they were getting into the Galaxy.

'Well, I'm not sure. I know he likes her, but Augusta had really drawn him in. Even Michael had never seen him like that before. Cobbold certainly hadn't, not that he would notice anyway. Let's see what happens with Mother Nature and a few glasses of pink bubbly.'

'Will Curtly and Gillian be a mummy and daddy?' asked Poppy from the back seat.

'Umm, not sure. Too early. Perhaps,' Sean answered uneasily.

'It's just that Tyson's mum told him Curtly was giving Mrs

Francis a good seeing to, and if they weren't careful Mrs Francis might have a baby.'

'Oh, God, did she now?' Sean stuttered. 'Where does Tyson live then?'

'Up Ladyman's somewhere.'

'Thought as much,' Sean guessed before lowering his voice to a whisper as he turned up the volume on the radio. 'Can't those scumballs go to another school? That's just not age-appropriate at all.'

Amelia smiled. 'If you'd left the Knights Tempest alone, perhaps you might've got your wish.'

'Ha bloody ha!'

Poppy raised her voice from the back. 'What's a good seeing to?'

'Ah!' said Sean. 'We're nearly here now. Remember to ask your mum tonight.'

'You bloody chicken,' Amelia mouthed as Sean got out of the car.

The girls raced for the buzzer at the side of the impressive gates. Daisy fell as they got close. Bryant wasn't sure whether she tripped or was pushed to the ground, but she had burst into tears.

'It's not fair. I want to push the buzzer.'

'I tell you what,' started Bryant the diplomat. 'Poppy, how about you push the buzzer and Daisy does the talking?'

'Yes,' shouted Daisy, jumping on the spot and forgetting the pain of the fall.

'All right,' Poppy agreed reluctantly.

The imposing gates swung open and the trio strolled down the driveway, the gravel crunching under their feet. The girls bounced on ahead and then dropped back to Dad's side. The big gun stared down the drive toward the incomers and Bryant felt Daisy clutch at his leg.

'What's up, sweetheart?' he asked.

'Does the gun work?'

'I shouldn't think so. I think it's too old.'

'Does Toby's granddad have a sword?'

'I don't think so, but he might do. Why?'

'Toby said his granddad is a knight, and knights have swords, 'cause they need them to kill dragons. Don't they?'

Toby charged out of the front door, plastic cricket bat and tennis ball in hand. 'Come on, girls, let's go play cricket. I'll be Alastair Cook and you can be the useless Aussies, 'cause they play like girls.'

'My God,' exclaimed Bryant, staring beyond the lad running at them with bat and ball. His mind started to work overtime, but he couldn't make a link with what he'd just seen.

'Ah, young man! You must be the intrepid reporter my daughter-in-law has been telling me all about.' A man came out after the boy with his hand outstretched. 'I'm James Walters. Sean Bryant, I assume?'

'Yes, sir, indeed. Pleased to make your acquaintance.' The two men shook hands.

'Dear fellow. The honour is entirely mine. How long have you got? I have a bottle of gin and some refreshing tonic water. Will you share one or two with me? I love to hear tales of derring-do with a glass in hand. Poor old Susan, I'm sure you'll understand, is far from good company at present.'

'Susan?' enquired Bryant then realised he meant Sue-Beth. He remembered her mentioning that her in-laws preferred her given name. 'Of course, I understand.'

'Toby, take the girls out to the back garden. I'll ask grandma if she can bring out some lemonade.'

Bryant was stunned at the quality of the finishes in the house, every nook and cranny as clean as a pin. Sir James showed him through to the drawing room. Sue-Beth was in an armchair. Bryant stooped to peck her on both cheeks.

'How you doing?' he asked quietly.

'Getting there slowly, thanks. I won't make it tonight, if that's all right.'

'That's fair. We'll catch up another time,' he said with sympathy. 'Nice vista.'

He went and stood in the French doors and stared out at the green and gold patchwork ahead of him. In a far field a combine harvester was unloading into a trailer. There was dust rising on the horizon that suggested other similar activities were in progress. The retired general approached from behind and planted a tumbler full of gin and tonic in his guest's hand. The first slug revealed significantly more gin than tonic. He caught a hint of a smile from Sue-Beth; she'd told him what a rogue her father-in-law could be. He took the next chair to hers and decided he must pace himself, bearing in mind the barbecue later on.

'Now then, tell me all about it. Right from the start.'

And that's exactly what Bryant did. From the black van that changed to a white van mid-journey; from the guest suites of Plantagenet House to the gruesome prison block and its story; from the escape through to the return and on to the liberation of prisoners and the arrest of guards.

'And all because of an article you were writing a few weeks ago,' the general observed.

'Apparently. An awful lot of luck, though. I just stumbled across the people at the same venue. Strange bedfellows was all I thought. If they hadn't abducted me, I'm sure it would've been in the paper and by now it would be old news.'

'And what about that murderer in Norway? You knew him as well?'

'Not really. I just happened to meet him in a toilet and when his face popped up on TV, I remembered it.'

'And fancy that! Two of you from tiny little Oakshott involved.'

'That's true, but until I met her under an oak tree at Plantagenet House, I'd never laid eyes on her before, let alone talked to her.'

248

'Incredible! Incredible!' Sir James clapped his hands. 'More G and T?'

Bryant put his hand over the glass and then shook it. 'I'd better not. We're having a barbecue tonight for our wedding anniversary.'

'Excuse me if I do then,' Sir James guffawed. 'And what of this Lionheart fellow? Apparently they know who he is now.'

'So I read, but I'll learn more tonight. For what it's worth, though, I think they've got the wrong person.'

'You do?' asked the host, pouring himself another tumbler of drink. 'I might as well make the most of this. Cheers, again!'

'Yes, I do. They're convinced it's a man and it appears the trip to Norway has confirmed this, according to some of the papers. But my sources are not disclosing anything to me at this time. For what it's worth again, I think it's the porn star, a very manipulative woman. She's not in custody, though.'

The conversation drifted away from the news story of the moment and onto everyday matters that eventually left Sir James snorting and snoring in his chair. Moving away from the Knights and Plantagenet House brought Sue-Beth more into the conversation, and Bryant sensed a lightening of her mood.

The three children appeared, Poppy's face like thunder.

'We've been playing all this time and he won't let us have a bat.'

'You have to get me out first,' Toby protested indignantly.

'Come on then,' said Bryant. 'Your mother and I will come out and make the numbers up while granddad has a nap.'

The five went out and played cricket for an hour or so before all decided they were tired out and made their way back inside, to be told that granddad had come over all peculiar and taken himself off to his bed for an extended gin and tonic induced sleep. The Bryants bade farewell to Lady Isobel, Sue-Beth and Toby and set off for home.

After strolling at Daisy speed along the quiet country lane toward the airfield, Poppy made an announcement.

'Toby said his granddad does have a sword, but he's not sure he uses it for killing dragons.'

'I didn't believe him; Mummy said boys are always like that,' Daisy contributed.

'Like what?' Dad requested, expected some nonsensical gender-dividing answer.

'Tell fibs to show off to girls,' Daisy retorted.

'He said it was in the locked shed,' said Poppy, trying to justify her earlier statement.

At home, Amelia was busy preparing salads and desserts for the evening barbecue. Bryant still found it hard that the usual patter of paws on the wooden floor was not there to greet him. He went into the kitchen to greet his wife with a peck on the lips, promising to help out in an hour or so. First, he had to go and write a few more words for his article. The last bit was a lie, but he needed to buy some time in the study with his laptop.

'Okay, hun,' said Amelia. 'But can you just get the beer and wine and put it in the fridge. I got orange juice for Duncan. Is that still what he has?'

'Yeah, I think so. I think there's some coke in the garage. I'll get that as well.'

After he'd loaded the refrigerator he made for the study.

'Oh, by the way, Duncan is bringing Tanya tonight. I said they could stay in the spare room.'

In the study, Bryant replayed and replayed news footage of the scenes outside the gates at Plantagenet House. He drank coffee after coffee and was growing frustrated that he couldn't find what he was looking for. He started to lose concentration and like a shopper who'd missed a vital ingredient, had to retrace his steps until he found the right place.

Then, bingo! He found it. He froze the action immediately and joined his wife to continue the preparations for the evening. Amelia remarked that he seemed like the cat who'd found a secret hoard of top-quality cream and wasn't going to share it out with any old alley cat like her.

The children were having an afternoon snooze, so the parents stole the moment to share a bath with a bottle of pink bubbly and ready themselves for the arrival of their guests.

A few good friends from the village were joined by Duncan and Tanya. Gillian was escorted by Richardson, and Jones brought his boyfriend, Peter. Before the evening's proceedings were under way, Bryant took the HST members through to his study. Drinks in hands, they listened with intent to his theories and what he proposed to do with the information, now he'd cracked the code. Together with the freeze-frame picture, and in the absence of any better suggestions, they drew up a plan.

Champagne, pink and white, flowed after using it to toast the happy couple and too much food was eaten after Poppy had stood and said grace. As the assembled guests picked up their cutlery to begin the feast, Poppy reminded them that they all needed to say an extra prayer for Elsa. Coloured lanterns marked out a rough square on the lawn and dancing took place under the stars.

Amelia and Sean decided to leave the clearing up until the morning. Getting ready for bed, he folded his clothes and put them over an arm of a chair. From the en suite, camouflaged by teeth brushing, Amelia said, 'She's going for the jugular tonight.'

'Who is?'

'Gillian, idiot. Who else do you think I mean? She's a bit tipsy. She said she's going to lay herself on a plate for him.'

'Oh, I see.'

'Is she making a mistake?'

'I don't know. But I don't think he wants pushing too hard. Anyway, he's got a job to do tonight.'

'Is that what you went off to discuss earlier?'

'Yep.'

'What is it then?'

Bryant went through every detail. Amelia asked the

occasional question. After lengthy discussions about their own future roles in the matter, the romance that started in the bath earlier, and continued on the makeshift dance floor on the lawn, petered out and the anniversary couple went to sleep.

Gillian missed with the first attempt at getting the key in the lock. Yes, she felt a tiny bit drunk, but wasn't sure whether it was that or the anticipation of a sordid evening ahead that caused her to miss the mark. Richardson calmed her hand and helped her guide it home. Inside the small hallway, she kicked off her shoes, went through to the kitchen and reappeared with an open bottle of chilled white and a couple of glasses.

Richardson, after drawing up plans with the others, had only had the one drink, so without question he could handle a couple of glasses of wine. Gillian placed a CD in the DVD player while he poured the wine. The air outside had cooled but the small lounge had retained the heat from the day. Gillian removed her pullover allowing the blouse underneath to ride up to reveal her bra. Richardson was facing away from her, so she held the pose long enough for him to turn and catch a glimpse of the undergarment. The blouse was already unbuttoned low enough to allow a full view of her cleavage as she placed the jersey on the back of the armchair. Katie Melua sang as Richardson brought the wine across and relaxed into the corner of the sofa. Gillian nestled in beside him, her fragrance filling his nostrils with a sensuous wonder. He could feel a reaction to her closeness, but knew he must resist.

'Look, um, Gill, do you mind if we have a little chat?' he said, defending himself against the temptation flooding through his veins. He placed his arm around her shoulder and hoped it wouldn't send the wrong message.

'What is it, Curt?' she responded in a low breathy whisper, allowing the warmth of the words to play in his ear. 'I'm ready for you and I want you.'

'Look. The truth of it is, I can't think of anything better than to get naked with you. It's true you're a stunningly attractive woman and I'd be happy to be part of your life, but I grieve for Augusta.'

'I did wonder, but I feel a fire burning inside. I can't hold it off. She must have been special.'

'I'm not really sure if I'm honest. We were only friends who enjoyed each other's company.'

'You weren't lovers?'

'No.'

'Would you like to have been?'

'Oh God! I don't know. I'm a love-maker not a bloke looking for a quick shag. If we had been, part of me would've died in that bomb blast. But it didn't and it's left an empty feeling. I want to fill it with you, but I need time.'

'How long?'

'I don't know. A day, a week, a month, maybe even a year. Who knows? Will you wait until I'm ready?'

I didn't realise blokes were like this, she thought. 'Yes,' she said after a while. 'Yes, I'll wait. You're too good a man to give up on. We'll be friends, yes?'

He drew her close and kissed her on the cheek.

'Yes, we will. Ah! And there's another thing. I have to go on a job tonight.'

Richardson, like Bryant earlier, went on to tell about the discovery and how they needed to go and find more evidence. He was waiting for a call from Jonah to say the coast was clear and, just as soon as it was, he'd be on his way. He joked that if he'd been in the throes of deep passion he might not have been able to draw away to a call of duty, even though it could end the Knights Tempest once and for all.

It wasn't long before the mobile phone came to life in his pocket.

'Duncan. All right?'

'Michael's in position and reckons it's been quiet for a good half-hour. Are you ready?'

'Yeah. Be out in a sec.' With that, Richardson wriggled himself free of Gillian's grasp, leaning over to kiss her smartly on the lips that had a seductive taste of wine. He hoped it was not for the last time, but that would be up to her. He lowered his hands to her blouse and did up her buttons. Most blokes would think him nuts; married or not, most would have succumbed. Her eyes glistened in the low light.

'Wait for me, please?'

'I will.'

Cobbold dropped Richardson off. He stood still, adjusting his vision to the darkness and waiting for the tail lights to disappear around the bend in the road. Silence soon enveloped him, forcing his ears to be alert. Rummaging in hedgerows could be heard. Richardson was amazed at how much life there was in the night.

'Psst!'

The sound came from behind him. A man emerged from the darkness carrying an assault weapon. The blackened face couldn't hide the gleaming teeth of Michael Jones.

'How goes it?' Richardson asked.

'All clear. Quiet as Villa Park when they go down a goal.'

'Huh! I'll get the picture to start with and then skirt round the back. You can give me cover wherever I am.'

'No worries. Synchronise your watch to mine. I have one twenty-two... Now, you won't need any more than twenty minutes. Meet here at one forty-two. Oh, and another thing, there are security lights at the back, but don't worry, they've been on a few times but there's no reaction from the house. They're obviously used to wildlife turning them on.'

20

Bryant, Cobbold and Richardson sat at the former's kitchen table drinking coffee. Empty plates that had contained cooked breakfasts were pushed to one end.

'This'll do; it's absolutely damning,' said Cobbold, studying some pictures taken in the early hours. 'Now, as we were saying, all we have to do is entice her here.'

'Not a problem,' said Bryant. 'I'll ask Amelia to text her, making out the girls want to play with Toby again. That's the easy bit, though, because then I'll have to persuade the girls to actually play with him. They weren't over enamoured yesterday at playing cricket all day long. Once that's done, we'll have her to ourselves and can hit her with the evidence.'

'Okay,' agreed Cobbold. 'But tell her to come in her own time. We don't want to spook her.'

Bryant returned after persuading Amelia to send Sue-Beth a text invitation to come for coffee and let the girls play with Toby again. Amelia would bribe the girls to do as they were told.

After an hour, Cobbold received a text from Jones – still positioned in a small copse near the Walters' home – to say Sue-Beth and Toby were leaving and headed toward the village. An hour and a half after Amelia had sent the invitation, Toby was in the garden playing with dolls, having struck a bargain that cricket would be introduced to the itinerary after twenty minutes.

Sue-Beth sat at the kitchen table with Bryant, who had his

laptop with him, and Richardson. Cobbold had left so she didn't feel overcrowded and intimidated.

'This all looks a bit formal,' Sue-Beth said nervously as she took a seat.

'God! It's not meant to be,' said Richardson. 'We're probably more nervous than you are. Having said all that, though, we have a rather disturbing discovery to put to you.'

'Oh?'

'Yes. Sean will take up the baton first of all. I'm afraid to say he's out-detected the detectives in this instance. Go for it, mate.'

'Right then,' Sean began, clearing his throat as if about to address a huge gallery rather than just two people. 'You see this picture?' He brought up a picture of a Range Rover driving past the gates at Plantagenet House on the day of the liberation.

'Yes,' said Sue-Beth.

'Well, you watch.' Bryant clicked down a key which turned the still image into a moving picture. 'Watch this. As you can see, the car is making cautious progress, almost as if it doesn't want to be noticed but, thanks to a bloke pulling a trailer, it's hindered slightly. Bonk! There you go.'

'Christ!' said Sue-Beth, the enormity of the images sinking home. 'That looks like my father-in-law's car. Please tell me it isn't.'

Richardson and Bryant exchanged uneasy glances which Sue-Beth immediately picked up on.

'My God!' she exclaimed and sunk into her chair, disbelieving. 'My God!'

'That on its own isn't proof,' said Richardson. 'As you can see, that isn't Sir James driving. Have you any idea who it is?'

Bryant zoomed in, but the image wasn't digital and the face pixelated as it became too large.

'No idea,' she said, slumping back again.

'That's not the end of it, though,' continued Bryant. 'Yesterday, when I brought the girls round, I noticed Sir James's Range Rover had a sizeable knock on the rear nearside wing that would be in perfect alignment with where it collided with the trailer. As seen here by a photograph that Dwi... I mean Curt, took during the night. Also, Toby mentioned to the girls that his granddad kept a sword in the outbuilding that joins onto the garden. I dismissed the idea at first because they'd been harping on about Sir James being a knight and knights needing swords to kill dragons. Then a thought came to me, and after discussing it with the powers that be, Duncan, Curt and Jonah, we decided to do a search of the building.'

'Which I did last night,' Richardson put in. 'And over in the far corner, under a pile of innocuous-looking tarpaulins, I found a locked wooden chest. When I opened it I found the sword, as you can see from this photo.'

Richardson placed the photograph on the table in front of Sue-Beth. 'And, as you can see from these other photos, there was also chainmail, a surcoat with the cross of St George and this helmet, like the ones used by Ivanhoe to joust.'

'That gear is what the Lionheart was wearing when I went to that gathering at Beardstock Manor, you know the one, the one Henriksen was at,' said Bryant.

'This isn't yet proof that it was Sir James,' objected Sue-Beth with less than convincing conviction.

'True,' agreed Richardson. 'But I suspect he never thought he'd be caught, so I expect his prints will be all over it. Then, I believe we need to look into his visits to the families of soldiers killed in the recent wars in Afghanistan and Iraq, and I'm sure you'll find all visits to P House would align with these trips. It was a good reason for him to potentially stay out for days on end.'

'Just coincidence.' Sue-Beth was running out of objections.

'Possibly, I agree,' said Richardson. 'But once again, my suspicions suggest that mobile phone records will prove me right. There's probably more than one mobile involved, but we'll soon tell if they were together at any point.'

'My God! You know what. When I got home after Sean and me got away from P House he said something that has sort of haunted me ever since. The words keep coming back to me. Forgive me, my mind is all a whirl at the moment, but he said I wasn't expecting you back, or words to that effect anyway. In short, guys, you think he's the Lionheart, don't you?'

'I'm absolutely one hundred per cent sure of it,' Richardson went on. 'Another thing, when you think of it, who else could have had intimate knowledge that you and Sean lived in the same village? Not even you two knew that one. No one else could have made such a connection.'

Sue-Beth put a palm to her mouth.

'No. My God! We have to get back. Poor Isobel. She'll be beside herself.'

'Don't worry,' Richardson said calmly. 'We have those things covered these days. There'll be a team of support officers for her. She's as much a victim of this as Sean. She'll need you in the future, though. Best you keep out of it for now. You don't want Toby seeing his granddad arrested, do you?'

Sue-Beth blew out her cheeks and placed her hands over her face. She looked stunned. She was staggered. Having sat down with her son in the last few days to break the news that the man he called uncle had died, now she needed to work out how to let him know granddad would be going to prison, probably for the rest of his life. Why? Why on earth had he got involved in it? Sure, there had been clues, but most of these were only now manifesting themselves with twenty-twenty hindsight.

'Are you sure?' she croaked.

'Ninety-nine point nine per cent,' Richardson confirmed.

There was an uneasy atmosphere taking over the kitchen. Sue-Beth was visibly shaken by the revelation and would probably need counselling herself. The last few days had certainly had their fair share of trauma. Both men believed silently that this upright woman, who'd served Queen and country, had been dealt a shabby hand. They also recognised that if anyone had the strength to pull themselves back from the brink of adversity it was Susan Elizabeth Walters.

The atmosphere was punctured by the ringing of Richardson's mobile phone.

'Duncan. All done…? What do you mean?' Richardson got up from his chair and disappeared into the back garden.

Bryant sensed something had gone wrong but was more concerned with the plight of Sue-Beth. He reached out to offer a hand. She took it and clearly the human contact was just enough to breach the dam. A single tear coursed its way down her cheek. Soon there was another and then another, and then the dam crumbled and a torrent spilled over the edge. Gentle tears became uncontrollable sobs. She buried her head in Bryant's shoulder.

Amelia appeared with a couple of handkerchiefs.

'You poor thing,' she said, trying to console her new friend. 'I'm sorry. We don't have any tissues, probably used up by Sean during a bout of man flu. But here are a couple of his hankies. They're washed, I promise.'

A couple of truncated laughs could be detected through the sobs as she took the first of the proffered pieces of cloth.

Richardson came back into the kitchen with a face that told of a newly found £50 note but the loss of an entire wallet.

'I don't believe it,' he said. 'Jones and Cobbold have contrived to lose him. A couple of local detectives knocked on the door, only for Lady Isobel to tell them Sir James wasn't in. Cobbold told them not to search the house yet, but play it gently. Jonah swears Sir James never left by the front gate. I told Jonah he'd probably fallen asleep.'

'Bloody hell!' exclaimed Bryant. 'If he walked out of the back, he could've doubled back round to the airfield.' There was a part of Bryant, possibly the part comforting Sue-Beth, that wished him luck and that, with good fortune, he might well be on his way to a life of seclusion in Montenegro or somewhere Lady Isobel could join him later. Then again, Sir James was a tyrant in the making, up there with the worst of them. No. That wouldn't do. Executions had taken place at his behest and, in some cases, appeared to have been used for his own sordid entertainment. All Bryant's notions of sympathy vanished at the thought of his own neck in a noose.

'We've already covered that one. A car is there as we speak, plus the fact that the police helicopter operates from there.'

'I know where he'll be.' It was Sue-Beth who'd spoken. 'He'll have walked out the back which, as strange as it seems without a map, is the quickest route to the main road. He often does it. Then he'll have walked round the block until he got to the church. He'll have gone to see Nathan, possibly with a bottle of claret to drink his health. I know it seems bizarre but it keeps him sane. He always says a good chat with Nate can make all the problems in the world disappear. Funny, it's something they never did when Nate was alive.'

'This church here?' asked Richardson.

Sue-Beth nodded.

Richardson punched a couple of keys on the keypad and put the receiver to his ear. Just as he began to speak, there was a loud crack. The sharpness of the sound reverberated off every hard surface in the vicinity.

'Must be one of those bloody bird-scarers,' mused Bryant.

'No,' said Sue-Beth. 'I've heard enough of those to know exactly what it was.'

'So have I.' Richardson was already flying toward the front door.

Out he charged, speaking on his phone to Cobbold as he went. He scooted across the gravel drive onto Church Road and headed in the direction of the gunshot. Cobbold was trying to make himself heard above the frantic sprint – not so much heard, more understood. He was unsure of Richardson's mind owing to the death of Augusta, and had promised him a month's leave after this job was put to bed. The last thing he wanted was Richardson charging in gung-ho and joining the long list of dead heroes. There was no need; back-up was minutes away.

Just before the church gate, Richardson slowed to a walk, gulping air as he regained his composure. He proceeded cautiously, ducking down to almost crawl past the sign for the church near the gate and just behind a low stone wall. Peering around the gatepost, his suspicions were confirmed. The land rose slightly to the cemetery area to the north of the church and from his low position, he could make out the shoes of a man lying prostrate. It looked as if he was on top of a grave. He eased his gun from its holster and disengaged the safety catch. Slowly, he lifted his head above the rise in the ground. Each inch revealed more of the scene until he was fully erect. As it had seemed from his crouching position, it was a man lying on a grave. He slowly moved forward up the slight incline until he had an unobstructed view of the body. Spatters of red stained the brilliant white of the memorial cross at the head of the grave.

Gun in hand, he edged forward cautiously, not quite sure why, as the deed had been completed. At the moment he saw a gun on the ground between two graves he was aware of a figure moving quickly from the church porch. An older woman was scuttling along the path, headed for the gate. She screamed as she noticed Richardson and then screamed again, louder. Richardson turned to face her, seeing the fear in her eyes. The woman's legs buckled as he started in her direction. Years of training and life in the field had taught him always to expect the unexpected, but a feeling from deep inside told him this was exactly as it appeared. A man had blown his own brains out, an unsuspecting woman, maybe a cleaner, had been inside the church when the gun had fired and when she thought it safe she decided to make a run for it. She'd seen a huge black man carrying a gun inside a rural graveyard and a few yards further on, was what looked like a dead body. Now the monster was coming after her and, after all, she was the only witness.

Perceiving no further threat, Richardson returned the weapon to its holster. He held his hands out wide to each side and moved over to walk a line toward the woman, blocking her view as best he could. He could see she was a frightened mess, the blood having drained from her face and her limbs giving the support of a melting jelly. She didn't cry, but merely offered words to a greater being who must have been appalled at the carnage in his own peaceful garden.

'I'm a policeman, don't be frightened.' It sounded feeble.

'Please! Please! Don't shoot me.' Richardson realised her eyes were closed and she was unaware he'd holstered the pistol. 'I've promised Bert I'll take him to the hospital this afternoon. He won't cope if you kill me.'

'I'm not going to kill you. I'm a policeman. You're safe. I promise.'

He got to her, kneeled down beside her and took her around the shoulders, holding her quaking body.

'I'm sorry,' she said. 'You must think me a fool.'

'No, no, not at all. My name is Curt. What's yours?' Richardson's voice was soothing.

'Heather.'

'You've had an awful shock, Heather. You've been very brave. Is Bert your husband?'

'Yes,' she answered, as sobs of relief came. 'Of forty-two years.'

'I'll take the pair of you to the hospital this afternoon. Let's get you on your feet and get you to the gate.'

By this time, Cobbold and Jones had arrived along with half a dozen uniformed officers. Heather safely handed over, Richardson went over to the body. The exit wound through the top of the head was grotesque, blood and bits of brain spattered all over. In the middle of the cross, the headstone of

Colonel Nathan James Walters 1971-2005, a white envelope was fixed, curiously untouched by blood or brain. It was addressed to Colonel Nathan Walters MC. Richardson stared at the envelope. He was aware of Cobbold coming up beside him.

'Oh! What a nice young man! You've got 'em all charmed in this village.' Cobbold spoke sarcastically, having endured a minute or so of Heather pouring compliments on his officer.

Richardson paid no attention to his friend's teasing. He merely opened the envelope and scanned the letter within.

'What's it say then? Suicide note?'

'Kind of,' said Richardson. He read out the letter to Cobbold and now Jones, who'd joined them.

'My dearest son, Nate.

'Today was the last time I communicated with you across the love that fills the void from earth to heaven. I will join you shortly, my son. Keep a place for me at your side.

'We nearly achieved so much. I now know I probably panicked. It was clear the journalist, Bryant, was sniffing around but, as it turned out, he hadn't picked up the scent. I misjudged Susan, and I'm ready to answer to you when we meet. You chose well and she'll make a good mother to Toby. Who knows? The young man might read of my dream and think his grandfather right all along and the Knights will be reborn.

'Indeed, my son, there's still a flicker in the dying embers. You remember I talked of the other Isobel – not your mother, but Isobella who adopted the name to honour your mother – well, she managed to scramble her way to safety with me and is now safely tucked away with our many friends abroad. She's a good judge and reader of men and will know when to bring the Knights together again.

'Your mother, Susan and Toby are well looked after and will all one day join us at God's side, for that is surely where we shall be. He keeps sending messengers to this place and we all return having not completed our task. One day, he'll send us all together.

'You might think me weak for not seeing this through, but I believe Mr Bryant was on to me. He looked me straight in the eye when he said he believed that loathsome character Henriksen had picked the wrong person. His eyes were firm and sure and I knew then my time was up. He identified Isabella as the leader but there was a knowing glint in his eye that said it was me.

'I now have one deed left to me, my son, and that is to allow my lifeblood to mingle with your mortal being before making the final leap to join you in eternity.

'The love of a father for a son knows no bounds.

'Love you forever, your devoted father.'

Epilogue

Nearly three weeks after the death of the Lionheart, and despite protestations from many, he was laid to rest alongside his son in the family plot at Oakshott Church. The interest in the village subsided and before long, it was as if nothing had happened. Obviously, Sir James was missing, but the community had gained a new resident. A tall muscular man had taken up an invitation to move in with his lover. The kindling was now alight and with every day that passed, the flames spread with a growing intensity.

Gillian had heard the rumours from the tittle-tattlers at the school gate. But that's exactly what they had been before the summer holiday: rumours. Now, since the beginning of the new school year in early September, she had put things right in no uncertain terms. The rumours had been quashed and they were rumours no more. Now every word was true. For the time being, no word was enough to describe the passion that burned in the hearts of Gillian Francis and Curtly Richardson.

For the first time in his life, Richardson felt a part of something. He was part of the village community. He'd taken Gillian down to his rented home – correction: house – in the New Forest and together they loaded up a removal van which took his chattels to store in a barn in Oakshott. Gillian's television had been replaced with Richardson's fine up-to-date smart HD model and accompanying Blu-ray player. The rest would wait until they bought a home together. When asked, assurances had been given that Gillian would remain as the school's head. She would not walk away from the village that had given her a shoulder to lean on and the job she loved.

On the afternoon of the third Sunday in September, Richardson was sitting in the home dressing room of the Oakshott cricket pavilion, twiddling a bat nervously in his hands. While feeling the bat, he pondered how he'd got himself into this hole. The night before, he'd been in the village pub with Gillian, Sean and Amelia. It was a karaoke evening and, for some strange reason he now attributed to two or three pints of Adnams, he claimed that because he was of Afro-Caribbean descent he could sing like Bob Marley. After murdering 'Buffalo Soldier', he re-joined his party, drunken failure etched all over his face. Then the village cricket team captain had approached and he found himself bragging.

'Of course I can play cricket, man. It's in my blood. My middle name ain't Vivian for nothin'.'

Sean sat with his head in his hands, Gillian held a hand over her mouth and Amelia started to laugh. Another pint of the famous Suffolk brew and tales of some of his better innings started to be exaggerated.

The following morning, Oakshott won the toss and elected to bat. For some reason, and much to the amusement of Bryant, the captain asked Richardson to go in at three. After getting padded up, Richardson went and sat with his mate, who'd set up deckchairs on the extra cover boundary for the opening ball of the match. Just before 'play' was called, the two men were joined by the ladies who, for some reason, had all volunteered to help with the tea. As well as Amelia, Gillian and Sue-Beth, Toby was there with Poppy and Daisy.

'Holy shit!' Richardson exclaimed as the opening bowler unleashed the first missile of the afternoon. 'I never saw the bloody thing.'

The others laughed.

Richardson flinched when the second ball caught the

Oakshott number one under the chin. He went to the ground as if felled by a cannonball. After a few minutes of treatment it was evident he wouldn't be carrying on.

'Your turn, Curt,' came shouts from the pavilion. 'Good luck!'

A woman came over and took some orders for teas and coffees. 'I'll have tea, please,' said Richardson.

'I thought you were batting next,' said the tea lady.

'I somehow don't think it's going to have time to go cold,' Richardson responded as he left for the crease. Within ten paces he turned and headed back to his friends. He removed his helmet, tossing it to a surprised Bryant. 'I can't wear that thing!'

'You're joking! Have you seen how quick he is?' Bryant nodded in the direction of the bowler, who was already back at his mark, a full pitch and a half from the stumps.

'Not yet. I haven't seen one yet,' joked Richardson. 'Besides, Viv never wore a helmet! See ya soon.'

Drops of blood stained the ground where Richardson's predecessor had fallen. His intestines started to turn to water. He took his guard, surveyed the field placings and prepared for battle. He looked up to see the wiry young bowler start his approach. Richardson's knees wanted to buckle and he felt as if he was wearing boots of concrete.

'Oh shit!' Richardson muttered to himself as the ball flew past like a cruise missile before he'd even moved a foot. The bat was nowhere near the same line as the ball had travelled.

Richardson managed to negotiate his way to the end of the over with lady luck on his side. During the next over from the other end, the bowling was not so hostile, his batting partner, a young lad named Joe, scoring two runs from one shot. Then it was his turn again.

'Go on, Darren,' a fieldsman shouted encouragement to the bowler, who appeared to be fired up enough without anybody else's input. 'You'll get 'im this time.'

The first ball of the new over came at such a ferocious pace that Richardson barely had time to get in position. Just when he closed his eyes and expected a bone splitting crunch in the side of the face, he somehow got the bat in the way. Through no skill on Richardson's part the ball took off from the edge of the bat and earned him a fortuitous six!

He turned with a smug look on his face for the benefit of Darren. To his surprise, the bowler was standing only two or three paces away looking like a lion about to move for a wounded antelope.

'Bit o' luck there then, nigger,' he snarled at his opponent.

The N-word shocked Richardson. He hadn't really heard it, not least had it directed at him, since his early days in the police. Sometimes he'd been able to laugh it off as banter. This time there was no hiding the unmasked venom that accompanied it. Richardson didn't make eye contact with his adversary, nor make a verbal response. 'I'll take yer head off with the next one, nigger.'

'That's enough, Darren,' ordered the opposing captain and the bowler paced back to his mark. There he circled and started to move in for the kill. This time the ball was pitched fuller and Richardson placed his left foot down the pitch and felt a resounding crack through the handle as the ball sped away toward the extra cover boundary, just to the right of where his friends were seated.

He hadn't noticed before but Cobbold had joined the group with a woman in her late forties or early fifties. His thoughts were interrupted by the foul-mouthed bowler.

'Don't let that fuckin' thing touch the ball.'

It was too late. A dog just beyond the group of supporters had retrieved the ball and was bringing it back to the fieldsman, dropping it at his feet. A tear fell from the policeman's cheek and splashed onto the dusty ground.

'You okay, mate?' enquired the wicketkeeper and then, referring to the bowler, 'He'll calm down soon. Don't worry about him. You've got the beating of him anyway as he gets knackered.'

Richardson was aware of two momentous happenings in the last few seconds and neither was related to the pretentious bowler.

'Trust me,' replied Richardson, 'that's not what's bothering me. You see that dog. Despite being a bitch, she's got more balls than the likes of Darren will ever have. She took a bullet in the protection of her master.' He watched as the golden Labrador hobbled back to her family for much patting of the head, this greeted by firm repetitive tail-wagging. Whilst it was true that the sight of Elsa fielding the ball was an emotional moment; only Richardson knew the true reason for the tear.

He now had the feel for batting again and eventually, when he was caught out trying to hit a six, he strolled off to much applause from the pavilion and his friends. He'd scored sixty-seven runs. Instead of heading to the dressing room, he went over to his friends, who were all standing and applauding with vigour, none more so than the recently arrived woman whose beaming smile could have lit up the darkest of nights.

She stood to greet the new batting hero of Oakshott, who dropped his bat and gloves to the ground and joined her in an embrace of pure love – the love that a son would have for his mother or a mother for a son. This particular mother and son hadn't seen each other since before Dwight Carter had 'died' in prison.

The woman released herself and held her son at arm's length. 'Let me look at you,' she said with a strong West Midlands accent. 'You've changed. Where has my lanky and weedy son gone? He's been swallowed whole by this fine body of a man who stands before me.'

Tears cascaded down the faces of the long-lost relatives. It was probably doubly hard for his mother. First of all, there'd been the shocking disbelief when Cobbold had called to tell her that her Dwight had not actually died but been taken into the witness protection scheme and had thrived with his new identity. Then there was the pulsating nervousness of the prospect of reunion. Even a cynical old copper like Cobbold was moved to tears.

The pair chatted for the rest of the Oakshott innings. Sue-Beth, Gillian, Sean and Amelia joined the happiness. Jonah wasn't there to share in his friend's happiness, but Cobbold had assured Richardson the retired soldier had been informed of the planned reunion and wished them luck for the future. Oakshott managed two hundred and twenty-eight runs for the loss of eight wickets.

This proved to be more than enough as the visitors crumbled to one hundred and sixty-two runs all out. Richardson managed to get two wickets including the bowling of his nemesis, Darren, who disappeared back to the pavilion like a scolded dog heading for the seclusion of his kennel. In addition to the wickets, Richardson snared a catch at mid-wicket.

After showering, Richardson bought a huge jug of beer to share with his team-mates for his fifty, and a second one for his man of the match status. He enjoyed the company of his mother but, more than anything, he enjoyed the contentment of the love that was blossoming between him and Gillian. Above all, he'd been accepted into the village and made to feel as welcome as a prodigal son returning to his roots. He hoped he could persuade his mother to move and join him in the Suffolk countryside, but that debate was for another day. He was surrounded by warm friends and an even warmer glow radiated from within.

Out of the corner of his eye, Richardson saw Darren leave a throng of players standing at the bar to visit the toilets. He nodded to Sue-Beth. She placed her drink on the table.

'Excuse me,' she said. 'Need to see a man about a dog.'

'Me too,' said Richardson, and the pair followed in the direction of the bigoted bowler.

'Sorry, love,' said the slightly tipsy man as Sue-Beth

appeared at the door of the gents. 'Wrong one. Unless, of course, you'd like me to show you a good time in one of the cubicles.'

'I don't think so,' Sue-Beth answered in a threatening mono-tone. 'On both counts.'

'I don't understand,' slurred the bowler.

'Didn't think you were too quick on the uptake.' This voice belonged to Richardson who was heading menacingly towards him.

Darren tried to finish, shook off the excess and tucked himself up. He'd rushed things a little and a damp patch manifested itself around the zip area of his trousers. Without acknowledging the bigger man, he tried to slip past, but a well-developed forearm barred his path.

'Not so fast – I'd like a word,' growled Richardson.

'Oh, you played really well,' squeaked a less-than-confident Darren. 'No hard feelings about the sledging? Hey?'

'Guess what?' Richardson didn't wait for an answer. 'I don't like being called nigger.' His powerful forearms tensed as he grasped Darren's collar tightly and pushed him up the wall until he was touching the floor only with his tippy-toes. For a tall man, he felt light to Richardson's adrenalin-filled muscles.

'No, I understand. It was only banter.' Darren gasped out the words at the same time as trying to catch his breath. The black man's grasp was beginning to choke off the air to his lungs. 'I didn't mean any harm by it. Honest.'

'You know what,' said Richardson, sliding his opponent further up the wall, 'people like you make me sick. It's all a joke. It's not serious. Well, let me tell you something; your type of language is heard in every pub and bar, in every office and warehouse, and in every shopping centre and sports arena up and down the country. And to a man, and even woman, every single one of you says you don't mean it. It's a joke or it's banter or whatever. Then low-life, ambitious, would-be Hitlers or Napoleons hear what you say and take you seriously. And then, before you know it, hundreds are dead in Norway and others have died around Europe, including a special friend of mine.'

Darren listened. There was little more he could do. Breath was on ration and a feeling of nausea was rising from deep inside. His arms were free but, like a rabbit dazzled by head-lights, he was unable to move and like the rabbit he was beginning to fear for his life. His eyes willed the door to open and a saviour walk in. But nothing changed. The woman would probably stop anyone from entering. A moment of relief and air cascaded into Darren's lungs as Richardson briefly relaxed his vice-like grip. It tightened again.

'And, this lady here...' Richardson jerked his head in the direction of Sue-Beth, 'she lost the bloke she was going to marry. So, that's why I despise your low-level comments so much. But, you know what, I actually believe you. I do believe you didn't mean it, like most others who utter such tripe. The trouble is, Darren, there are people out there' – Richardson jerked his head again, this time toward the window – 'who do think you mean it and in your name try and rally a revolution based on these petty-minded prejudices. Niggers and gays, and spastics and greys have no place in the world of people like the Knights Tempest.'

Darren nodded. Richardson released his grasp and the captive fell to the floor, gulping in air like a thirsty man taking in water at an oasis. He looked up at the mountain of a man who stooped and helped him to his feet.

'The Knights are real, then?' Darren asked between generous portions of oxygen.

Richardson nodded. 'Yeah. They were, anyway. They're broken now, though.'

'Good speech,' Sue-Beth complimented him after Darren had left. She laughed. 'A little bit over the top to make sure the audience listens.'

'He won't change.'

272

'I think he will. There was true contrition in his eyes, along with the fear. The tears were genuine.'

'Course they were. All bigots are like that. Bullying bigots, that's what they are. Mouthing off about blacks and gays and disabled and... um... even old people. They have a craving to be returned to their Anglo Saxon world where only the most brutal of macho white men could rule the roost. Then, like all bullies, when a stronger argument is put forward and they're caught on their own, they crumble.'

'You mean a stronger bully,' she smiled.

Richardson smiled as well. 'Maybe. But, it all seems so futile.'

'What?'

'The war against right-wing bigotry. We'll never beat it.'

'Never give up trying, though.'

The pair went to leave the washroom when Richardson stopped and barred the way. 'Sue-Beth, what're your plans for the future?'

'Why? I haven't really thought about it.'

'Well, Jonah's thinking of giving it away and looking for an easier life. Peter's minted, so money won't be a problem. You see, I've spoken to Cobbold about you being my partner. You'll keep the police-stroke-army relationship going. What do you say?'

'I'm flattered, but I wasn't Special Forces.'

'Doesn't matter.'

'OK, if one of our jobs is to go after Willow.'

'It'll be extremely high on the agenda. Welcome aboard.'

Curtly Richardson will return for further operations.